WITH GREAT DISCRETION

A NOVEL OF FACTUAL HISTORY
ABOUT HEROISM AND THE CHEYENNE PEOPLE

BY

J. HOOLIHAN CLAYTON
AUTHOR OF *COMMENDABLE DISCRETION*

WITH ILLUSTRATIONS AND ENGRAVINGS
FROM HARPERS WEEKLY

DOG SOLDIER PRESS

TAOS

Published in March 2022 by
Dog Soldier Press, PO Box 1782,
Ranchos de Taos, NM 87557
dogsoldierpress.com

Graphic Design: book interior and cover
Ananda M. Sundari, Alchemy Arts
AlchemyArtsllc.com

Library of Congress Control Number: 2022933430
Printing: Ingram Sparks
Print ISBN: 978-1-7371362-4-8
eBook ISBN: 978-1-7371362-5-5

"…and in the managing of quarrels you may say he is wise, for either he avoids them with great discretion or undertakes them with a most Christian-like fear."

Much Ado About Nothing, Act II, Scene 3
- William Shakespeare -

Magna est veritas, et praevalebit.

"There are only a few of us left, and we only wanted a little ground, where we could live. We left our lodges standing and ran away in the night."

- *Ó'kôhómôxháahketa*, Little Wolf,
Principal Chief of the Northern Cheyenne people -

"I am here on my own ground and I will never go back. You may kill me here, but you cannot make me go back. You can starve us if you like, but you cannot make us go south. We will not go."

- *Vóóhéhéve*, Morning Star/Dull Knife,
Principal Chief of the Northern Cheyenne people -

Foreword

For generations, the *Tsétsêhéstâhese/So'taahe'*, the Northern Cheyenne people, lived and hunted buffalo with their allies, the Lakota and Arapahoe, on the Great Plains. As settlers encroached on Indian lands and discoveries of gold attracted waves of prospectors, gamblers and criminals into traditional hunting territories, violence escalated between whites and Plains Indians. After the conflict on the Little Big Horn, during which the U.S. Army suffered an inglorious defeat, America demanded retribution. General William Tecumseh Sherman was given military authority over all northern reservations and declared that the Indians would be prisoners of war. Soldiers guarded the agencies and there were rumors that all ponies and firearms would be confiscated. The U.S. Congress passed a law to steal the Powder River country and the *Mo'öhtávo'honáéva*, the Black Hills, directly in violation of the 1868 Treaty of Fort Laramie.

Meanwhile, Colonel Miles on the Tongue River and Colonel Mackenzie out of Camp Robinson were scouring the plains and mountains for Lakota and Cheyenne warriors and their families. On November 14, 1876, Mackenzie and four cavalry regiments attacked the Cheyenne village of Morning Star and Little Wolf on a fork of the Powder River. Fighting was fierce, but the people escaped, leaving much needed supplies, lodges and horses behind. The soldiers burned the Indian camp and took possession of over 700 head of ponies. The Cheyenne found refuge with

Crazy Horse's people, but resources were insufficient to support everyone and the winter weather was brutal. In the spring of 1877, the surviving people of the Northern Cheyenne tribal bands surrendered, believing they would remain on agencies with their Lakota relatives. Instead, they were sent to Indian Territory, far to the south, where starvation, disease and cultural devastation threatened to annihilate every last man, woman and child.

Prologue

The buffalo were cardinal. Those damnable Indians and their buffalo.   What the United States required was cattle; great herds of cattle to feed a growing population. And the plains would need to be cleared for the expansion of railroads and homesteading. Forthright enough then. Just like the heathen red man, the ascendancy of the buffalo would end. He would propose a strategy of extermination. A policy that would kill two birds with one stone. After all, the most expedient approach with which to induce redskins to come to heel would be to eradicate their main source of sustenance. Civilians and military personnel alike would be given permission to slaughter buffalo whenever and wherever they found it actionable. Ultimately, neither the herds of wooly beasts nor the tribes of savages would stand in the track of progress and civilization.

SHOOTING BUFFALO

1

He was in Omaha when Secretary of Interior Carl Schurz summoned him to Washington D.C. His original aim had been to collect his livestock and travel north to find Sitting Bull's band; to visit old friends, long missed. Instead, when he entered the depot and the ticket agent made note of his name, Charles W. Collins found he had an urgent telegram from Washington D.C., forwarded by Allan Pinkerton. Collins had been providing protection for the transport of a substantial quantity of railroad security bonds from Boston to Chicago and was now anxious to be shed of cities and congested masses of people. He was set to board a Pullman on the Union Pacific Railroad headed west.

Washington DC Jan 12 1879
To C.W. Collins c/o Pinkerton National Detective Agency Chicago Ill
Require you in Washington DC Vital Come at once
Substantial remuneration and no restraints on methods
C. Schurz
Honorable Sec. of the Interior

Collins debated whether to travel to the capital or just carry on to his intended destination. He could not imagine what Schurz might have in mind, given the man's animosity for former President Grant and all associates, but mercenary aspirations incited him to send a return telegram inquiring as to the nature of the proposed employment. He could, at least, consider all contingencies.

Not being acquainted with Omaha, C.W. questioned the telegraph operator about possible accommodations for the night.

"Friend, between the exorbitant price Mr. Marsh is currently charging for his horse railway, the roaming bands of feral and decidedly ferocious dogs, and the frozen mountains and valleys of mud in our streets, I suggest you rest here overnight," the man told him. "Morning would be the time to go exploring."

"Thank you. I will be just over there when a reply comes."

C.W. took himself over to a bench in a corner of the small depot. It was empty of passengers due to the lateness of the hour. Using his carpetbag as a foot rest, he tipped his hat over his eyes and slipped off to sleep. In the early morning, he was awoken by the arrival of an immigrant family of what he took to be Bohemians. There appeared to be three generations of them, including six children. They settled across the depot from him, but were raucous with scolding the younger offspring, distributing food and arranging articles of clothing.

Abandoning hope of additional sleep, Collins contemplated an idea he had been formulating during the waking hours of his train journey from Chicago. Now grown weary of his farm on the Pacific coast, he planned to purchase ranch land near Deer Lodge in Montana Territory. He could raise cattle, some chickens and perhaps a few blooded horses. He desired solitude and wide-open spaces. His misanthropy was becoming acute of late and a location distant from large human populations would suit him perfectly. Therefore, a profitable assignment from Secretary Schurz would not go amiss, as long as it did not offend his sensibilities.

By early morning, a reply had come from Schurz. In response to C.W.'s inquiry, he flatly refused to delineate the commission via telegram, insisting that confidentiality demanded their meeting in person. Collins took this to mean secrecy or subterfuge. He purchased a first-class ticket for a berth on the ten o'clock express train bound for Chicago. From there he could board a Burlington and Ohio Pullman to Washington.

Not wanting to leave the depot now, he procured a copy of the *Omaha Daily Bee* from a newsboy who had come in with a growing throng of passengers gathering in the building. From his bag, Collins took out an apple and a hunk of cheese, making this his breakfast. A citified young man sat beside him on the bench and began perusing the back of his paper, even going so far as to pinch a corner of the page with a thumb and forefinger to steady it. Collins lowered the newspaper and looked at the man askance.

"Purchase your own," he said quietly, "or depart."

Shrugging sheepishly, the youngster got up to seek alternate seating arrangements. C.W.'s subsequent neighbor appeared to be an older drummer of taciturn nature. He found this vastly more suitable. Resuming his reading, he happened upon an article about Cheyenne Indians breaking out of a reservation in Indian Territory. Some of them had been captured and held at Camp Robinson on the White River. The report included acrimonious rhetoric involving butcheries, imaginary or real, and demands for the U.S. Army to protect the worthy citizens of the state. The editor, one E. Rosewater, was expressive with lurid details and melodramatic modifiers. It was all too familiar to Collins. He turned his attention, instead, to the newspaper's prolific advertising, learning of the benefits of St Jacob's Oil, the great German remedy for rheumatism, as well as the fact that Sheeley Bros. Packing Company now had telephone connections. J.B. Detwiler offered the largest stock of carpetings in the West and Byron Reed & Co. was the oldest established real estate agency in Nebraska. For such concerns, white Americans were willing to vanquish the indigenous peoples of the continent. It seemed to be a rather cockeyed exchange.

It was snowing when the express train left the depot and crossed back into Council Bluffs, traversing the Missouri River by way of the engineering marvel of the Omaha Bridge. Collins settled in his berth, stowing his carpet bag and relaxing into the comfortable upholstery and ideal warmth of the compartment. The windows fogged up and he wiped an opening with his sleeve. A curtain of fluffy snow obscured most of the view of the mighty river, so he turned back to his newspaper. He could hear a couple of gentlemen nearby discussing the recent yellow fever outbreak in New Orleans and the projected National Board of Health legislation that would be proposed during the 45th session of the U.S. Congress. Apparently, the men were not in favor of having a body of the federal government in charge of preventing the introduction of contagious diseases into the United States. According to one of the men, enforced quarantine would restrict trade and negatively affect the economy.

Well, Collins thought to himself, it is always about money, never about common good or general welfare. A quote of Plato's came to mind. "Power and fortune must concur with prudence and virtue to effect anything great in a political capacity."

He began reading an article about the so-called "Black Exodus" to the western territories from southern states. The South was alarmed that, after cheating blacks out of their earnings and removing their rights as free citizens, ex-slaves were emigrating west to seek improved prospects. According to the report, colored laborers were being recruited by railroad companies in the interest of replacing Chinese workhands. Having been with the Freedman's Bureau after the Great Rebellion,

C.W. could well imagine that working on construction gangs, in extreme weather conditions and battling impossible terrain, still had to be preferable to the restrictive and barbarous tribulations of the post-Reconstruction South. Of course, railroad magnates, such as Jay Gould of the Union Pacific, would be exploiting them to the fullest. Out of the frying pan and into the fire.

A baby began crying at the other end of the railway car. C.W. could hear the mother humming a lullaby. His thoughts turned unbidden to a memory from his time with Sitting Bull's Hunkpapa band. Soldiers had attacked the village on the Redwater River and they had fled, through freezing winter weather, leaving behind much needed blankets and food. That night they had sheltered in a box canyon and, sitting beside a fire, Collins had listened to a Lakota mother singing to her wounded and dying girl child.

The porter came by to offer coffee or tea and Collins was grateful for the interruption. Some recollections were best evaded at all costs.

GOING HOME

2

He was ushered promptly into Secretary Carl Schurz's office. It was grand and impressive with massive furniture and all the accoutrements of power, as with most administrative offices in the nation's capital city. An excellent copy of the Lansdowne portrait of George Washington dominated the west wall.

"Mr. Collins," Schurz said, "I appreciate your swift journey to Washington. Please, sit down."

C.W. took a seat in a chair near the desk. He held his black Stetson hat in his lap and brushed some dust from the crown pensively. "I admit to having been hesitant to come, given your well-known antipathy for President Grant."

The man adjusted his pince-nez. "I respect Mr. Grant and I have come to admire and acquiesce to the wisdom of his peace policy toward the Indian. Lately, I have heard of you and your...particular skills. Especially your circumspection."

"I am known among certain circles for my specific abilities. And for my loyalty to President Grant." C.W. held the man's gaze with his piercing blue eyes. "But I assume you did not request my presence in Washington to visit that particular issue."

"No, I most assuredly did not. I have quite another matter to discuss with you." Schurz got to his feet and paced a bit with his hands clasped behind his back. "A situation has developed and I need a man working for me behind the scenes. I require an operative I can trust and I have heard from reliable sources that I can trust you. I have also heard that you maintain certain sympathies for the Indian. These are desirable traits."

Knowing he was supposed to be complimented, but particularly unswayed by such tactics, Collins sat silently waiting for the man to continue.

"Perhaps you have heard of the Northern Cheyenne escape from the agency near Fort Reno in Indian Territory?"

Collins nodded in response.

"They have been committing depredations across Kansas and Nebraska. They eluded thousands of soldiers and civilians, fighting their way out of skirmishes and steadily making their way north."

"But I read a newspaper article only recently that stated the Cheyenne were captured last October and are being held at Camp Robinson."

Schurz came around the desk and leaned against it near Collins, hooking his thumbs in the pockets of his waistcoat. "Some of this is true. They actually split up into two groups somewhere near the confluence of the North and South Platte rivers. We think a chief called Little Wolf took many of the warriors and kept going north. We cannot find them. The others were apprehended and have been held at Fort Robinson since late October and have been treated well for the most part. But...there has been a development."

C.W. sensed Schurz's uneasiness. "Yes?"

"The post commander at Fort Robinson was replaced in December by a Captain Wessells. He is, you might say, a bit high-strung. I am afraid that...well when General Phil and I insisted the Indians return to Darlington Agency in the south and they flatly refused, the captain took measures that were...well they were misguided." Schurz retreated behind his desk and sat down.

"What did the Cheyenne want? To stay at Fort Robinson?"

"No, to go to the Red Cloud Agency that was recently moved north from proximity with Fort Robinson. It had been their original destination and they were unaware it had been relocated. Apparently, many have relatives there."

"And why was this an issue?" C.W. asked, frowning in perplexity.

Schurz became animated. "Just think of it, Mr. Collins...the entire reservation network would be placed in peril. Some of the Poncas have also left Indian Territory to travel north. Indians could just remove themselves and go where they wished, as the whim took them. It would be disastrous."

Collins smoothed his moustache and smiled acerbically. "Tell me, Mr. Secretary, why did the Cheyenne leave Fort Reno in the first place? This desperate journey of hundreds of miles was certainly not a whim."

"Something about insufficient food and medicine. Some such complaints," Schurz said dismissively.

"Of for...look I do not mean to be disrespectful, but starvation and disease seem to be very good motives for absconding back to home country."

Schurz sighed. "Very well, I believe there were reasons. And apparently, Crook had led them to believe that if they did not adjust to their new home, they could return north. It was entirely ill-advised on his part."

Collins crossed his legs, setting his hat on the unoccupied chair next to him. "No doubt. And what did this Captain Wessells do that was so foolhardy?"

"When they refused to comply with the order to return south, he locked them in a barracks building and withheld heat, food and water. He did this for several days." Schurz pulled at an ear and shook his head.

"I assume you did not know of this?" C.W. asked, not attempting to disguise his uneasiness.

"Of course not," Schurz replied with impatience. "I am not one to torture children and old people."

"No, you just consign them to indentured misery on a reservation in unfamiliar territory."

Schurz came to his feet. "Enough of this!" he said loudly. His German accent was now quite noticeable.

Collins calmly picked up his hat. Placing it on his head, he got to his feet and made for the door.

"Wait, Mr. Collins," Schurz entreated. "Just wait a moment. At least until I have told you everything."

C.W. turned, but remained near the door.

"I apologize for the outburst," the man said, his accent again in abeyance. "I am quite full of concern about these unfortunate events and it has unseated my composure. Please sit and hear me out."

Still lingering near the exit, Collins took off his hat.

"Mr. Collins, I assure you, if you are passionate about the injustice of the situation, you may be of help. Come, sit." Schurz gestured beckoningly.

Walking back to the chair, C.W. sat down again. "I will hear you out, Mr. Secretary. But I have heard of some of your blunders in regards to Indian affairs. I remain uncertain whether I desire to enter your employment in this matter."

"I understand, I understand..." Schurz said, resuming his chair, "but as I stated in my telegram, you will have no restrictions on your activities and I will remunerate you handsomely. Very handsomely."

"That is a point in your favor. Pray continue. Do the Indians remain incarcerated and starving?"

"No, they escaped the barracks five days ago."

Collins cocked an eyebrow. "There were no guards?"

"The Indians had guns," Schurz said, leaning back in his chair.

"It is peculiar that they had not been disarmed upon their capture."

"They had been disarmed. They had somehow hidden other weapons."

"What happened?" Collins asked.

"Many were killed. Others were recaptured. Around forty are still at large."

"Well, if you are asking me to hunt them down, you can think again. I will not do it."

Schurz put up his hand in appeasement. "No, no, not that. There is quite another issue. I have heard a rumor that Phil Sheridan is appointing military officers to investigate the entire debacle. I want my own man on the ground, as it were."

"And?"

"You no doubt have heard of General Sherman's interest in transferring control of the Office of Indian Affairs to the War Department. Sheridan is also campaigning vigorously for this handover. He has been exceedingly critical of my reforms of late." Schurz removed his glasses and rubbed his eyes. "You may not think much of me in the way of protecting Indian interests, but I assure you, if the military gets its way, their strategy of pacification will be merciless."

Collins nodded. "And so you want me to investigate and report directly to you." It was a statement, not a question.

"Yes. And if you can acquire intelligence that will arm me in my efforts to keep the Indian Bureau within the Department of the Interior, that would be greatly beneficial."

"I will not be asked to prevent further disaster? Only to investigate and report to you?"

"Yes, that is all. Of course, I have already given you permission to act upon your own discretion. All I ask is that you do nothing to give me away or bring my authority into question. I would prefer that it would seem you were employed by some private entity. Or even the

Pinkertons?"

"Allan and I are not currently on the best of terms," C.W. said, grinning. "But he owes me a favor and I will send him a telegram requesting that I may use the cover of his agency."

"Ideal. Then you accept my commission?"

"I do, but only with the proviso that I may leave your employ if I find it offends my conscience in any manner. I will not be signing documents."

"No I quite understand," Schurz said, standing up. "And I wish to keep our association entirely clandestine. You must send all communication to my private rooms. My wife and I are currently residing at the Willard Hotel. Address all correspondence to Herr Burschenschaft. Here, I will write it down." He scribbled a note and handed it to C.W.

"Very well. And expenses?" Collins came to his feet and slipped the paper into his vest pocket.

"I will make a draft available today at the National Savings Bank, but not through my secretary. Go directly there. Also, I will send a letter of credit to whatever location you request in future. I am hopeful that you will depart with all possible haste."

Collins donned his Stetson. "I intend to leave today."

"Excellent, excellent." Schurz smiled in a tight-lipped manner. They shook hands.

"I believe the best plan would be to begin at Dodge City and follow the trail from there. As you say, I am not intended to prevent any subsequent calamity and so there is no haste."

"Some alacrity is recommended. Troops out of Fort Robinson continue to pursue the Indians. But yes, your mission is merely to discover as much as possible about all relevant occurrences and the activities of military personnel."

"Very well," Collins said. "I will be in communication

as soon as I learn anything." He gave a cursory salute and left the office without further ado.

POWER STRUGGLE

3

His horse and mules were boarded in a Denver livery stable, having been sent there in anticipation of his journey north. Collins wired instructions and sufficient funds so as to have his animals, gear and tack loaded on a boxcar to connect with the new Atchison, Topeka and Santa Fe railway out of Pueblo, Colorado and onward to Dodge City, Kansas; his current destination.

Having arrived back in Chicago, he boarded a Pullman Palace Car on the C.R.I.&P. From there to Dodge City, he would have complete privacy with his own porter and every luxury. During a layover of a few hours in the "Windy City," Collins had purchased a heavy bearskin coat, a long silk scarf, two pairs of heavy twilled duck canvas waist-high overalls, a union suit, a top-quality bedroll, woolen gloves and stockings, a new Winchester repeater and a canvas dog tent. Although the prices had been exorbitant, he felt certain the items were far less expensive than they would be in Dodge City. C.W had had a belly full of suffering privations while fulfilling employment in remote locations.

He slept most of the journey; slept and read the pile of newspapers he had purchased in Chicago. The landscape was unremarkable, although he did enjoy a few sightings of deer and antelope. Once he thought he espied a small band of Indians on horseback. No more majestic and imposing herds of buffalo, however. Not since General William Tecumseh Sherman, Commanding General of the U.S. Army, had applied his proven "scorched earth" tactics to the Great Plains. In the war, he had severed enemy supply lines and demoralized civilians through hunger and privation. To produce a similar effect for his Indian adversaries, he and his pal, General "Little Phil" Sheridan, actively promoted the tourism of wealthy sportsmen and European potentates in a stratagem of slaughter. Military personnel were also actively encouraged to participate in the wholesale bloodletting, as buffalo were killed for hides and sometimes only for their tongues, considered a culinary delicacy by troopers, officers and dandies alike. Vacationing businessmen shot them from trains by the hundreds as a novelty adventure. White men spilled from the cities and saloons to become "buffalo runners," spreading across the plains as parasites through the guts of a dog. The seemingly inexhaustible herds were vanishing.

After two more days of travel by rail, C.W. was prepared to be delivered of trains. The land stretched interminably out the window as his conveyance slowed and came to a halt. A remarkably disagreeable odor hit him the moment he exited the railway carriage at the Dodge City depot. The stockyards to the east of the siding sent up a pungent aroma that mingled with the overpowering stench emanating from buffalo hides stacked in voluminous mounds across the tracks. Collins observed a group of men operating machinery that baled the hides into bundles for transport. Huge ricks of buffalo bones were also positioned along the tracks ready for transport to become fertilizer. Carnage made industry. He tipped his porter and asked him to send his baggage to the Elephant Livery Stable down the way, the establishment where his livestock were to have been boarded upon arrival.

Collins retrieved his carpetbag and made his own way across the tracks to the stables, through patches of filthy snow and puddles of slushy mud, to see if his animals had yet arrived from Colorado. He also intended to lodge there himself, as he had heard this was also a service provided by the famed proprietor, Hamilton Bell. It was easy enough to find the imposing structure, a large building with an enormous painting of an elephant on the false front, between the words "livery" and "stable." A teeming hub of activity, the yard was populated with buggies, delivery wagons and various equines. Collins wended his way to what appeared to be an office, off to the side of the barn. Inside, a tall man was berating a stable hand.

"Dammit Jules, you had better be quicker about mucking out the stalls of a morning or you, by god, will be finding employment elsewhere. No more damn excuses you little reprobate!"

The boy, who appeared to C.W. to be about 12 or 13 years of age, stood his ground. "How is it I am the only one to blame? Archie does little enough and I work my ass off!"

"Sass me again and I will give you the road!" The man took a half-hearted swing at the youngster, who dodged the hand nimbly. "Now get the hell out of here and get back to work."

Collins stepped aside as the boy pushed past him, grinning. He turned to the man who had seated himself behind a desk in a corner of the cramped room. "Are you Mr. Bell?" he asked.

Another worker stuck his head in the door. "Same rates as yesterday?" the fellow asked.

"Same," was the answer. He looked at C.W. "I am Hamilton Bell...call me 'Ham.' What can I do for you?"

"I am expecting the delivery of livestock from Pueblo for Charles Collins. A buckskin colored gelding and two mules, one fairly good size."

"Fairly good size you say? The beast could carry a

grand pi-anny on its back without breathing hard. They are here a'right. Just yesterday. You must be Collins?"

"I am."

"Your animals and all your possibles are housed in the back of the barn."

"Glad to hear of it. I will be departing tomorrow and would prefer to put up here, as well."

"We have a small room available upstairs. A bit fragrant above the barn, mind." Bell removed his derby hat and smoothed back an abundance of brown hair.

"Perfectly acceptable. I have had the rest of my baggage sent here from the depot as well."

"I will look for it."

C.W. moved his carpetbag from one hand to the other. "Meanwhile, I will go see to my animals. Afterwards, might you recommend a nearby destination for a meal?"

"Fancy or hearty?"

"Steak."

"Beatty and Kelley's place, next to the Alhambra. Just up the road there," Bell said, tipping his head toward the northwest. "Ask anyone the way. I should also mention that firearms are not allowed within the city limits. Due strictly to the trail herds and those damnable Texans."

"Never carry one," C.W. prevaricated. His .45 Colt revolver was safely ensconced in his valise. The new .30 .30 Model 73 Winchester carbine was in its scabbard among his baggage, wrapped in the bedroll.

"Alrighty." Ham got to his feet and put his hat on. They walked out of the building into a stiff wind gusting from the west. The perfume of the stockyards and hides were mercifully blown away from town. "I need to find out if this fella Collar showed up yet with my load of hay. Find me when you have eaten. Will set you up with a room."

"Thanks." They shook hands.

Bell headed around the side of the barn and C.W.

entered the dim interior, redolent with horses, grain and manure. As his eyes adjusted, he noticed the boy, Jules, pitching hay to what looked to be a blooded thoroughbred stud horse. Collins made for the back of the momentous structure, admiring the sturdy pens, clean bedding and the robust horses and mules populating the building. At the end of a row of stalls, he found a large pen opening into a small corral through a door on the south side of the barn. Ulysses, his gelding, had his nose stuck in a hay bunk against the wall, standing beside Molly, his beloved mule. Outside in the corral, he could see Joey, his other mule, lying stretched on his side in the weak winter sunshine.

All his gear and tack were stacked neatly just outside the enclosure. Collins made a quick inventory and noted that all seemed to be accounted for, except his baggage from the train. He would check on that after a meal. He placed his carpetbag with the rest of his belongings and stepped through the gate to enter the pen. He squeezed between Molly and Ulysses, who stopped eating and allowed him to hook an arm under their jaws and pull their heads close to his chest in an embrace. They snuffled him with velvet noses and Ulysses yanked on his sleeve with his lips. He spoke fondly to them, always grateful when they recognized him after an absence. Molly leaned her forehead against his shoulder, almost knocking him off balance.

After spending some time with them, he let his animals return to their hay. He slipped past to visit the herculean mule asleep in the corral. Standing away from the animal, he cleared his throat loudly. The mule's eyes opened and he raised his head slightly.

"Hey big fellow," C.W. said, smiling. "Come say hello."

Joey came to his feet ponderously. He shook himself with vigor then made his way toward Collins. He stood an impressive seventeen and a half hands tall, but was gentle as a puppy. Not for the first time, Collins was pleased to have discovered this creature, abandoned and starving on the outskirts of Carson City. He had brought the animal back to health with care and plenty of feed. The roan mule considered him with large and expressive eyes, as if reading his thoughts.

"That is the biggest danged mule I ever see'd," came a voice from the barn.

C.W. turned to see a heavy-set young man with a tow head and dirty face leaning on the side of the pen, watching him.

"He is large, there is no doubt about that."

"Mister," the boy said, warming to the subject, "I have see'd a right smart of mules since I came to work here, but I ain't never see'd no mule like this one here." He aimed a nod at the animal.

Finding he was quite hungry, C.W. walked back through the pen and out the gate. "You will take care of my stock whilst I am gone?" he asked, slipping two bits into the boy's hand. "And guard my belongings here?"

"Shor will, mister. No worry."

"Your name?"

"Archie. Archie Cole."

"Well then, thank you Archie."

"Yessir, yessir," Archie said, nodding enthusiastically.

Collins walked out into the escalating breeze, skating across the prairie and making the vanes of the windmill, hard by the barn, spin volubly. He pulled down his hat and made his way toward the town itself, crossing the tracks and a main thoroughfare. Over the wind, he could hear the lowing of cattle in the railyard enclosures, waiting for transport to the slaughter houses of Chicago and beyond.

4

Walking northwest toward the main part of town, he passed a hardware store and a group of men by a liquor and cigar emporium. Collins asked directions to Beatty and Kelley's restaurant. He was informed that his destination was just a few doors farther down the rutted and manure strewn street. Music from a squeeze box and boisterous laughter spilled out into the thoroughfare from the saloon next door, but the eatery was fairly quiet with only a few patrons populating the generous room. He sat in a corner with his back against the wall and placed his hat on a chair beside him. A wiry man in an apron walked over.

"Coffee mister?"

"Yes and a rare steak, two eggs, fried potatoes and biscuits."

"Got everything but the biscuits. Sold out this morning."

"Okay. No biscuits."

Collins pulled out a two-day-old copy of the Chicago Daily Tribune from his jacket pocket. His coffee arrived. It was lukewarm but passable. Absorbed in his reading, C.W. did not notice a man approach his table. The redolence of alcohol alerted him to the fellow's presence. He looked up.

"I do not appreciate you standing over me and breathing on me," he said. "Kindly go away."

The grimy individual swayed a bit as if riding out a small earth tremor. He did not depart nor speak. Collins presently discerned a supplementary unpleasant and unidentifiable fragrance emanating from the man. He stood up.

"I requested that you depart my vicinity. I will not do so another time."

The waiter hurried over. "Shadler, what the hell are you doing pestering my customers?" he asked, attempting to shove the man away from Collins' table. This produced little effect as the man was much larger and quite obstinate. "Sorry mister," the waiter said. "He is drunk and ornery."

"He is required to be drunk and ornery elsewhere."

Shadler, for that was his name, pulled a large skinning knife from a boot. He finally spoke. "You eastern fops are ruining the hunting," he said, slurring his words and waving the knife in the manner of conducting an orchestra. "Hows 'bout I skin you an' sell your hide for shoes?"

C.W. stood calmly, sizing the man up. The waiter commenced tugging on Shadler's belt to pull him away. The buffalo hunter made a lunge with his knife. Collins dodged, put out a foot and dropped him like a beef. A tall and stringy man came into the premises and sauntered over to retrieve the knife and help Shadler to his feet.

"Shithead has been guzzling hooch perpetually for three days," the tall man said to no one in particular. "Been in a bad mood since '76 when the herds began playing out. Blames the en-tire world." He supported the drunkard out the door and C.W looked through the window to see him throw Shadler into a half-frozen mudhole down the road and walk away.

"I cannot tell you what is more impossible to deal with," the waiter said. "Buffalo hunters, Texas cowhands, soldiers or freighters. Wish I had never come to this festered country. I will get your food."

Returning to his table, Collins sat down and began perusing the other restaurant patrons. Two appeared to be gamblers or perhaps confidence tricksters. They were deep in conversation across the room and had barely shown any interest in the altercation with Shadler. A group of four men occupied a large table nearby. They appeared to be local merchants and, as the topic of conversation was the creation of a citizen's committee to protect law-abiding citizens north of the "deadline," this did, indeed, seem to be the case. They were categorically animated in their enthusiasm, but had not bothered to lend aid when a dispute had transpired in plain sight. All talk and no do. Collins had heard somewhere that there were more than a few impressive law men currently employed by the town and speculated as to the reasons why a citizen's committee of do-gooders would be necessary as well.

His food arrived and he ate heartily. Collins generally did not care to eat much when travelling by train. Being confined and inactive for prolonged periods did away with his appetite, so he had had no significant meal for a good while. The steak was excellent and not cooked more than he liked. He read while he ate, particularly interested by the report of a meteor falling near Sioux City, Iowa. According to the paper, it appeared as a long stream of blue and yellow flame, exploding before impact and shaking buildings in the locality. He was fascinated by such occurrences, frequently contemplating the vast reaches of space beyond Earth and never tiring of gazing at the stars with a sense of wonder. Not being religious, C.W. remained unencumbered by irrational mythologies attempting to explain all fantastical phenomena. He preferred conundrums and enigmas over uncompromising explanations and faery stories. And he was always baffled by the anger that came with devout religiosity, as if it were pure affrontery to think for oneself. It was the one area where he and his devoutly Catholic mother had never agreed.

Collins had noticed a tonsorial parlor on the east side of the restaurant. He settled the bill for his meal and stepped next door for a shave. On entering the small clapboard building, he instantly caught a reassuring whiff of bay rum. The barber stopped sweeping the floor and looked up. The gentleman sported a stiffly waxed and curled moustache with close-cropped muttonchops. He appeared markedly dapper.

"Welcome. What can I do for you?"

"Shave please," Collins answered, removing his hat and hanging it on a hook by the open door. He sat in the only chair, a well-worn leather and brass affair mounted on the floor.

"Hair cut?"

"No just the shave."

"Trim your moustache and side burns?"

"Side burns," Collins said, settling back as the fussy man adjusted the chair to a reclining position. "I do the moustache."

"Very well." He fetched a hot towel out of the back of the tiny shop and wrapped Collins' face, then began stropping a straight razor and humming.

"Any Indian trouble lately?" C.W. asked through his towel.

"Beg pardon?" the barber asked, removing the cloth and briskly applying frothy soap onto Collins' stubbled whiskers.

"Indian trouble lately?" Collins knew barber shops were frequently a hub for gossip.

"Oh my goodness, no. Not since the scare last September with those Shay-annes sneaking through here off the reservation. Stretch your chin for me, please. We were all petrified, I can tell you."

Having already noted the fact that this barber was

rather delicate, Collins wondered bemusedly whether perhaps he had been more alarmed than some. The man had a gentle touch at any rate and Collins suffered no nicks or scrapes.

"But there were no actual incidents?" he asked, while the barber wiped soap from the razor on a towel hanging from his belt.

"Not really, not in town, but it was terrifying to think we might have all been scalped in our beds." He finished shaving C.W. and, taking the towel from his belt, he wiped away residual soap. "Cologne?"

"Just some bay rum."

The man took a blue bottle from a shelf and splashed a generous amount of liquid in his hands. He rubbed the cologne into Collins' face and hair. "There. How is that?" he asked, cranking the chair back to an upright position.

"Most excellent." Collins said, getting to his feet.

"Care for a bath?"

"Not today. How much for the shave?"

"Four bits."

Collins pulled two quarters from a pocket and handed them over. "Thank you." He fetched his hat.

"We have a very nice bathhouse in the back. Especially now when there are no trail herds coming into town. Nice and private."

"Okay. Might see you later." Collins walked out the door and back into the hostile wind, cooler now that evening was approaching.

HIDES AND BONES

5

Hamilton Bell was in his office when Collins returned to the livery stable. A small sheepherder stove in the corner was ablaze and he went over to warm his hands.

"Well, fella, did you find a steak?" Bell asked.

"Yes. It was quite acceptable."

"Cup on that table yonder. Help yourself to coffee."

C.W. took a tin cup that looked passably clean and filled it from the pot on the stove. He sat in a straight-backed chair near the door. "Thanks."

"Good you got out of town afore it got disorderly. Best to keep shy of some of the types what come out after dark."

"And the law?"

"Law is around but never enough. Even with the gun-totin' rule."

"Mind my smoking?" Collins asked, setting his cup on the floor and taking out his pipe and tobacco.

"Naw. Just not in the barn. Too much in there wants to burn."

Collins packed his pipe from the leather pouch he had purchased in Chicago. "I thought this time of year would be quieter without the Texas herds coming in."

"Some. Plenty occurs however. Hell, we even had a woman shot down last October." Ham took out a cigar.

"In a shootout?" Collins asked. He brought out his match safe from a jacket pocket and offered a light. Then he lit his pipe and puffed on it briskly.

"Asleep. In the mayor's house," Bell replied, producing billows of smoke from the cigar. "Hey crack that door a mite."

C.W. complied, glad to let in some fresh air. The cigar was rank and cheap. "She was killed by the mayor?"

"Naw...here is the story. The gal, Dora was her name, had a sweet voice and could dance a bit. She showed up last summer and played at the Comique. Was damn popular and right pretty. Stayed at Mayor "Dog" Kelley's house with a gal what worked for Kelley in his saloon. Anyways, a kid, one Spike Kenedy, was gunning for Dog and rode up to his house and put four bullets into it. One slug hit Dora and done for her. Dog was over to Fort Dodge and not even there."

Collins helped himself to some more coffee. "Why was this Spike gunning for Kelley?"

"Some folks think it were 'cause they was both sportin' Dora."

"What happened to the kid?"

"Bassett and Earp and some of the others chased him down and kilt his horse out from under him. He were right shocked to discover he had slew Dora, thinking all the while he had snuffed ol' Dog. He were acquitted at any rate."

"Acquitted? How could that be?" Collins asked, incredulously.

"Mebbe 'cause it were an accident. Mebbe 'cause his daddy is one of the biggest damned ranchers in Texas and brings his herds through every year."

"'Nothing emboldens sin so much as mercy,'" Collins said, quoting Shakespeare.

"Well if you are saying he is still a wild cuss, then most particularly. And with nobody daring to say ought about him 'cause of daddy. Paid for the funeral though. Everything shy of a twenty-one gun salute and all."

Getting to his feet and banging out his pipe on the fender of the stove, Collins said, "There is precious little justice in this world...especially for women." He placed his cup back on the table, briefly wondering whether the vessels were ever actually washed.

"Damn right. Shame about that gal. Made my point though. Plenty of law but never enough." Bell stood and yawned mightily. "You will be wanting to see that room?"

"Please."

Ham lit a hurricane lamp and led the way out the door and into the barn. They ascended a narrow staircase just to the left, climbing into the dim heights of the building. There was a kind of entresol against the east side of the structure with a line of five doors down the walkway.

"This first one here is empty," Ham said, opening the door. "Cost you six bits over the boarding bill for your livestock."

"Fair enough."

The small room did reek a bit from animals, but appeared to be clean enough. He would need his bedroll for the bare rope bed that took up most of the space. There was a conductor's lantern on a corner table, the only other furniture in the room.

"Jules keeps these rooms passable. No heat though, 'cept for the lamp. If you need to piss, just go down and use one of the manure piles below. Shitter is out back. Wash off at the windmill." Bell left him unceremoniously and could be heard clumping heavily down the steps.

C.W. lit the lantern and, climbing back down to ground level, he moved quietly through the barn so as to not disturb any of the livestock. He came to the pile of his gear outside the pen where his animals were housed. Beside the mound of his possessions, he could make out the sleeping form of Archie. Apparently, the lad had taken his duties as guard quite seriously. Collins gently shook the young man, who sat up rubbing his eyes.

"You back then?"

"As you see. Did my baggage arrive from the train?"

"Yessir. It be right over there."

"Excellent. Well, if you have a room to go to, you no longer have to bed down here."

"Makes no mind where I sleep. I just as soon keep watch on your goods. You paid me for it. 'Sides, I like bein' with this here mule." He jerked a thumb at Joey, standing just inside the gate, his head drooping in slumber.

"Suit yourself, then. I will be taking my bedroll and my bag and leaving you to it."

Archie returned to his nest, fashioned from saddle blankets and straw. Collins dug his bedroll out from under his tent and other trappings, retrieved his carpetbag and made his way back to the stairway and his room. He set the lantern and his bag on the table and unrolled his bedding, removing his Winchester repeater carefully and leaning it against the wall. He took off his city duds and rolled them up tightly, intending to attire himself the next morning in the more practical clothing stashed in his bag. He donned his new union suit in the chill of the room, found his volume of Shakespeare and slipped between the sougans, warming up quickly beneath the weighty quilts.

He opened his book to *Coriolanus*, a play he had not read in a while, turning to the beginning of the third scene of Act II. He read a bit aloud to himself: "Ingratitude is monstrous, and for the multitude to be ingrateful were to make a monster of the multitude; of the which, we being members, should bring ourselves to be monstrous members." Collins loved the bard's wit and alliteration. There were no authors to rival him and he had been reliable company on many adventures. He read for a while longer, then smiling and drowsy, Collins depressed the side lever on the lantern and blew out the flame.

6

Arousing himself in the predawn, Collins lit the lamp and dressed in the sturdy and serviceable clothing he had chosen for the trail. He packed up his bedroll, again secreting his carbine within. He made his way down the shadowy staircase, tussling with the unwieldy bedding and his bag. He found Archie was still asleep beside the pen, snoring softly, so he quietly deposited his belongings and slipped away. Outside the barn, early light allowed him to avoid stepping in manure or twisting his ankles in potholes as he headed to the stock tank to splash water on his face. The livery office was dark, although he saw that Jules was coming from behind the building with a wheelbarrow and a pitchfork. The wind had died down during the night and the dawn was frigid but calm.

"Morning," the boy said, nodding.

"Good morning." Collins retrieved his Stetson from a nail on the windmill trestle and wiped his face on the sleeve of his woolen frock coat. "I need to purchase supplies. Can you recommend an establishment?"

"Zimmermann is your best bet. A might spendy, but he will have whatever a guy might require. His place is just up on Front Street. Biggest building along there."

"Thank you. I will head over there. By the by, your pal Archie is asleep in the back by my animals, if you need to find him."

"Stupid bugger is always sleeping," Jules said in disgust and wheeled his cart into the barn.

The day was dawning clear as C.W. crossed the railroad tracks and strolled down Front Street toward the largest structure he could make out. A couple of dogs trotted by him, appearing to be on some mission or other, known only to them. A bay horse, saddle and all, ambled leisurely down the street. Angling across the avenue, careful not to trip on frozen ruts, he stepped up onto the shabby narrow boardwalk that lined the margin of a row of false front buildings. Just down the way was a twelve foot post with a wooden cut-out of an oversize Sharps carbine mounted on top. The effigy indicated he was probably at his destination. A lamp shone in the building and the door was unlocked when he tried the handle.

Inside, a gentleman in bright blue suspenders and stockinged feet was stretched out on a counter. On hearing Collins enter, he sat up and swung his legs around to dangle above the floor. "Back misery," he said with a German accent. "Hard surface gets it straight." The man pulled on a pair of boots that lay nearby on the counter top and jumped down.

Walking over to warm himself by the pot belly parlor stove in the middle of the large room, C.W. waited for the fellow to pull himself together. The building was crammed full with dry goods of all types and sizes, leaving barely enough room to maneuver.

"Frederick Zimmermann at your service," the man said, coming over to where C.W. was standing. Zimmermann had voluminous side whiskers that reached past his shirt collar.

"Charles Collins," he responded, nodding a greeting.

"I require a few supplies for the trail."

"At your service, at your service," the German said, rubbing his hands together. "But if you are planning on going after the buffalo, I am afraid there are almost no more. And this is a poor time of year to go out on the plains. *Gefährlich*...Dangerous with blizzards and men who are not sociable. Men who will rob and kill you. Desperate men."

"Thank you, I appreciate the warning. But I am not hunting, only travelling through."

"Still...oh well you appear to be a man who is clear in his own mind." His manner altered to become all efficiency. "*In Ordnung,* let us make a list of supplies and I will seek to fulfill all your requirements."

"Most excellent."

They went together to the main counter and Zimmermann stepped behind to pull out a ledger and stub of pencil. Collins provided him with an inventory of items he wanted, including all food stuffs, extra ammunition, tobacco, Gayetty's paper, safety matches, a pig iron skillet, collapsible canvas buckets, coffeepot, coffee grinder and a small hurricane lantern with fuel. With an extra pack animal, he could afford to bring along some luxuries for the journey. He noticed a display of Arbuckle's coffee behind the counter and it made him smile, thinking of his friend from earlier days.

As he sauntered around the store, while Zimmermann began collecting the requested goods, C.W. found a couple of back issues of *Harper's Weekly*, an old 1866 Department of Interior public survey map of Kansas and Nebraska, a shiny new Green River knife, some bandage material, opium tablets, aspirin tablets, a new toothbrush and dental powder. He added all this to the growing quantity of items on the counter. He even discovered a small folding table behind a barrel of pinto beans.

"This for sale?" he asked.

"Everything is for sale, *Herr* Collins. But it will cost you one dollar. A sportsman from England sold it to me and the wood is mahogany. It is a rare article."

"Add it to the tally, if you will."

"There is also a folding chair. Four bits."

"I will take that as well."

Mr. Zimmermann's eyes seemed to fairly glisten in anticipation of such a lucrative sale during the off season of January, when no trail herds came to town and his business was mostly local. Collins felt unequivocally decadent indulging in these extravagances, but the idea of a comfortable camp every night appealed to him. Joey and Molly would suffer no hardship in splitting the load between them.

Having explored the entirety of the store, Collins decided to go back to the stable and arrange for grain. "I am going to fetch my animals so as to have them ready to load when we have completed our transaction," he told Zimmermann. "Do you require a deposit in assurance?"

"*Nein, nein,* we will have all prepared and organized in anticipation of your return."

"Many thanks."

"*Es ist nichts,* my friend.

As Collins was leaving the premises, a couple of women entered, one dragging a young child by the hand. He tipped his hat and held the door for them. The woman with the child smiled timidly, but neither thanked him. These were the first females he had seen in Dodge City since his arrival. Front Street had become more active with wagons, horses and men. The wind was blowing again and he drew his hat down tight and folded up his coat collar against it. Back at the Elephant Livery Stable, he found Hamilton Bell in his office, eating a plate of bacon and eggs. The smell of food reminded Collins he had not yet eaten.

"Coffee over there," Bell said, shoveling a forkful of egg into his mouth. "You look less of a dandy this morning," he opined through his food.

"Thanks." C.W. found his cup from the night before and filled it. He sat down and blew on the coffee, too hot to drink.

"Sleep okay?"

"Very well. Good bed."

"Plan to stay another night? Will hold the room for you." Bell wiped his plate with a hunk of bread and stuffed it in his mouth.

"No, I am leaving today. I need a sack of oats for the trail."

Bell took a sip of coffee and swished it through his mouth to clean his teeth. "Can do. Should take four, considering the size of that mule."

Collins grinned. "One will do. I also wanted to see if you would be willing to provide some information."

His companion took on an air of caution. "Information?"

"I was just wondering about the conflicts with Indians that occurred last September."

"No need for worry, Mr. Collins," Ham said, relaxing back into his usual informality. "They was all captured up north."

"Right. But I am more interested in the particulars of the violence."

Squinting his eyes again in suspicion, Bell asked, "Now why would this interest you, 'specially? It were a tragedy and no mistake. What exackly is your business here in Dodge anyhow?"

C.W. could see there was to be no casual inquiry with which he could access important intelligence. Citizens of isolated regions usually kept their cards close to their chests and it was clear that residual acrimony at the recent proximate Cheyenne raids lay just under the surface. "Mr. Hamilton, I am currently employed by the Pinkerton Agency," he dissembled. He had already alerted Allan Pinkerton that he would be using the agency as cover, with his approval or not.

"My mission is to investigate all claims of loss and depredations."

"Then you are here to lend aid to them what were

attacked?"

"In a manner of speaking." C.W. finished his coffee, stood and refilled his cup. He waved the pot at Hamilton, who nodded.

"All along the route north, in fact," he added fallaciously and poured the man another cup of coffee. Experience had shown him that the truth could frequently lead to repudiation. He was an innately honest individual, but was able to equivocate with the best of them, when called upon to do so.

"Well then, I will tell you. It were some excitement and plain out and out murder 'round here back last autumn. Them injuns broke out down south and needed horses and supplies and they was desperate and plumb irate." Collins could tell Ham was rousing himself for the recitation.

"They attacked cow camps and took or kilt horses and kilt plenty of fellas that was workin' out there on the plains," he continued. "There was farmers and young'uns and stock men all kilt. Why they even done for an ol' colored cook working for Chapman and Tuttle."

"Did the military pursue them?" C.W. asked, sitting down again.

"That damn Captain Rendebrook out of Fort Reno had 'em pinned down on Turkey Springs near the Cimarron, aided by some of our boys from up here but the injuns got the best of him and the soldiers had no water and got so thirsty they drank horse piss. 'Round three of them troopers was kilt. That is when the bloody-minded heathens come up this way and commenced raisin' hell." Ham took a slug of coffee. "We done drove 'em off, though. We hit 'em at Bluff Creek and again on Sand Creek. Dave Driskell even brung back a scalp. We could of put paid to them redskins had the soldiers been more sprightly. Would of saved them folks up on Beaver Creek."

"I thank you, Mr. Bell, for your concise recollection

of events. About how many were killed around here do you think?"

"Injuns or whites?"

"Whites."

"In the end, only about four," Ham said a bit sheepishly, no doubt thinking of his earlier exaggerations. "That is including the colored cook. Some went missing that was never found, though. But there was a sight more up north on the Sappa. Quite a few whites done for up there and women savagely outraged. Word was maybe five injuns was kilt all told in the raids 'round here. Not enough for sure. Army should of wiped 'em out years ago, along with the buffs."

"Were there any further conflicts prior to the incidents you refer to on... what was it? On Beaver Creek or Sappa?"

"Redskins murdered folks up there on both Sappa and Beaver Creeks. But yeah, sure enough, before that there was another fight. Big fight...about eighty or so miles northwest of here. Officer named Lewis brought around 250 troopers from Fort Dodge and braced 'em in a canyon."

Collins stood and placed his cup on the table. "And what was the outcome?" he asked.

"Lewis got kilt, but the soldiers got back all the loot them injuns had stolen. Bunch of horses too. Put 'em on foot and sent 'em running. Now the army has got the savages at Camp Robinson, I hope ol' Phil takes and hangs 'em all, like they done in Minnesota back in '62."

C.W. opened the door. "I will be packing up now. Will you figure my account and I will settle with you on my way out? And may I get Archie or Jules to lend a hand?"

"I will send one of 'em to you."

"Thank you, Mr. Hamilton. And thank you for your hospitality."

"You bet."

Walking out of the office, C.W. saw that the boys were

busy with men wanting feed or to lease a buggy or some other business. Ready to depart forthwith, he walked into the barn and headed for the pen with his gear and livestock. Again, he was struck by the complete and utter hatred that white settlers held for Indians. It twisted his stomach. They would not be satisfied short of absolute extermination or panoptic subjugation. As surely as the British government had sought to rid itself of the Irish during the Great Famine, the U.S. government would justify the total destruction of America's indigenous populations. Perhaps one day the tables would turn, he thought to himself. *Filleann an feall ar an bhfeallaire.* Treachery returns to the betrayer. One could only hope... for he had suffered ignominy and loss on the altar of such contempt.

7

As he rode out into the short grass prairie, aiming northwest from Dodge City and away from the Arkansas River, his first hour or so was occupied with bringing the gelding back into obeisance. The mules were calm and undaunted, but Ulysses spooked and shied at every bird, clump of brush and gust of wind. Collins swore at him a few times, but knew his horse would line out after he recollected the habitude of journeying. The animal had been sedentary for far too long.

His hat was drawn down tight against the squalls that assaulted them; sometimes bringing gravelly snow, stinging his face and causing Ulysses to tuck his rump and crow hop. The horizon was featureless except for the occasional line of shrubbery and stunted trees that mapped out a distant spring or seasonal creek. The cold blue sky was vast and patterned with low-slung clouds, sporadically obliterated by opaque veils of fleeting white-outs that then passed on as ghosts, scudding toward the eastern reaches of the plains. Straw yellow grama and buffalo grasses, stretching in all directions, were painted with drifts of scintillant snow, glittering in the intermittent sunlight.

The going was slow due to the shenanigans of his horse and the fact that Collins did not care to push his burdened pack animals too hard. Their loads were not untoward, but he always chose to pamper his livestock when possible, knowing the occasion could potentially arise when swift flight was desirable. As Zimmermann had cautioned, he might very well encounter disagreeable men who harbored bad intentions, especially now the buffalo herds were being hunted to extermination and concomitant sources of revenue were drying up. Bearing this in mind, the .45 caliber Colt was strapped over his frock coat and his Winchester carbine was slung in its boot on the offside of his saddle. C.W. was not one to court unwanted company nor to trust in the milk of human kindness.

Through watery eyes, squinted against the unrelenting wind, Collins could see recurrent expanses of bleached buffalo bones, scattered across the winter landscape as relics of the tragic slaughter perpetrated over the past ten or more years. Bone pickers would, no doubt, come again in spring and summer, like carrion eaters cleaning up a battlefield where the dead had been left untended. Sodbusters could augment their meager livelihoods by scouring the prairies for grim effluvium of the once boundless herds of magnificent beasts, selling bones for as much as eight dollars a ton, if the market was sound.

The grasslands he now traversed no longer flourished with myriad forms of animal life. It was an empty desert, a forsaken knacker's yard. He remembered the scene of carnage two years before, up on the Yellowstone, and the grief he had witnessed among the Lakota peoples, starving and inconsolable. Buffalo carcasses had been strewn across snow-covered terrain, bloody and stripped of hides and tongues. Sitting Bull had foretold of a death-wind that would take the heart of the people. It was rapidly coming to pass, spawned by the dregs of white society, coughed up onto the Great Plains with big-bore Sharps rifles in hand.

Reining Ulysses in on a small rise overlooking a span of shallow coulees, Collins took his compass from a coat pocket. He wanted to maintain a northwesterly course so as to make his way to Fort Wallace. From there, he could send a telegram to Secretary Schurz, as well as gather more information pertinent to his commission. The horse was settling down now. He stood passively while Collins took his bearings. Joey tried to get his head down for a mouthful of dried grama, but the lead rope was too short from where it was tied to the pigging string on Molly's packsaddle. She mildly raised a hind leg as warning for him to halt his tugging. He jerked his head up.

Collins put away his compass and nudged Ulysses onward. The mules lined out again in their dogged fashion. He could tell from the position of the sun that he had only a couple more hours to travel before he needed to make camp. He hoped to navigate as far as the Pawnee River, or at least one of its tributaries. His animals required water and so did he. He was used to more northern climes, where water was plentiful. Kansas was arid country. The map he had found at Zimmermann's store was outdated, but handy for showing possible water sources in unfamiliar territory.

The wind gave a mighty gust, nearly taking his hat. He pulled it down tighter and proceeded across undulating contours, watching for prairie dog burrows and old coyote dens that could collapse under his animals. He had lost a horse once that way in Wyoming territory. A piece of ground, undermined by a badger hole, had given way from under him and his mare had broken a leg, forcing him to shoot her. He had been left afoot and heart-broken. He had no desire to repeat the experience and he knew that prairie lands could appear deceivingly benign, in more ways than one.

A movement to his left caught his attention. C.W. narrowed his eyes and studied the object, seeming to float effortlessly across the landscape. As it angled nearer, he identified a buffalo wolf, lighter in color and more stout than a coyote, with distinctive black markings. He had heard these wolves were disappearing as summarily as the buffalo herds they haunted. Ulysses caught a whiff of the animal and snorted restively. Collins reached to pat his neck reassuringly, telling him that all was well. The creature faded into a gully ahead of them, seeming to dissipate as mist into the earth.

At last, he thought he could make out a consequential delineation of trees far ahead. He aimed his horse at it and picked up the pace so as to have plenty of light to set up camp. He approached the water course cautiously, more wary of humans than any other beings. As he eased his horse down the incline to the bottoms, Collins spotted a sandy clearing among narrow leaf cottonwoods, box elder and willows. There seemed to be plenty of dried grasses for the horses, dispersed among the trees and brush beside a narrow channel of water. He suspected he had not made it as far as the Pawnee and that he had come upon a minor stream. He could find no trace of recent human activity and so decided he would make camp in this protected alcove of vegetation.

Collins dismounted and eased all the cinches on his stock. He dropped Molly's lead rope, knowing she would stand and Joey would stay with her. He tethered Ulysses to a nearby tree branch and stepped away to relieve himself and reconnoiter a bit more. The sheltered riparian area smelled rich with pungent willow and wet soil. The creek showed ice along the edges but ran free in the middle, swift enough to remain thawed in moderate winter temperatures. Here, the frigid wind was mitigated and he felt relieved to have escaped its unrelenting assault. He returned to his animals and unsaddled his gelding, turning him loose to roll the itch from his back. He unloaded each of the mules in turn, then unsaddled them as well, hobbling Joey and Ulysses as a precaution. Molly had proven she would remain steadfast in her constancy, staying close to hand at all times. His horse and mules picked their way to water, drinking long after a hard day's ride.

He strung a rope between two sturdy trees and set up his tent. He tossed his bedroll inside and placed the table and chair just outside. He organized his other gear, filling the lantern with fuel and setting it on the table. He had stowed all food items in panniers, so he removed what he required and lashed the food packs up in a tall tree. Experience had taught him to be vigilant, even if most of the dangerous mammals of the southern plains had been substantially eradicated. While gathering branches for a fire, C.W. noticed a piece of roseate flint in the side of a cut bank. He pulled it out and realized he had found an intact, finely worked spearpoint. It was an object of great beauty. He took it back to camp, stowing it safely in his shaving kit, wrapped in a spare neckerchief.

With sufficient wood, he built a fire, filled the coffeepot and put it on to heat. He filled one of the canvas buckets with grain and walked it around to his animals, giving a good portion to each one. Joey attempted to steal a mouthful from Molly, but she bit his neck and he stepped away. Collins grinned, amused by the fact that despite Joey's immense size, Molly was always dominant. When she had finished her share, Collins scraped a last bit of grain from the bottom of the bucket and held it out for his jack mule in consolation. There was something very endearing about the fellow and he spent some time rubbing the mule's ears and forehead.

His livestock wandered off to forage among dried sedge and switch grass. C.W. made coffee and fried up a piece of salt pork with a potato. Night was falling and he ate at his table in the light of the hurricane lantern. He smoked his pipe for a while, enjoying the dying campfire and thinking about the day. After he had washed his dishes and scrubbed his pan with creek sand, he checked on his animals one last time and moved his table and lantern into the tent. Placing his Winchester and revolver close to hand, he rolled out his bedding and removed his coat, vest and blouse and, lastly, his Wellingtons. The bearskin coat made a comfortable pillow and the hefty bedroll was abundantly warm. He slipped off to sleep easily, knowing his mules would alert him to unwanted visitors.

8

It was still dark when Collins awoke. He was startled to find an unaccustomed pressure against his side. He reached for the match safe he had secreted under his bedroll, hoping fervently that a polecat had not joined him in slumber. Lighting a match, he saw that his new companion was some sort of nappy canine, snuggled against the side of his bedding. He scorched his fingers as the match burnt down. He cursed and struck another match to reach up and light his lantern. The dog lay very still, its eyes trained on his every move.

"What the hell?" Collins said aloud, sitting all the way up and examining the motley creature, dirty dappled white with black ears. It appeared to be skin and bones and was not very large in size.

"Where did you come from?" C.W. asked the dog. Its ears perked in response, then pinned back against the head as if in anticipation of a beating. He reached out a tentative hand and the animal cringed a bit, but did not retreat. With knuckles showing and fingers down, he put his hand close enough for the creature to smell. The dog watched him closely then moved almost infinitesimally to take a sniff. Slowly he opened his fingers and laid them softly on the dog's forehead. They remained locked in this impasse for a few minutes, then the animal pulled back and touched its tongue lightly to the tip of a finger. Collins smiled and reached slowly to gently stroke the petite head.

"Well, my new friend, I suppose you have come for some food?"

The dog bellied forward a small distance along the side of the bedroll. It wagged a truncated tail uncertainly, keeping its eyes trained on Collins.

"Okay, okay," he said soothingly. "But I need to get up now."

He slowly extracted himself from the heavy bedding. The dog recoiled and ran from the tent. Slipping on his clothing, boots and the bearskin coat, Collins picked up the lantern and went out to see if the dog had departed as inexplicably as it had arrived. He noticed the animal lying by the pile of saddles under a cottonwood tree. He suspended the lantern from a branch, thereby illuminating his small camp.

"There you are. Not polite to run off before breakfast is served."

Again, the dog cocked its ears at the sound of his voice. Loosening the tether, C.W. lowered his panniers to the ground. He took out a loaf of bread, wrapped in paper, and broke off a hunk. He tossed it in the dog's direction, causing it to bolt into the darkness. Collins sighed, stuffed the remaining loaf in his pocket and went to build a fire. He stepped into the tent to retrieve his matches and when he returned, the dog was chewing on the bread. He lit the fire, filled the coffeepot from the stream and put it on to boil. Early light was breaking in the east and he could see the silhouettes of his horse and mules standing together not far away along the creek bottom. He returned to his panniers, found a can of milk and poked a hole in it with his knife. Fetching an extra tin plate, he poured out the milk, then crumbled more bread into it. He placed it a few paces from the dog.

Collins ground coffee beans and threw them into the pot. Then he fried up some more of the salt pork and opened a can of beans to add to the pan. He sliced a piece of bread for himself, then tossed the rest of the loaf toward the dog, who had cleaned the plate and had now taken up a position closer to the fire. He could hear his horse and mules stirring, hobbles clinking, and looked over to see Joey reaching a nose out to smell the dog. It jumped up and ran over to lie beside Collins' chair by the fire. He put a hand down to stroke the dog's head and it did not flinch or run away. He rubbed its ears and scratched its sides. The dog rolled over on its back submissively and he could see it was a female.

"So you are a little girl," he said. "About time we had another lady around here, hey Molly?"

The mule looked over as if she understood his words. He felt something crawl on his hand and he pinched it between his fingers. It was clearly a flea. He got up and grabbed the can of kerosene and an extra pigging string. Making a noose of the rope, he slipped it gingerly over the dog's head. She stayed very still until he tugged her away from the fire. She came easily enough and he led her to an exposed patch of sand. Opening the can, he poured some of the paraffin on the dog's back, working it into her coat with a rag and making certain to reach every part of her small frame. She sneezed a couple of times, but now appeared to be willing to allow whatever he saw fit to do with her.

In the strengthening daylight, he could see that part of her tail and tips of her ears had probably frozen off, similar to the way he had seen it happen to young calves up north. He walked to his packs to get a bar of glycerin soap. He went down to the creek to wash his hands. Back at the fire, the dog was again beside his chair, stinking of paraffin. Taking the rope, he led the dog to the water's edge and lathered her thoroughly with soap. Picking her up, he placed her in a shallow backwater and rinsed her off, convinced now she would let him handle her and trust him not to harm her. He decided to keep the dog until he could find a home for her. He simply could not bring himself to leave a starving animal behind on the remote prairie. He took her to the tent and used a saddle blanket to dry her off.

Removing the rope, Collins let the dog go and went to eat his breakfast. The dog came over to watch him eat, eyes following every forkful. When he had had sufficient nourishment, he scraped the rest onto the dog's plate, chiding himself for being too weak-kneed to withstand a begging canine. She studiously consumed every morsel, then lay down beside the plate, licking her lips. He washed the dishes and packed up camp. The dog stayed close but kept out from underfoot.

C.W. filled the bucket again with oats and grained the horse and mules, then saddled the animals and began loading his outfit. Knowing the dog would be too weak to keep up on a long day of travelling, he built a platform of his tent and bedroll on Joey's packsaddle and covered it with the bearskin coat, hoping he could coax the animal to ride. When he was all set to depart, he went to where the dog was lying and carefully lifted her into his arms. She held herself stiffly as he moved toward Joey and set her onto the packs. She jumped down immediately and sat looking at him.

"Dammit, dog," he said, not sure of what to try next. He could tie her up on the packsaddle, but then she could strangle herself when he was not paying attention. He decided to let her follow along as best she could. He needed to keep moving.

Tightening the cinches one final time, he swung into the saddle. The dog became agitated, making tiny whimpers and running back and forth alongside Ulysses. The gelding snorted and bowed his neck. C.W. got an idea and, dropping Molly's lead rope, he rode over beside an embankment. The dog ran up the bank and dove onto the saddle with Collins. He had a small struggle with

Ulysses to convince him everything was acceptable, but the horse finally calmed and he rode back to his mules and snagged Molly's rope. The dog perched comfortably on his saddle in front of him, as if she had always ridden there.

Climbing out of the creek bottom, he checked his compass and headed again in a northwesterly direction. A chilly breeze was picking up, ruffling the dog's fur. He asked her how she was doing and she licked his hand. He thought he had better give the creature a name. *Geal* meant "pale-colored" in the Irish, so he thought he would just call her Gal.   Willing of her company now, he caressed her head and told her she was pretty. She watched the horizon attentively, as if on guard.

The sky was cloudless over the great enormity of the southern plains and there was little enough to see as the journey dragged on. A raptor rode currents of air, high above in the distance. He sang all the verses he could remember of *The Dunlavin Green,* while the rising wind blew the song from his mouth across the limitless expanse of lonely grasses. And the wraiths of Irish rebels rode alongside them, not quite at home in the state of Kansas.

SLAUGHTER

9

Abruptly, the land gave way to a narrow sandstone canyon, through which a modest stream wound. Collins followed an animal trail into the expanding gap of trees, low cliffs and dense dried undergrowth, ever alert to his surroundings. In a clearing by the creek, he dismounted and led his stock to a wide, open pool of spring-fed water, looping the reins and lead rope loosely around the saddle horn. He lifted Gal from the saddle so as to not startle his gelding. The animals lined up to drink while he took out his map to discover their location.

From what C.W. could make out, he was on Ladder Creek somewhere near Punished Woman Fork, which would eventually feed into the Smoky Hill River to the north. Then, it seemed, if he followed the river to the west, it would take him directly to Fort Wallace. It was too early to camp, so he tied Molly's lead rope hard and fast to the saddle and led Ulysses along the creek bottom, working the stiffness from his legs and giving the dog a chance to explore. A faint scent of smoke put him on his guard and he tied his animals to a tree and retrieved the carbine from its scabbard. Quietly, he made his way beside the stream, keeping away from dried brush and leaves that could betray his approach. Gal stayed on his heels, instinctively aware that stealth was required.

Collins came around a bend in the creek to a sheltered place of juniper trees beneath a steep bluff. A brief wisp of smoke rising faintly above the tree tops drew him toward the hidden camp. Turning to look at the dog, he knelt and placed a hand on her back to push her to the ground. Naturally timid, she retreated to a nearby cluster of willows and lay down, her eyes trained on him. He moved closer, hunched over and placing each foot carefully, until he could see the fire and a crude brush shelter nearby. There was no one evident in the camp.

With a crawling sensation on the back of his neck, he turned suddenly to the sound of the dog growling. A few paces behind him stood an emaciated young Indian man with one thigh bound in strips of hide. The boy had a nocked arrow pointed straight at him. Collins held the Winchester away from his body, barrel pointed upwards. He shook his head forcefully.

"Okay, okay," he said, putting his other arm out with the hand open. "I am only passing through."

"Why were you looking for me?" the Indian asked in well enunciated English, keeping the arrow aimed at Collins.

"I was worried about running into buffalo hunters. I only came to see who was here. Let me go back to my horses and I will leave."

The boy shifted uncomfortably on his injured leg.

"Who are you? Why are you worried about buffalo hunters?"

"My name is Collins. I am on my way to find out about what happened to the Cheyenne people who went north."

Lowering the arrow a bit, the young man eased himself onto a nearby outcrop of sandstone. There was perspiration on his brow. "Why do you care about this?"

"I was asked to find out so the truth could be told." C.W.'s arm ached from the strain of holding the carbine out to the side. He took a chance and lowered the butt to the ground.

"Put that gun away from you."

Collins complied, tossing the rifle gently down on a dried mound of fescue grass. He noticed the dog had bellied closer and was watching the Indian intently.

"Why should I not just kill you?"

"Maybe I can help you," Collins told him. "Maybe you need food."

The Indian huffed contemptuously. "I could just kill you and take your food. And your horses."

"This is true," Collins said with a grim smile. "But you are sick and need help. Besides, that is the worst bow and arrow I have ever seen. I doubt you could kill anyone."

Sighing, the boy threw down his weapons. "Kill me. I do not care anymore. It is true. I am sick and hungry and have been hiding here for many, many days. I do not care."

Picking up his Winchester, Collins walked over and stood beside the young man. "Go back to your camp. I will come with food and medicine. What is your name?"

"*Séavóněske*. Woodchuck."

"Very well, Woodchuck. I will be back very soon."

Retracing his steps with Gal following behind, C.W. found his horse and mules where he had left them. He led them back to Woodchuck's camp. The boy was re-clining on the ground by the dying fire. He appeared to be completely resigned to his fate and did not bother to look up at Collins' approach. Unsaddling the gelding, C.W. ground-tied him and went to loosen the cinches on his mules, letting Molly's lead rope drag on the ground, but leaving Joey secured to the pigging string. He had not yet made up his mind about staying to camp. He took some bread from a pannier and knelt down beside the boy.

"Here is some bread. May I look at your wound while you eat it?"

"I will wait."

Collins gently unwrapped the strips of hide and gingerly picked some small pieces of fungus from the injury in Woodchuck's thigh. The smell of corruption was strong as he revealed what was undoubtedly a bullet wound. The Indian lay with eyes closed, silent and grave.

"How old is this?"

"Many days old. Maybe three moons. I have put medicine on it...otherwise I would be dead."

Whatever the nature of the fungus, it had kept gangrene from setting in, but the bullet was still in the muscle of the thigh and the infection would never heal as long as the projectile remained. "I see that the medicine has helped. But I should take the bullet out. Will you let me do this?"

"If you wish it."

"I wish it. Eat your bread."

Getting to his feet, Collins went to unsaddle and hobble his animals. He was committed now to helping this young man, who would die without aid. He went to fill his coffeepot with water from the creek and brought it over to the stone hearth, adding wood and blowing on the coals to rekindle the fire. The boy had eaten the bread and was again lying on his back.

"I am going to use my knife to take out the bullet," C.W. told him. "I have some medicine that will dull the pain. Do you want it?"

"No."

Throughout the procedure, Woodchuck did not flinch or make a sound. Thankfully the wound had festered and brought the lead slug closer to the surface of the thigh muscle. When he had it out, Collins washed the wound with soap and hot water. The boy gave him some more fungus from a pouch around his neck and he crumbled it into the lesion. He cut strips from one of his blouses and bound the leg, finishing by rewinding the strips of hide for additional protection, leaving room for the injury to drain.

"How do you know these skills?" Woodchuck asked.

"From a war between the whites that took place a few years ago."

As the sun began to set behind the sandstone bluffs above them, Collins grained the livestock, put up his tent and set about making coffee. He fried more salt pork and added beans. Gal had disappeared and returned with an opossum. She lay under a juniper tree, killed and ate it. Woodchuck was lying quietly by the fire with his eyes closed. Collins filled a plate with food and took it over to the Indian.

"Woodchuck...here. Eat this. I know it is not the best, but you need to eat."

Sitting up, the boy accepted the plate. "I am grateful."

After filling a plate of food for himself, C.W. sat on his folding chair by the fire. "You speak excellent English. Where did you learn?"

"I learned." Despite his hunger, Woodchuck chewed slowly and thoroughly.

Collins handed him another hunk of bread. "I am headed for Fort Wallace," he told the boy. "You cannot go there."

"No."

"Will you tell me what happened?"

After a long pause, Woodchuck said, "I was with the *Tsétsêhéstâhese,* the Cheyenne people, who left the agency in the south. There was a battle near here. We had come very far and had taken plenty of horses and supplies, but the soldiers caught up with us and stole everything. There was a running escape and I was hit by a soldier bullet. One beloved woman was trampled. I buried the woman near here and I stayed behind so I would not be a burden. I have been here ever since, hiding. At first, I was able to snare animals to eat, but when winter came I starved. I have been staying alive on tubers and rodents. I never learned how to make a proper bow or arrows."

Collins poured them both a cup of coffee. "You are Cheyenne?"

"Yes."

"Where can you go?"

"When I am able, I will go back down to the agency in the south. I have relations there."

"I am sorry I cannot help you to get there."

"Do not be sorry. I will heal now. I have my life back. It is enough"

"How will you make it through all the settlements?" Collins asked.

"There are ways. It is how the *Tsétsêhéstâhese* made it this far from Fort Reno."

"I will leave food with you. As much as I can spare." Collins said.

"Why are you helping me? Why do you not want to kill me the same as the other *ho'evoto?*"

C.W. smiled, assuming he meant other white men. "It is difficult to explain. I have learned to see what is happening to Indians from their perspective."

"How did you learn this?"

"I learned."

10

It was with great difficulty that Collins rode away from Woodchuck's camp. The young man insisted he leave only half of the food he intended to leave and that he depart the vicinity early in the morning. He flatly refused the offer of warm clothing. Collins had spent enough time with the Lakota to know that personal choice must be honored and that every person's fate was so determined and accepted. He supposed it was the same for the Cheyenne people.

In parting, Woodchuck had given him a round stone, smooth and worn, the color of red clay. "This has no qualities," he told Collins. "But I have kept it for a long time. It feels good in the hand."

Riding north along the west side of Ladder Creek, with Gal seated in front of him, he was saddened by the thought that he would never know the boy's ultimate fate nor whether he made it back to Indian Territory without being caught by some of the righteous denizens of Kansas. This prospect caused disquiet and he turned his attention to a flock of Canada geese gathered in a wide pool. The birds were not inordinately concerned by his presence and called back and forth amongst themselves.

An unaccustomed hissing to his left made him glance up at a sandy rise on the edge of the narrow valley. There, in majestic authority, stood a large gander keeping watch. The sight made C.W. smile in admiration. Gal was excited by the geese and whimpered softly.

"Easy, girl," he told her. " 'One touch of nature makes the whole world kin.' "

They travelled the length of the shallow canyon, then climbed an easy grade as the stream meandered into open land, bounded by fewer trees and thinner vegetation. No longer obstructed by the sandstone rimrock, the wind hit in full force, scourging them relentlessly. Clouds were assembling on the horizon and C.W. hoped they did not threaten intemperate weather.

The day passed in a monotony of tedious, lifeless terrain, occasionally broken by groupings of bones and skulls or an infrequent decaying buffalo carcass. Even along Ladder Creek, there seemed to be a dearth of fauna. The stream was mostly frozen and the denuded trees along its banks offered limited shelter. Again, Collins' spirits were made melancholic by this wasteland devoid of living beings. He finally noticed a great horned owl watching them from a skeletal cottonwood tree about midday, but he could not suppose what the creature hunted. Perhaps nocturnal animals were more prolific along the creek.

His mind wandered, meditating upon Woodchuck and the fierce individual liberty that seemed to invest all Indian peoples with whom he had ever associated. The greatest standard of true democracy he had as yet encountered was found among groups of Indians, if the actual measure was complete freedom of individual choice. Some of this drive for self-determination could also be found in Irish republicanism and this made sense to him, since both the Indians and the Irish had societies founded on a long history of tribes and clans. Unfortunately, the desire for complete independence, Collins mused, also gave rise to warring factions within the social order, along with the consequential inability to successfully band together against a common foe. In Ireland, this impediment had presented difficulties since the Norman invasion and, later, during the Tudor conquest. For the indigenous peoples of the Americas, European encroachment was often aided by one Indian tribe turning against another.

Having read a book by Bernal Diaz del Castillo, a soldier with Cortés, Collins was aware that the success of the Spanish conquistadors had had much to do with Mexican tribes fighting with them against the Aztecs. He was also aware that the Pawnee were scouts for the U.S. Army against the Lakota, the Crow had scouted for Custer and many Apache men had been providing reconnaissance for General Crook in the Southwest. Only brutal hierarchy seemed capable of sustaining authority and control over large populations of people. The British Empire was an excellent example of this. And the British were still proving that Irish peoples could be made to fight amongst themselves. *Divide et impera.* Divide and rule.

Snow struck early in the afternoon, coming sideways with icy, stinging pellets. Collins looked for some sort of protection from the assault and found none. Gal wedged herself behind the swells of the saddle and Ulysses pinned his ears back, tossing his head in agitation at the onslaught. C.W. bent over the horse's neck, wincing against the driving sleet and desperately seeking some minor shelter for his animals. After an infinity of misery, he finally spied a cut bank ahead and dropped into the creek beneath it. Due to low water, there was a narrow sand bar at the base of the eight foot bank. He lifted Gal to the ground, dismounted and gathered the horse and mules into a group, speaking reassuringly to them. Even Molly seemed to have been disconcerted by the sustained barrage of wind and biting snow.

With barely enough room to stay out of the slushy water of the stream, Collins perched on a tree root that had been exposed by erosion. Gal tucked herself under his knees. They were in a decidedly compromised position and the only hope was that the storm would abate before nightfall. So much for comfort, he thought grimly. He sang an old Irish song, *The Croppy Boy*, to calm his animals. Some of the lyrics seemed appropriate, given his earlier reveries. *My own first cousin did me betray. And for one bare guinea swore my life away.*

Beginning to shiver from the chill of their damp retreat, C.W. was heartened by a noticeable weakening of the storm. In a short while, the snow abated and, after tightening the cinches and wiping his saddle with a sleeve of his coat, he swung onto Ulysses. Gal climbed the bank and vaulted into Collins' arms. The gelding seemed to be adapting to the dog's presence and barely recoiled from her flying leap onto his back. Collins moved them north through Ladder Creek and back up into the stiff breeze still blowing from the west.

He calculated, from the halo of the sun behind a blanket of murky clouds, that they still had some time before sunset. Easing the horse into a faster walk, they travelled quite a distance until coming to a confluence with another stream. The area offered a thicker growth of trees and underbrush, providing a windbreak. Despite remaining daylight, Collins chose a small hollow for a campsite and unloaded his livestock with alacrity. He rubbed them down with a saddle blanket, gave each of them a good ration of oats and picketed Ulysses and Joey. He dug beneath the trees for dry wood to start a fire, then gathered more to stack in a pile nearby. He pitched his tent and arranged the campsite before making a meal. By this time, the sun was down.

Exhausted, Collins slept hard. Despite this, he woke before sunrise and stepped out of the tent to relieve himself. The dog followed him into the wintry air of predawn. Fully awake, he checked on his horse and mules and began packing his gear. According to the map, he was nearing the Smoky Hill River and, if so, could make Fort

Wallace by the end of the day. He had hoped to shoot a deer or antelope by now and had not purchased a sufficient quantity of meat beyond the salt pork. He was anxious for a change of diet and for news from Secretary Schurz and the officers at the fort. The day was barely breaking as he rode back into the open prairie, heading steadily northward toward the river. He thought he could hear gunfire far off in the distance.

As the sun ascended to mid-morning in a cloudy sky, C.W. noticed a wagon on the northeastern skyline. Not particularly desiring to meet up with anyone, he began angling in a more westerly direction, knowing he would still encounter the Smoky Hill River. Coming over a small rise, Collins rode right up on two men intent on skinning a freshly killed buffalo. One of the men wore a heavily stained hat with the brim pushed up and displayed a full beard, thick and crusted with some type of substance, possibly food or blood. He was thickset and bulky. The other fellow was more or less clean-shaven, gaunt, and was adorned in a tattered derby hat and filthy patchwork leather coat. Ulysses snorted at the smell of blood and both men jerked to their feet, clearly ready for any eventuality.

"Whatt'er you after?" the big man asked gruffly.

"Nothing," Collins answered, resting his hand on the butt of his Colt.

"Then why'r you here?" the hunter asked, combatively.

The gelding danced around uneasily and Collins had to rein him in. Gal growled almost inaudibly. "My purposes are just that," he said.

"What?"

"My purposes."

The wagon was moving nearer. Collins did not care to contend with a third or fourth member of this unsavory company. He could smell them now, despite a stiff breeze, and he badly wished to depart.

"Air you bein' cute?"

Apparently, the slender man did not speak or was not allowed to. He contented himself with squinting malevolently at C.W.

Collins nudged his horse forward. "I am leaving," he said, purposefully abrupt, knowing this would further confound the pair of dunderheads.

The wagon had almost arrived. While holding the lines of a distinctly undernourished team of rawboned horses in one hand, a grizzled old man had a large caliber rifle aimed unswervingly in Collins' direction, the barrel supported by one knee. Thoroughly belligerent now, Collins jerked his Winchester from its scabbard. He summarily levered a round into the chamber, cocked the hammer and pointed it at the driver.

"I am leaving," he said again flatly. "Do not attempt to stop me or I will kill one or more of you."

"Hey Digger, get shed of that gun," the big man yelled, waving his bloody skinning knife. "You air gonna get us kilt."

Collins rode off to the northwest. Wrapping his reins around the horn, he pulled his Colt and turned in the saddle to keep both his carbine and revolver aimed at the mangy assemblage. The group stayed motionless as if frozen, watching him steadily as he moved away. Knowing the reach of a Sharps Big Fifty rifle, such as the one held by the wagon driver, he did not experience relief until he descended into a shallow coulee and used it for cover to travel out of range. If those men and Shadler, back in Dodge City, were authentic specimens of the buffalo hunter breed, he thought as he put distance behind him, then the wholesale slaughter of the great herds was made that much more heinous.

11

Fort Wallace rose out of the plains, its unimaginative architecture looking like so many children's toy wooden blocks. A few wind-blown leafless trees dotted the area around what looked to be the officers' quarters, but the remainder of the fort was open and without even a nod at protection from ceaseless gales. There were quite a few buildings, more than Collins had expected, and a fair population of cattle, hogs and horses roamed the locale or sheltered in the lee of structures. He had forded the Smoky Hill River without difficulty, it being short of water and mostly frozen, and found the outpost by its profile on the otherwise unfettered skyline.

A few troopers were lounging around the east side of a building, hunkered down out of the ubiquitous and numbing wind. Collins rode over to ask directions to the post adjutant's office. One of the soldiers cheerfully directed him to the northeast corner of the parade grounds. Angling across the open and deserted clearing, he dismounted in front of a modest L-shaped building and tied his animals to the hitching rail at the front, easing their cinches. He pushed Gal gently to the ground and told her to stay.

After knocking, he walked into the office. A fussy looking officer was seated to the right of the adjutant's desk, behind which sat a beefy man with captain's insignia.

"Yes?" asked the captain.

"I wish to speak with the post commander, if possible."

"What is this regarding?" asked the other officer.

C.W. noticed he was a light colonel. "Are you he?"

"I am Lieutenant-Colonel Van Voast."

The man was balding, with a receding chin and moist, pouting mouth. He gave the general impression of asthenia and lack of mental vigor. Collins had heard of Van Voast. He had been shunted from one remote frontier post to another and was known to be accident prone and an inveterate busy body. His presence in Fort Wallace seemed to be an indication of the army's failing interest in the site's continued usefulness.

"My name is Charles Wolfe Collins. I am currently employed by the Pinkerton Agency to investigate the escape and capture of the Cheyennes."

"And why would the Pinkerton Agency be interested in those renegades?" Van Voast asked perfunctorily.

Collins noted that he had not been invited to sit. "We have a client who is interested."

The adjutant had been observing him closely. "The U.S. Army does not answer to clients," he told Collins disparagingly.

He smiled. "Perhaps not, but this client is fairly illustrious and I am certain you are acquainted with the political influence of Allan Pinkerton."

Van Voast came to his feet, apparently agitated. "Come, come, gentlemen. Let us be amiable. The evening is upon us and we can billet you in the unoccupied laundress quarters. I assume you have a horse?"

"A horse and two pack mules."

"Well the stable is just south of your lodgings. Make use of it and feed your animals accordingly. Captain Wheeler here can show you. Please come to dine at my quarters on the northwest corner of the parade grounds as soon as you are settled." Van Voast turned to the adjutant. "See to our guest, Captain."

"Yessir." The man did not salute his superior officer.

"Excuse me, Mr. Collins. I have some business to attend to."

Van Voast exited the office, closing the door loudly behind him. C.W. thought the man seemed not quite in command of himself.

"You frightened him," Captain Wheeler said.

"What?"

"Any hint of a potential slur on his character terrifies him."

Collins decided that the captain was not a particularly pleasant individual. "I see. Well, then I would appreciate you directing me to my quarters."

Captain Wheeler pushed past and went out the door, deliberately not pausing to wait while C.W. gathered up his animals. Gal came out from under the porch of the building and followed as he led Ulysses and his mules after the adjutant. When he caught up with him, the officer pointed to a rough lumber shack with a few shingles missing from the roof.

"You can billet here. The cavalry stable is down there and you will find hay in the north barn. That is the mess hall and kitchen over there."

Wheeler walked away before Collins could ask about the post trader or possible supplies from the quartermaster, as he had intended. He opened the door of the habitation and looked in. He found one room with a badly rusted Franklin stove, a solitary broken window and holes in the planked floor chewed through by pack rats. The place smelled strongly of rodents. A narrow iron-framed bed, with several broken springs, occupied a corner.

Collins decided he would rather be hanged by his thumbs than spend a night in such surroundings. He walked around to the leeward outside wall of the hovel and unloaded his gear and unsaddled his animals. With Gal on his heels, he led them to the stables, found an unused and fairly clean pen in a corner of the barn and filled the hay bunk from a mound of hay piled loosely nearby. Most of the stalls were filthy and generally empty. The balance of the cavalry mounts seemed to be roaming freely about the fort.

It occurred to him that the overall condition of the post appeared to be dilapidated and in need of repair. The soldiers he had so far encountered were partially out of uniform, disheveled and looked to be predominantly unwashed. Van Voast and Wheeler, as officers, were presentable enough, but C.W. suspected they were the exception rather than the rule. He knew from experience that remote forts tended to slip the moors of discipline and slide into the unruly manifestations of pervasive ennui.

Back with his belongings, he prepared a makeshift camp. Without trees, he was unable to pitch the tent. There was no available firewood, but he could do without it for one night and he intended to depart the next day. He brushed off his clothing, tied Gal to a packsaddle with a pigging string and patted her head reassuringly. He filled an enamelware bowl with water from his canteen and placed it nearby. The sun was swiftly setting, so he carried the hurricane lantern with him as he walked across the parade grounds toward the well-lit dwelling he surmised was the post commander's quarters. A man in civilian clothing was standing by the door awaiting admittance when Collins climbed the steps to the porch.

"Good evening," the man said. "I am Assistant Surgeon James Finley."

Collins held out a hand. "I am Charles Wolfe Collins."

The door opened and a young orderly invited them in. Lt. Col. Van Voast was standing by a fireplace with a glass of wine in his hand. Captain Wheeler was seated in a library chair off to the side. Collins found it interesting that more officers were not present.

"Hello, hello," Van Voast said. "Roger, fetch them

some wine."

"I would prefer coffee if you have it," Collins told him.

"Of course...Roger, some coffee for Mr. Collins, if you will. And Finley?"

"Coffee for me as well, please sir."

The orderly left the room. Collins placed his hat on a sideboard and took a seat in an oak rocker. The surgeon found a stuffed armchair.

"Is this your first time to Fort Wallace?" Finley asked conversationally.

"It is."

"And where do you hail from?"

"Ireland."

"Thought I picked up an accent," Wheeler said disagreeably.

"But you have been in America a long time, have you not?" the surgeon interjected quickly.

"I have. Since '49"

"Did you fight in Mr. Lincoln's War?"

"I did."

"I was in medical school at Rutgers."

"A worthwhile endeavor, nonetheless."

"How do you find your accommodations?" Van Voast asked Collins, interrupting the discourse.

Collins glanced at Wheeler, who was watching him slyly. "Acceptable."

The orderly returned without the coffee. "Dinner is prepared," he said.

They all moved into a small dining room and seated themselves around an oval table covered in a lace tablecloth. A plump woman, probably an enlisted man's wife, served dishes of hominy, beef steaks, stewed apples, stale bread and mashed turnips with onions. It all looked rather unappetizing, including the meat, which was cooked thoroughly and dry as whang leather. Collins thought the fare to be outstandingly dreary, considering the fort was in close proximity to the Kansas Pacific Railway and therefore had access to finer comestibles. The plates were passed around and everyone began to eat. The orderly finally brought cups of coffee to C.W. and the surgeon.

"So tell me, Mr. Collins," Van Voast said, stoutly working at cutting up his steak. "What do you wish to know about the Cheyenne renegades?"

Taking a sip of coffee to help wash down a bite of beef, Collins said, "I wanted to know if they passed near here. Did you engage them?"

"My men of the Sixteenth Infantry were relentlessly scouting the area around the post after Colonel Lewis engaged the Indians southwest of here on Punished Woman's Fork. I had a supply train fully loaded with provisions equipped and ready should they encounter the brutes, but they slipped undetected across the tracks and headed north to ravage and murder poor settlers around Oberlin." He wiped his mouth energetically with a linen napkin until the thick bristles of his moustache protruded out in a roof over his wet lips and weak chin.

"I had heard that Lewis was killed?"

"He died in the ambulance en route to Fort Wallace. They brought him to us already deceased."

"I was not assigned here yet," Surgeon Finley told him. "I came in November. Colonel Lewis was brought in last September, I believe."

"Yes and a terrible tragedy it was," Van Voast said. "He was well-liked and respected. His body was sent home to his family in the state of New York, escorted by a member of General Pope's own staff."

"Those redskins paid a hefty price though," Captain Wheeler told him. "A couple of scouts found where they had hidden their horses and supplies. Captain Mauck, the second officer in command, ordered all the ponies killed and the packs destroyed. The Cheyennes may have escaped, but they had almost nothing with them when they left."

Collins felt ill, thinking about the slaughtered horses and the desperate people and especially about Woodchuck. "Yet they were able to pass by here unobserved?"

"It was a stroke of luck, that is all," Van Voast said defensively. "They are shrewd and cunning as nocturnal animals."

"They will be punished," Wheeler said. "There is talk that several of the murdering heathens will be sent for trial at Fort Leavenworth."

" 'Forbear to judge, for we are sinners all,' " C.W. quoted.

"That was Shakespeare, was it not?" Surgeon Finley asked, seemingly glad to change the topic of conversation.

Collins nodded. He asked, "Would it be possible for me to purchase some food stuffs here?"

"Mr. Clark is the post trader," Finley told him. "He has a place just to the northeast of the row of officers' quarters."

"Excellent. And I also need to send a telegram. Is it possible to send one from the post?"

"Your best bet is to go to Wallace Station about two miles west of here," Wheeler told him tartly. "It would be the most expedient as that is the location of the telegraph office."

The meal proceeded in idle conversation of weather, fear of another cholera outbreak and history of the fort. Collins brought up the topic of Custer and the court-martial that resulted from his leaving Fort Wallace without permission. It had been yet another transgression that Custer had nimbly dodged with the aid of his friend, Phil Sheridan. Van Voast seemed loath to criticize the man and Wheeler appeared to admire him. In the end, the discussion turned to the discovery of the fossilized monster, *Elasmosaurus*, by the post surgeon Turner back in

1867. C.W. knew about it from his friend, Captain Myles Keogh, who had been the post commander at Fort Wallace at the time.

"Yes, the fossil is housed in the Academy of Natural Sciences of Philadelphia," Finley told him. "I periodically search the area for more specimens, but alas, have been unsuccessful."

"You would be better off studying your Bible," Wheeler told him. "It is blasphemous to believe there were creatures on Earth prior to man."

Collins smiled to himself, thinking he could have prophesied the choleric man's desultory truculence. A mean spirit and a closed mind were predictable companions.

12

A small shadow materialized from under the porch as Collins took his leave from Van Voast's residence. He jumped a bit, startled, until he recognized Gal, dragging a length of the rope with which he had secured her. He lit the lantern in the shelter of the building and proceeded back across the parade grounds. Donning the bearskin coat against the growing chill of the evening, he arranged his saddles, tent and gear into a barricaded platform on which to spread out his bedroll. Digging out another can of milk, he filled the bowl for Gal and added crusts of bread he had secreted in his pocket from dinner. He then took the lantern and made his way to the stables to check on Molly, Ulysses and Joey.

His livestock were quiet and drowsy in the cramped stall. Collins looked them over briefly, threw more hay in the bunk and then returned to the lee of the shack to bed down for the night. Gal snuggled in next to him, curling up tight on the saddle blanket he arranged for her. The pounding of the wind rattled shingles on the roof above and whined eerily through the abundant gaps in the walls of the building, making it difficult for sleep to come. The stars were blurred by wisps of cloud that glided swiftly across the sky in ethereal legions. Far away, coyotes yipped and barked and one lone wolf answered.

There was a faint aura of light on the horizon when Collins awoke. He packed up his gear, hoping to find coffee at the nearby mess hall. He went to check his animals and refill the hay bunk. He replenished a water trough in the stall with buckets hauled from a stock tank outside the barn. He found an old currycomb and brushed down the horse and mules, talking to them and checking for saddle sores and girth galls. He called Gal over and groomed her as well. She wagged the stump of her tail exuberantly.

Outside, it was brighter and there was only a slight breeze blowing. Collins visited an adjacent privy, then wandered over to the mess hall. Gal sat and watched him go inside. No one was about, but he heard clamor coming from the kitchen in the back. He walked over and glanced in. There was a rotund man, attired in a private's uniform and apron, feeding kindling to a sizeable wood range. The sight of a coffeepot on the stove cheered C.W. considerably. He cleared his throat. The portly fellow swung around abruptly.

"Holy thunderation! Who in the fuck are you?"

Collins could not help chuckling at the comical expression on the poor man's ruddy countenance. "Pardon my sudden appearance. I did not mean to alarm you."

The cook wiped his weathered and beardless face with a corner of his untidy apron. "Well I sure as hell am awake if I were not before. Give a fellow some warning next time."

"I am genuinely sorry," C.W. said contritely. "In truth, I am sincerely anxious for a cup of coffee and it may have made me overeager."

"I can understand that, for sure. Grab a cup from over there and help yourself."

Collins poured some coffee and took a seat on a rough-hewn stool by the stove while the private busied himself with peeling a mountain of potatoes.

"My name is Corky Brown. Private Brown as is."

"I am Charles Collins. I am on my way north and stopped to see the commanding officer."

"Old Boasty Voasty? Nothing he could say would be useful. He has only a puny kinship with the truth."

"Is that so? I take it you are not fond of him?"

"Nobody at this post is fond of him." Brown paused to scratch his balding head with the tip of his knife. "The man is a buffoon."

"He was not long on information either." Collins got up to refill his cup. "Mind if I smoke my pipe?"

"Nope. Have at it."

Sitting down again, C.W. filled his pipe and lit it. "Were you here when the Cheyenne came through last autumn?"

"I was. Back then I was a first sergeant. Now I am as you see." Private Brown shrugged. He took an enormous frying pan from a peg on the wall and placed it on the stove, then dropped in a lump of bacon grease he spooned from an old can.

"You were a sergeant?" Collins asked. "What happened?"

"Van Voast happened. When them damn Indians snuck past us in the dark and he missed his chance at glory, there were quite a few of us that got busted down in rank."

"You were demoted because the Cheyenne were not captured?"

"Yeah. Old Voasty and Wheeler were back here guzzling who-hit-john with Colonel Davis while the rest of us was out patrolling the area and guarding the railroad tracks day after day." Brown began to slice up potatoes and toss them in the pan, making the grease sizzle loudly. "Nevertheless, they got through us and then massacred all the homesteaders up north. Van Voast and Colonel Davis took it real personal and laid the blame on any of us who was on duty when they slipped by. I imagine Voasty caught some shit off his superiors after he had postured around and made claims to stopping them savages dead in their tracks when they came near the fort."

"Ná tabhair taobh le fear."

"Pardon me?"

"Trust not a spiteful man. It is an old Irish proverb."

"There is truth in it, sure enough."

"Still, busting you down in rank hardly seems fair, given you did your best."

"Been in the army for a long damn time. Nothing about it seems fair." Brown scraped at the potatoes with a spatula.

"Were you in the war?"

"Was in the 13th Indiana Infantry Regiment. '61 to '65. That your dog?"

The back door of the kitchen was cracked open to let out some of the heat from the big cook stove. Gal had found her way around the building and was poking her head through the opening.

"She is mine."

"I like dogs. Always had them when I was a boy."

Collins put his spent pipe in a coat pocket, stood up and placed his cup by a wash basin. He could hear soldiers entering the mess hall. "Thank you for the coffee."

"You want breakfast? Be glad to feed you."

"I want to get over the post trader's outfit. Could I perhaps come back for some leftovers?"

"Sure. There is always something. Will have scraps for the dog too."

Collins went out the back door and walked north in the direction of the row of officers' houses, with Gal following close behind. The sun was now up in a cloudless sky, but a rising breeze took away any warmth it provided. He headed toward a stone building that stood off by itself. Smoke blew sideways from a chimney. He climbed the steps and walked in the door, closing it behind him and leaving Gal to wait for him outside. A makeshift door in the back of the store opened on leather hinges and a tall, angular man walked out.

"Hello," he said, holding out a hand to shake. "My name's Alfred Clark. You looking for something in particular?"

"I am looking to purchase bread and meat, for the most part."

"You are in luck. Mrs. Babik, a corporal's wife, just brought in several fresh loaves and I bought an antelope off of a nester yesterday."

"I would like to purchase as much of each as you can spare."

"I will pack it up for you. Look around while you wait." Clark returned to the back room.

Warming his hands by the stove, Collins glanced around the room. There were shelves stacked with air-tights, tea, sugar, woolen blankets, molasses, canned milk, tobacco, shaving soap, pickles and tins of soda crackers and biscuits. A worn countertop was strewn with a variety of knives, poor quality clay pipes, trinkets and a nickel-plated derringer. All manner of enamelware basins, galvanized pails and barrels occupied the floor. The premises appeared to offer the customary sutler wares of ambiguous value. Now that the Kansas Pacific ran through close by, Clark was probably not thriving in local trade. Collins figured he must be selling liquor on the side. Most of them did.

Clark returned carrying a bulging flour sack and a tied paper bundle. "Here is your meat," he said, setting the flour sack down on the counter with a thud. "It is double wrapped in waxed paper, so it cannot leak blood. And here," he added, laying down the paper package, "is four loaves of bread. It was all I can spare."

"I will also purchase some hard cheese, jerked meat and some dried apples, if you have them."

"Sure do. Wait a tick. Have to get it out of the cellar."

In a short while, Clark showed up again with a small

wheel of cheese coated in wax and a cotton sack each of dried apples and jerky.

"How much do I owe you?"

"Let us see here...I will give you the meat for fifteen cents a pound, so at five pounds that is seventy-five cents, the bread is ten cents a loaf, apples are ten cents a pound and cheese is eighteen cents a pound." Clark did his figuring on a scrap of paper. "All told, that is a dollar and seventy-five cents. Will throw in the jerky as it is a trifle stale."

Collins thought the provisions were a tad expensive, but handed Clark two silver dollars. The sutler dug around in a cash box and gave him two bits in change.

"Where you headed?" Clark asked.

"North."

"Well, good luck to you and thanks for the trade."

"Glad to have the meat. Was tired of salt pork."

Outside, Gal was no where to be found. C.W. whistled and called, but could not find her. He began walking south toward his camp, his arms loaded with bundles, saddened by the thought he may have lost his little companion. He stowed the meat and other food in a pannier and hung it on a rusted spike, previously nailed into the siding of the shack for some purpose or other. He did not want the pack rats or other scavengers to get into his supplies. Quite hungry, he decided to return to the mess hall to find some breakfast.

13

"I really kind of feel sorry for those Indians," Private Brown told Collins. They were sitting at a slab table in the corner of the kitchen, drinking coffee. Collins had just finished a plate of fried potatoes and a thick slice of ham.

"That so?" he asked, warily.

"Yeah. First, they were sent down to Indian Territory and nearly starved to death. Then they were hunted like dogs all the way north and finally were locked up and starved again."

"You heard about that?" C.W. asked, taking out his pipe.

"We all heard about it. Damn shame, little children and all." There came a sound of insistent barking by the back door. "I think your dog is out there."

Collins went to open the door and found Gal outside, wagging her tail avidly. He was more pleased to see her than he cared to admit. "Where have you been?" he asked her, noting a trace of blood on her muzzle.

"Let her in," Brown told him, filling a plate with scraps.

Collins beckoned the dog inside. The cook took the plate to her and set it on the floor. She hesitated, looking at Collins.

"Good girl," he told her and leaned down to push the food closer to her. She ate swiftly, licking the plate thoroughly, then lay down by C.W.'s chair.

"I could use a dog like that," Brown told him.

"I found her out in the middle of the prairie. Skin and bones, but she does know how to hunt." He relit his pipe. "I have gotten used to having her now."

Brown put more wood in the stove and damped it down. "As I was saying, the troopers really had no reason to shoot all of those poor Indians down just 'cause they broke out and tried to run for it," he said, refilling their cups and returning to his chair.

"No. It was shameful." Collins was mildly surprised to find a soldier with such unconventional opinions. "What do you think would have happened if the 16th could have caught them near here?"

"Van Voast would have behaved just like most of them. Too many of the officers out west are eager to make a reputation. They want to return east with a good story to tell. Custer was that way."

"You ever serve under him?"

Brown took a big drink of coffee. "Naw. My company was strictly assigned to duties down south until '77. Have heard enough from troopers who knew him, though. Figured he got what was coming."

"He sacrificed an assemblage of worthy men, even if he deserved his own fate," Collins said, getting up to knock the ashes out of his pipe in the stove. "I lost a good friend." Unwelcome memories of the battlefield came back to him. He regained his chair and changed the topic of discussion. "The Colonel Davis who was here last fall...was that Colonel Jefferson C. Davis?"

"It were."

"He is the officer who shot General Nelson back in '62."

"I had not heard of it."

"He was not punished, due to the war, but he has been under a cloud since."

"Like I said, all these officers have somewhat to prove. Does not do much for the rest of us."

"No, ambition tends to scapegoat. As Shakespeare wrote, 'vaulting ambition o'erleaps itself.' Well, I should be going," C.W. said, retrieving his Stetson from a peg on the wall. "Thank you for the breakfast."

"Sure. Hey, let me pack up a little ham for you and the dog." Private Brown wrapped a rather large slab of the meat in a towel and gave it to Collins.

They shook hands at the door and Brown patted Gal on the head. She moved away timidly.

"Hope you get reinstated soon," Collins told him.

"Probably a cold day in hell, but maybe when Van Voast gets shipped off somewhere."

Back at his meager camp, Collins added the ham to the other food in the pannier. Clouds were building and he wanted to be on his way so to send a telegram to Schurz. He was packing his gear when Finley, the assistant surgeon, found him.

"I heard Van Voast sent you over here," he said. "That was a cruel joke."

"Short on hospitality, anyway. I am currently headed for Wallace Station."

"I came by to invite you to stay at my quarters at the hospital. They are humble, but better than this."

"Very kind of you, but I need to send a telegram and keep traveling."

"I have heard you are with the Pinkertons?" Finley leaned against the wall of the shack, out of the wind.

"I am." Collins continued to organize his belongings.

"Sounds rather official."

Collins stopped his packing and looked at the surgeon judiciously. "I am seeking useful information. Anything that pertains to the journey of the Cheyennes through Kansas."

Finley crossed his arms and studied Collins. "It is possible that a few soldiers were not as vigilant as they might have been."

"What? When?"

"When the Indians came through."

"Is that so?" C.W. observed him with curiosity. "Are

you saying some of them turned a blind eye?"

He hesitated before answering. "Maybe I am saying that some of the troopers were more compassionate than others. That contemporary procedures of the War Department may not appear to be entirely just, in every happenstance."

"And they confided in you?"

"Perhaps...thinking I might be sympathetic."

"And you are trusting me with this information?" Collins asked wryly.

"It may be useful."

"Perhaps. Perhaps it would be more useful if I could speak with one of these soldiers."

"I believe you have already met one of them," Finley said, with a slight smile.

"Brown."

The surgeon nodded.

"Perhaps I *will* stay another night."

Finley left and returned with a couple of enlisted men who hauled Collins' tack over to the stables, leaving the food pack safely suspended on the leeward wall of the old laundress quarters. Finley suggested he turn his animals into a larger corral so they could move about more freely. Then, with the other men's assistance, they transferred the rest of his belongings to the hospital and Finley's quarters. Along the way, they passed soldiers employed by various duties, such as digging a new privy hole near a barracks building, chopping firewood and shoveling manure from the parade grounds. The surgeon paused to speak to a couple of troopers and seemed to be on friendly terms with all of them. A young private passing by sought to play with Gal, but she dodged behind Collins.

A small stove lent welcome warmth to Finley's quarters in an annex of the hospital. The day had become raw and flurries of snow had begun to blow through the grounds of the fort. Inside the main room of the hospital, a group of men were playing cards. There was a great deal of joking and ragging involved in the game.

"Just put your belongings down over there," Finley told Collins. "I will have an extra cot brought in."

"Are any of those men actually ill?" C.W. asked.

"A couple of busted limbs, a toothache, various respiratory complaints. Some of the boys are just visiting. Beats the hell out of being exposed to the elements or hanging around the barracks when off duty. Boredom is the greatest enemy of these fellows."

Collins had come to realize that Finley was one of those entirely reasonable men. It seemed that every situation was dealt with in an even-handed and logical manner, tempered with a degree of kindness.

"Come, let us go speak with Private Brown," Finley said, banking the fire in the stove. "I believe he is expecting us."

"He sent you to me?"

"He did."

They stepped back into the blustery late morning, the surgeon again greeting the men they passed en route to the enlisted men's mess hall on the east side of the fort. A group of hearty souls were playing a game of base-ball on the southern end of the parade grounds, occasionally pummeled by bouts of sleety snow. Collins remarked on the overall lack of hygiene and neatness of habiliment he had observed among the soldiers.

"Yes, it is a constant source of frustration to me. That and the theft of my medicinal stores of alcohol. Lieutenant-Colonel Van Voast is singularly ineffectual in promoting personal cleanliness or instilling military discipline," Finley told him, shaking his head.

"I assume this would cause more health issues for you to contend with?"

"It does indeed. Especially during the winter."

Finley led the way into the kitchen.

"I have brought Mr. Collins back," he said.

Private Brown was dicing onions, tears streaming down his leathery cheeks. "Help yourself to coffee. I am almost finished with this beastly task."

Finley and Collins filled their cups and sat at the table out of the cook's way.

"Bring your dog?" Brown asked, scraping onions from the cutting board into a big pot of beans on the stove.

"She is outside."

"Well, let her in, dammit. I like that critter."

C.W. went to the door and called to Gal. She followed him to the table and lay down beneath it.

"What happened to her ears?" the surgeon asked.

"They were frozen, I think. I only found her a few days ago. She found me, truth be told."

"Poor girl," Finley said.

" 'A friend should bear a friend's infirmities.' "

"Shakespeare again?"

"Again."

"What is this about infirmities?" Brown asked, coming over to sit at the table. He leaned down and tossed a piece of bread to Gal.

"Mr. Collins knows Shakespeare," Finley told him.

"So I learned. By god, that is admirable. He is too much for me."

Collins smiled. "I cannot imagine anything being too much for you."

"I will take that as a compliment."

"As well you should."

Cradling the heavy chinaware cup in his hands, Collins asked, "Was there some information you wished to impart to me?"

"Well...I was not entirely frank with you before. 'Fin' here told me you are with the Pinkertons. What exactly are you wanting to find out?"

"I am merely gathering intelligence regarding the truth of what happened to the Cheyennes as they fled north," he said. "The truth that may not necessarily agree with the official military version."

Brown sighed deeply. "Poor buggers, running for their lives and never given a chance to rest."

"The Indians?"

"They lost everything in the battle with Captain Lewis. All their horses, their food, everything. We heard it from the soldiers of the 19th that came with Lewis in the ambulance."

"And so some of you chose to lower your guard during the patrols along the railway?"

Brown looked over at Finley. "A few of us were over toward Monument, assigned to join the 4th Cavalry in an attempt to stop the Cheyennes from continuing north. Van Voast and Davis wanted the accolades and so did Captain Mauck, who had taken over from Lewis. Colonel Dodge was somewhere about, but later it turned out he had not strictly followed orders and Davis blamed him for letting the Indians slip by. There was a bit of a stir, I can tell you."

"I heard that Van Voast and Dodge had been at each other over who should take command." Finley interjected. "Which is why General Pope sent Davis here."

"Many of the soldiers were wanting to wreak violence of their own, afraid it was their last bid to engage any Indians and bragging about taking scalps and..." Brown shrugged. "Well you can imagine."

"I can indeed," Collins said.

"A few of us were down the line farther east. It was night, but we caught the sound of movement. We just agreed right then and there that we had heard nothing and moved back west away from the place. They got through and we claimed ignorance. It was better than allowing the slaughter of women and children."

"They had heard most of the fleeing Cheyenne were women and children," Finley said.

"That is what we heard from the soldiers with the ambulance," Brown said, nodding. "That there were only a few warriors."

"Van Voast must have suspected something if he demoted some of you," Collins said.

"Mauck was the one to put the blame on us, but he had no actual proof. Voasty used it as an excuse to deflect from his own empty bombast. I do not regret what we did. None of us do. We just feel sorry for those folks that got massacred up north. I know one of the sergeants with the 23rd Infantry under Dodge. They got there right after it happened and he told me it was entire devastation."

"The Indians were desperate," Finley said. "If they had not lost all their supplies and horses in their fight with Captain Lewis, then they might not have attacked the homesteaders."

"Quite possibly," C.W. agreed.

"Now we are receiving reports that the troops out of Camp Robinson are picking the rest of them off piecemeal," Finley said. "There have been running skirmishes since they broke out."

"Do you think we did wrong in letting them get past us?" Brown asked, ruefully.

"I believe you weighed duty with compassion and that is never wrong."

Finley observed Collins thoughtfully. "May we assume you will not make any report that could damage Private Brown's military profession?"

"Such as it is," Brown said, sardonically.

"Certainly not," Collins said. "My interest only lies in reporting any information not included in official accounts. And I would not want to destroy such an illustrious career," he added with a smile.

"Too right," Finley said, laughing. "Corky loves being a cook."

"It is preferable to working in that pest hole of a hospital."

The sound of men coming into the mess hall ended their conversation.

"Will you stay to eat?" Brown asked.

"We will leave you to your duties," Finley told him. "I will take him to dine in the pest hole."

Brown grinned. "Fair enough."

Collins and Brown shook hands.

"Good luck to you," Brown said.

"And to you."

FORT WALLACE

14

"It is rather unusual that a group of soldiers chose altruism over personal recognition and military obligation," Collins said, as they leaned against the wind, walking back to the hospital. He noticed that the baseball game had broken up.

"The Cheyennes were lucky that Brown's companions were of the same mind. One defector and all would have been lost."

Back at the hospital, they arrived in time for the noon meal, placed upon tables at the end of the long room. A couple of patients were served in their beds by the steward, a very young man named Private Oscar Davis. The meal consisted of corn bread, baked beans with side meat and stewed apples with raisins.

"Do you have problems with scurvy?" Collins asked.

"Used to, in Arizona Territory, where I was posted before. I have learned to encourage vegetable gardens, with limited success, and the regular consumption of fresh meat, onions and vinegar. This post did not have assigned mess cooks until the last couple of years. Prior to that, according to my predecessor, enlisted men served in the capacity for ten days at a time and much chaos ensued."

"I can well imagine."

After the meal, Finley and Collins took cups of coffee and retired to the surgeon's quarters, where they could converse freely.

"Where is your dog?" the surgeon asked.

"Outside."

"You may bring her in, if you care to. It appears to be snowing again."

Collins opened the back door and whistled. After a moment, Gal came around the corner of the building, her coat matted with snow, and yipped excitedly when she saw him.

"Come on girl," he called. She cautiously entered the room and lay down by the door.

"I had a dog, a little spaniel, when I first arrived here, but he was kicked in the head by one of the horses last December," Finley told Collins.

"Sorry to hear it."

"Army life is vastly improved by having a dog," the surgeon said, almost wistfully.

"Tell me more of the series of skirmishes that have been taking place since the breakout at Camp Robinson," Collins said, settling back into his chair and taking out his pipe.

"We have been receiving intelligence that soldiers of the 3rd Cavalry have been engaging the Cheyenne at various places as they flee toward the north. They have killed or captured more Indians and several troopers have been wounded or killed."

Collins shook his head, pulling on his pipe thoughtfully. "There cannot be that many of the Indians left. I simply cannot understand why they will not just let the survivors go."

"They are going so far as to burn any cavalry horse that is slain, to keep the starving Indians from eating it."

"God's teeth... *Mairg do bhíonn i dtír gan duine aige féin.*"

"What is that?"

"It is the Irish, the Gaelic language. Woe to him who is in a country where there is none to take his part."

"There may have been some sympathy for the plight of the Cheyennes before Decatur County, but after the depredations there, all compassion evaporated."

"And yet what worse crimes have been committed by the military and civilian governments against the Indians."

"True. It seems you have witnessed some of these crimes?"

Collins nodded. "I have. And only recently has the utter destruction of the buffalo herds been made entirely evident to me. The brutality of manifest destiny knows no bounds."

" 'Man's inhumanity to man makes countless thousands mourn.' "

"You know Burns."

"A very little. But the quote does seem fitting, for even within my own profession there are barbaric men. For example, I have been acquainted with a few post surgeons who seek specimens of dead Indians for anatomical research...virtual grave robbers who dissect and extract skeletal remains. Post Surgeon E.B. Mosely, up at Fort Robinson, is known to be exceedingly grisly and it has been reported to me that he has secured the heads of some of the Cheyenne people who fled the barracks and were killed on the parade grounds. He has boiled the flesh from these gruesome trophies and intends to ship the skulls to the Army Medical Museum in Washington."

"Whenever I have determined that I cannot be further confounded by human cruelty," Collins said, "I am once more shocked by some new revulsion."

"It seems we remove their humanity in order to treat them as less than human."

The two men sat in silence for a moment, lost in their own thoughts and listening to the wind rattle the windows. Suddenly, there was a commotion in the main room of the hospital. They could hear excited voices and acclamation. The steward came running into the room.

"They caught 'em, they caught 'em!" he exclaimed.

Gal jumped up and began barking.

"Calm down, Davis," Finley said. "What in the hell are you saying?"

"The boys of the 3rd Cavalry! They ran the savages down!" The young man pranced about as if the floor was on fire. The dog retreated under Collins' chair, growling.

Collins came to his feet and walked to a window. "Do you mean the Cheyennes?" he asked quietly.

"All dead, or nearly. Caught 'em in a hole up north of the fort yesterday morning. Captain Wessells was wounded and around six soldiers were killed, but they got 'em. They are done for and no more murderin' of white folks."

Finley and Collins exchanged looks.

"Davis," the surgeon said, "you need to calm down. Where did you hear this?"

"It is all over the post. Message came in and Captain Wheeler spread the news."

"I am certain he did," Finley said under his breath. "Okay, get back to your duties."

The steward came to himself. "Yes sir," he said and left the room.

"I will need to ride over to Wallace Station to send a telegram," C.W. told Finley, tucking away his spent pipe.

"It is only about two miles to the northwest. Angle a little north and you will find the railroad tracks. You can easily get there and back before supper. And I can keep your dog safe with me."

"I would be grateful. I must go as quickly as possible."

Collins knelt and stroked Gal's head. He retrieved the long silk scarf and bearskin coat from his pile of belongings. Then he went out the door, almost sprinting through the fort toward the stables. He caught up Ulysses, saddled him hurriedly, donned the coat and tied his hat down with the scarf. Joey brayed loudly as he led Ulysses away from the barn. He mounted and kicked the gelding into a lope, crossing the parade grounds and skirting the row of officers' quarters into open country.

The terrain around the fort was predominantly flat and the horse seemed content with escaping the confines of the stables and attendant lack of activity. Collins slowed the animal to a trot, not wanting to push him too hard. The wind slowed their progress with its incessant resistance from the west, but despite this, Collins found the railroad quickly and followed the tracks west into a moderately populated town. He located the telegraph office without difficulty and dismounted, securing his gelding to a post.

Inside the cramped building, he greeted a squat red-headed man behind the counter and requested a blank. He reached into an inside pocket for his bill book, wherein he had slipped Schurz' instructions for sending a telegram.

> Wallace Station Jan 23 1879
> To Herr Burschenschaft
> Report 3rd of Cav
> caught Cheyenne twenty-second instant
> Killed most Please advise how to proceed
> Will return for reply tomorrow
> CWCollins

"Send this to the Willard Hotel in Washington D.C.," he told the operator. "How much?"

The man took a pencil from behind a rather large ear and counted the words, making a tally. "Two dollars and ten cents."

Collins gave the man a gold eagle. "I will return tomorrow morning," he said. "I will be expecting an answer. My name is Charles Wolfe Collins."

The operator nodded and handed him his change. "I

will look for your reply, sir. Never fear. Exciting news about the soldiers up in Nebraska, is it not?"

"News?" C.W. asked, not wanting to discuss it.

"That the Cheyenne are mostly done away with. The troopers out of Camp Robinson finally paid them back for their crimes up on the Sappa."

"Oh, I see," he said noncommittally. The man seemed crestfallen at his lack of enthusiasm.

Outside, he tightened his cinch and swung into the saddle. He rode through town, surprised by the number of buildings and apparent population. The Kansas Pacific Railway was probably bounded by small boom towns similar to Wallace Station, prospering from homesteaders, sightseers and cattle ranchers. Small wonder, he thought, the Indians hated the railroads so fervently. They brought commerce and growing numbers of white inhabitants. He even remembered hearing a story of a band of Cheyenne warriors who successfully derailed a Union Pacific freight train back in '67. Courageous, but, in the end, futile.

15

Back at the fort, Collins spent time with his animals in the stables. He rubbed Ulysses down thoroughly, even though he had kept him to a walk most of the return trip from Wallace. He brought the mules back inside the barn, grained them from a bin of oats, brushed them and filled their bunk with hay. Molly shoved him repeatedly with her nose while Joey rested his head on his shoulder, almost bending him over double. It seemed they were all anxious to move on, including C.W.

Outside, the day was dying in pale rose and slate blue colors drawn along the skyline. Skiffs of snow sketched the windward sides of some of the buildings and the temperature was dropping. He entered the hospital to find another unruly game of cards taking place. Finley was attending to a patient on the other side of the spacious chamber. Collins went into the surgeon's quarters and found his dog lying by the stove. She wagged her stubby tail so ardently that her entire body shook. He knelt down and patted her head and rubbed her ears.

"She was not pleased with me," Finley said, coming into the room.

"How is that?" Collins asked, getting to his feet.

"She desperately wanted to follow you. I only was able to calm her down a short while ago. She is very devoted and yet you said you found her just recently?"

Collins nodded.

"She is a good little dog. Any more news in town?" the

surgeon asked, pouring a cup of coffee and handing it to C.W.

"Thanks," he said, sitting down. "I really only spoke to the telegraph operator. It seems he was delighted with the outcome."

"Predictable, I suppose." Finley took a seat, opened a tin box on a nearby parlor table and brought out a Parejo cigar. "May I offer you one?"

"No thank you. I prefer my pipe."

Slicing off the end with a pen knife, Finley lit the cigar and smoked with obvious relish. "What are your plans now?" he asked.

"I will leave early in the morning and return to Wallace Station. I am expecting a telegram. From there, I will travel north."

"I have the impression that there is more to you and your sojourn here than you have articulated. I wish you would tell me what precisely you are searching for, but I suppose you cannot."

"I am under strict orders to tell no one."

The dog barked softly. They heard footfalls approaching and Captain Wheeler entered the quarters unannounced.

"So it is true. You are still here," he said, going over to the stove and looking at Collins.

"As you see."

Finley was frowning at the intrusion.

Wheeler held his hands out to the heat. "Lieutenant-Colonel Van Voast was wondering what other information you wish to discover. There really is nothing else, now the heathens have been brought to ground."

"Is he ordering me to depart?" C.W. asked without emotion.

"See here, Wheeler," Finley said, coming to his feet. "I do not appreciate you barging into my quarters without an invitation. It is simply not done."

There was a pause as the captain contemplated the surgeon with disdain. "As adjutant," he finally said, "I have absolute authority to go where I damned well please...without having to request permission from some sissified croaker."

Finley started forward, but Collins rose and stepped between him and Wheeler. "What in the hell are you about?" he asked the captain.

"Simply this," he said with the hint of a derisive smile, "Van Voast wants me to inform you that he requests your presence this evening in his quarters."

Collins gazed steadily down at the man from his greater stature and returned the mirthless smile. "For what reason?"

"He desires to know the true nature of your mission and the name of your client. He is in command of this post, after all."

Finley walked over and regained his seat, crossing his legs and relighting his cigar, now apparently quite calm. "He does not have the prerogative to mandate Mr. Collins' attendance," he said nonchalantly through a cloud of smoke.

Collins also returned to his chair and sat down. "You may tell him I am leaving in the early morning and will not be venturing forth this evening."

Captain Wheeler stared at him. "I could have you placed in the guardhouse."

"You could," Collins said, taking out his pipe and tobacco pouch. "But you need to be very clear on one point." He packed the bowl of his pipe with great deliberation.

"What point?" Wheeler finally asked impatiently.

"Pinkerton has very influential allies and therefore, by proxy, so do I. You might remind Van Voast of that. From what you have told me, this may have quite an effect."

Wheeler stood staring at him ineffectually, plainly aggrieved. After a long moment, he spun on his heel and left without another word.

"What do you suppose he will do now?" C.W. asked.

"Most probably report to Van Voast that he could not find you. I do not believe he will want to admit to having been circumvented," the surgeon said, grinning.

"What an unpleasant fellow. Pray, what have you done to annoy him so?"

"I thwarted him in his efforts to severely discipline an enlisted man for drunkenness. Wheeler can exhibit a most pronounced predisposition for cruelty."

"That I can believe."

They discussed various topics until Davis informed them that supper was being served. They repaired to the dining tables in the hospital. The food was again bland and unimaginative, but Collins was no stranger to dire hunger and was seldom one to eschew a hearty meal. He managed to pocket some scraps for Gal. One of the patients seated near him held forth in a prolonged rant about the necessity of "giving the Indians an overdue lesson in manners." He was a particularly unappealing and ignorant lout with pustulous carbuncles all over his face and neck.

Collins quickly wearied of the man's harangue and retired to Finley's room. He was reminded that the frontier regulars of the U.S. Army in the western states and territories were not generally the best and the brightest. Meager pay, strict and occasionally harsh discipline, and a pervasive lack of creature comforts did not attract the upper echelons of society to the departments of the Missouri, Platte or Dakota. Too frequently, the enlisted force was comprised of poor urban immigrants, criminal classes, deviants and drunkards. Unquestionably, the average level of education lent itself to bigotry and gullibility in the ranks. It was a state of affairs that did not bode well for Indian populations of the Great Plains.

In the morning, Collins arose before dawn and organized his gear. He made his way to the stables in the early light and saddled his animals, tying Joey to the pigging string on Molly's saddle and leading them to the deserted laundress quarters to fetch the food pannier, relieved to find it undisturbed. Returning to the hospital, he tethered his stock and found that Finley had made coffee. Together they loaded his belongings on the saddles, adjusting the packs for balance and securing everything with diamond hitches. After drinking his fill of coffee and saying his farewells to the affable surgeon, Collins checked his cinches one more time, gave Gal a lift up and swung onto his gelding. The sun was barely visible as he rode out of Fort Wallace heading north toward the railroad tracks.

FRONTIER TOWN

16

Wallace Station was quite barren of activity when Collins rode up to the telegraph office. He secured his animals and tried the door. It opened and he found the same red-headed operator napping on his arms in front of the apparatus.

"Hello," he said.

The man roused himself, stretching and yawning. "Oh, sorry. Always want to be on hand for the last and first trains of the day, but this does not allow for much sleep." He finally looked at Collins and recognized him. "Oh yes, you received a reply late yesterday evening. Here it is." He handed the telegram to Collins.

> Washington DC Jan 24 1879
> To C.W. Collins Wallace Station
> Received report of Cheyennes in northwest Nebraska
> Investigate truth of depredations in Kansas
> Dull Knife Little Wolf missing
> Require you to find them
> Herr Burschenschaft

"Any reply?" asked the operator.

"Not at the moment. Can you tell me how to find Oberlin?"

"You have to ride north, cross the north fork of the Smoky Hill River and then angle northeast to find the south fork of Sappa Creek. You can follow that right up to Oberlin."

"I thank you."

Collins walked back into the chilly morning and found Gal sitting in front of the building, as if trained to do so. He slung her up onto the saddle, tightened all the cinches and mounted up. He rode out of town as people began to appear on the streets and around the hotels and other establishments. One P. Robidoux had an impressive business housed in a large and rambling structure. He nodded at a couple of men lounging by the door as he rode past.

"Hell of a mule," one of them commented. "Big as a house."

Collins smiled and gave a two-finger salute. He headed out of town, due north as the telegraph operator had directed, and as soon as they were clear of the buildings, the wind again made its presence abundantly known. Gal sneezed and burrowed deeper between the saddle swells and his lap. He turned up the collar of his frock coat and snugged down his Stetson. His continued journey would, no doubt, offer more discomfort and monotonous terrain. A locomotive whistle blew in the distance, heralding another load of goods and people traveling across the prairie to all points west.

The miles rolled along in predictable fashion, amidst the inevitable scarcity of wildlife. In one protracted area, he crossed the leavings of an immense prairie fire that must have burned the year before. He was aware that plains Indian tribes would occasionally set fire to expanses of prairie so as to revitalize the vegetation and attract birds and other wildlife. Since most of the Indians in Kansas had been relocated or killed, he doubted this was other than the remains of a natural fire or one accidently set by a careless homesteader. Or perhaps cattlemen attempting to drive off squatters.

As he rode, C.W.'s thoughts went to Wheeler and men of his ilk...bullies who sought to bend weaker or more courteous men to their will. This need to dominate and influence others seemed to be rather common in the military, a fertile field where bullies could not only prosper but find respect and advancement. He was able to identify many an example within his own acquaintance, not the least of which was Phil Sheridan. It was difficult to decide, he reflected, whether he predominantly despised tyrants or their lackeys. An oppressor was to be scorned and resisted, but a lickspittle was contemptible. Opportunely, both types were frequently the authors of their own ruin. As Petrarch had written, "Man has no greater enemy than himself."

A delineation of stunted trees became visible up ahead in the late morning. The sky remained cloudless and the day had warmed considerably. Collins rode toward the trees, doubting that he had reached the north fork of the river so soon. He only hoped there was open water for his animals. As he neared the shrubbery, he heard a distinct turkey call. Through a gap in the scrub, he could see a small stream and he rode down to it, dismounting and leading his animals to drink. Gal darted around the creek bank, sniffing and reading ciphers invisible to C.W. He secured his horse to a snag and wrapped Molly's lead around the saddle horn. Pulling his Winchester from the scabbard, he moved as silently as possible toward the direction of the turkey call.

Gal crept behind him as he tracked through the brush, placing each foot with intention. At last, he glimpsed a small flock of wild turkeys through the undergrowth. He cocked the rifle, aimed at a large tom and fired. The dog spooked and took off back along the creek and the turkeys scattered. He broke through the thicket and retrieved his kill, heavier than he expected for the time of year. Retracing his steps, he found Gal huddled by the mules, visibly shaking. He put down the turkey and called her to him, kneeling down to caress her head and speak comfortingly. After the dog had calmed, he cleaned the bird, tied it to Joey's packs and continued on his way, using the compass to maintain his northerly course.

As he traveled, he chewed on jerked meat and hardtack from a supply stowed in his saddle bags, occasionally giving morsels to Gal. The prairie rolled out in front of them in seeming infinity and he unexpectedly descended into memories of his mother and their terrible experiences during the great hunger and subsequent emigration. They had arrived in New York City with almost nothing, having barely escaped starvation, where their struggles continued as they fought for a place in the overcrowded Irish slums of the vast metropolis. Finally, his mother had found a position as cook in a wealthy Catholic household and he took to sweeping out saloons and running errands until he joined the nascent New York Metropolitan Police Department, shortly after the Great Police Riot. As a policeman, he gained a reputation for fearlessness and integrity, especially during gang riots between Irish immigrants and nativists. He was later assigned to a detective unit where he remained until the war.

Around the middle of the afternoon, Collins noticed the silhouette of what he took to be a covered wagon on the skyline. He did not particularly desire to encounter more buffalo hunters, but the conveyance and its owners were directly situated in his path. He tugged the side of his frock coat behind his holster to ease access to the .45 and continued on his way. As he drew near, he saw two figures sitting in chairs by a campfire, one noticeably wearing a dress. Relaxing his guard to a degree, he headed toward the wagon. There was a team of stout draft horses picketed nearby. Ulysses whinnied at them and one answered back. As he rode closer, a man, tall and lean, stood and waved.

"Hej," he said. "Hello."

"Hello."

The woman now stood up. She was almost as tall as the man and rather pretty and he saw there was a small girl hiding behind her skirts.

"Our *vogn,* wagon, has broken," she said.

Not really wanting to be held up, but unwilling to abandon this small immigrant family, he hesitated. He could not place the language or the accent.

"Do you need help?"

"Nej. We are waiting for another wheel," the man said. "My *bror* has gone to Wallace."

"Come, spise, eat," the woman told Collins, beckoning him with her hand. "We have *kartoffelkager.* We welcome you." She bent down to tend to an iron pan on a grate by the fire.

"Clara means potato cakes. She makes them very well. *Venligst,* eat with us."

Seeing that it would be discourteous to refuse, C.W. lowered the dog to the ground and dismounted. He tied his animals to the back of the wagon and eased their cinches. He reached around in one of the panniers until he found a small jar of peach preserves and took it over to the woman.

"Mange tak skal du have," she said, smiling and accepting the jam.

The little girl was attempting to get close to Gal. The dog was dodging around the people, fire ring and chairs in an attempt to avoid the child. Collins called her to him.

"I am Aksel," the man said, bringing another chair. "Aksel Rasmussen. This is Clara, my *kone,* and Inger," he added, gesturing toward the girl. "Sit."

"My name is Charles Collins." He went to the chair and sat down. Gal crawled underneath him and Inger came over to sit nearby. Clara busied herself with handing out plates, while Aksel handed him a cup of coffee. Collins found it to be quite strong and sweet, with a cinnamon flavor. He noticed Aksel watching him, so he smiled and nodded in approval.

"Where are you coming from?" he asked.

"Salina...in Saline county," Aksel told him, sitting down. "It is too *overfyldt,* crowded, now. We are going to homestead in Nebraska."

"I hope you have luck."

"And what are you doing out here?" Aksel asked. "It is a very empty road."

"Traveling through. I thought perhaps I would go to Deadwood in the Black Hills," he prevaricated.

"So, you look for *guld,*" Clara said. "Hard work is better. That is how you will be rich."

"Now, now," Aksel said to her. "It is not for us to say what is better."

Clara shrugged and placed two crispy cakes on Collins' plate. He thanked her. "Are you originally from Sweden?" he asked, making a guess.

Inger laughed. *"Nej, nej,"* she said and laughed again.

Aksel scolded her in their language and the girl became contrite. "We are from *Danmark.* My daughter is *uhøflig*...rude. I am sorry."

While they ate, they spoke about homesteading and shared stories about immigrating and ship voyages. Clara was a teacher and explained her plans for a school in their new home.

Collins finished his coffee and cakes. "I must keep riding," he told the Rasmussens. "Thank you so much for the food. It was delicious."

"You must be very careful," Aksel told him. "There were recently terrible Indian attacks near here. Many men killed and women...*voldtægt.*"

"Yes, I have heard of this," he said, "I will be careful."

"This country will be much improved when all the

vilde mænd are killed or sent away," Aksel said, while Clara nodded in agreement.

"This is good country, a good place for a new beginning," she said. "For *hvid mænd.* Not for *halvnøgen mænd* with no god."

IMMIGRANTS

17

At his campsite, on the banks of what he was fairly certain was the north fork of the Smoky Hill River, Collins contemplated the defective empathy of so many individuals. He was thinking of the Rasmussens and how perfectly agreeable people could not seem to recognize that Indians were entitled to a place in America. It seemed ludicrous that Europeans had been flooding the Americas for hundreds of years, all the while displacing the original people without remorse. Perhaps, he thought, as he gathered more wood for the fire, he could empathize with the Indian plight due to his intimacy with the oppression of the Irish by the English. Thinking on it, he could not recall any history wherein Denmark had been conquered. In fact, the Danish had been some of the fiercest Vikings, according to his recollection of history, which meant they themselves had been aggressive conquerors. Many of the brawniest, blonde Irishmen had Danish blood.

The encroachment of poor white immigrants into Indian lands had been a feature of North American history since the first indentured servants landed on the eastern shores. He supposed that empathy was not a bedfellow of desperation. Still, he mused, while plucking the turkey and Gal rooted around in the pile of feathers, *ní bhfaghann dorn dúnta ach lámh iadhta...* a shut fist gets only a closed hand. Many a frontiersman had suffered dire consequences when encroaching upon Indian lands. Ironically, wealthy easterners seemed to have the greatest sympathy for the Indians, and yet they really had no clear understanding of the vexed complexity that arose from interactions between profoundly incongruent peoples.

Collins skewered the turkey on a pole he had shaped for the purpose and suspended it between two forked branches driven into the ground on either side of the fire. He sat on his chair and smoked his pipe while he turned the bird over the coals. Joey and Ulysses jangled their hobbles as they drifted from one clump of dried grasses to another, while Molly stood contentedly, dozing with her eyes half-closed. The dog was off somewhere, hunting. The wind had died down as the evening advanced. A coyote yipped somewhere off to the south.

When the turkey was sufficiently roasted, C.W. ate a leg and shared a piece of breast with Gal, who had returned without sign of having had success in her expedition. He left the rest of the carcass over the dying coals, adding damp willow bark to produce smoke. The sun was down, so he was unconcerned about attracting unwanted human guests, and he had not seen bear sign in days. The dog could ward off any other visitors. He made a little brush and saddle blanket shelter over the smoking coals and retreated to his tent and bedroll and was soon fast asleep.

Finding the bird nicely cured the next morning, he wrapped it in pages from one of his Harper's Weekly magazines and stowed it in the food pannier. The odor of meat had fascinated local coyotes most of the night and he and Gal had lost a good bit of sleep. The aggravation had been worthwhile, he decided, as it meant extra victuals for the trail, especially since he had no wish to spend an inordinate amount of time in settlements until he reached Camp Robinson. Oberlin was a necessity, but he hoped he could interview survivors of the Cheyenne raids swiftly, being certain the general sentiment would be entirely vitriolic toward the Indians.

Back out on the trail, Collins consulted his antiquated map and checked his compass. He rode in a more northerly direction, so as to not miss the south fork of Sappa Creek. If he too precisely followed the telegraph operator's instructions, there was a risk of running into the south fork of the Saline River or the north fork of the Solomon and ending up far off his intended course. The Kansas plains were infuriatingly repetitive and bereft of distinguishing landmarks, although indigenous tribes, no doubt, knew every mile intimately. He could well imagine, though, how many overly confident prospectors and emigrants had gone astray and left their bones upon its seemingly infinite bosom.

As the morning wore on, he began to notice the infrequent outline of remote sod houses on the horizon, their distant profiles resembling abandoned loaves of bread, alien to the sweeping terrain. One of the structures boasted a solitary tree, exaggeratedly bent toward the east by the remorseless wind. The landscape was otherwise lifeless with the exception of two vultures that hovered overhead for a good while, as if considering the possibility of his failed survival. Once he espied a large herd of cattle far off to the west.

Around noon, C.W. descended a low rise and sighted a meandering course of trees in the near distance, following a northeasterly path. He angled down toward the waterway, surveying the terrain for possible danger from humans or otherwise. Finding a backwater pool of open water, he dismounted and allowed his stock to drink while he wandered a little upstream, where the water ran more swiftly, and filled his canteen. Gal gave a short bark and took off after a prairie chicken that had been foraging along the creek bottom. It escaped in a furious beating of its wings, leaving the dog to trot back in defeat. Collins gave her a piece of jerky as compensation.

Crossing over and following the north bank of the stream in the assumption he was, indeed, on the south fork of Sappa Creek, Collins came upon a dugout, burrowed into a south-facing hillside and reinforced with rough wood planking. A four pane window and sturdy door enhanced the front of the structure and he noticed colorful curtains behind the glass. A stovepipe protruded from the dirt roof, from which a faint swirl of smoke rose. There was a sewing machine just outside the door next to a battered table and a couple of spindle back chairs.

Riding by, with no reason to interact with the occupants, C.W. noticed a small tow-headed child emerge from the door. He kept going, hoping there would be no delays.

"Hey," the boy called.

Groaning inwardly, Collins pulled up and turned in the saddle. "Yes?"

"Who'r you?"

Gal growled softly.

"Just riding past," he told the boy. "No need to concern yourself."

"That your dog?"

This seemed to Collins to be a distinctively foolish question, given that Gal was riding on his horse with him. "Yes," he answered patiently.

A hefty woman came out of the dugout, her drab dirty blonde hair framing a fleshy cheerless face. Her apron was tidy, as was the boy's attire. "Erhard," she called in a strong German accent. *"Komm her."*

"The dog, mama. I want to see *der Hund.*"

"Nein," the woman said, eyeing Collins suspiciously. *"Komm her."* She reached out and grabbed the child's arm roughly. *"Hören."*

C.W. almost inquired as to the name of the creek hard

by, but thought better of it and urged Ulysses to move on.   Molly hesitated a moment, as Joey had his head down nibbling some dried leaves on a squat bush and she had to lean into her breast collar to propel him forward. Collins heard the boy call out again as he angled his horse east along the stream bank, then climbed out of the bottoms to top out on the prairie above. The wind hit him with purpose, but was blowing from the southwest and so was slightly less intrusive. He turned up his collar and kept an eye out for additional dwellings, not wanting to meet up with other inquisitive nesters, either overly wary or starved for human commerce.

As the journey proceeded, Collins began to ruminate upon the number of Prussian immigrants he had come in contact with since he had first arrived in America. In New York City, they had been quotidian, especially as bakers and saloon keepers. There had even been an area of Manhattan called Little Germany. It still seemed as if every other individual he met was of German descent, including Secretary Schurz, Major General Franz Sigel of the Northern Army, many of the soldiers he had run into either during the war or out west, Villard of the Northern Pacific Railway, several influential men he had recently encountered in Chicago and St. Louis, Zimmerman in Dodge City, and now the woman in the dugout. He had read that Germans from Russia were coming to Kansas and Nebraska in growing numbers. They tended to gravitate toward farming. The German vote seemed to be influential in any region where they congregated.

In early afternoon, the wind died down and the day became rather warm for late January. There seemed to be a greater abundance of birds, rabbits and raccoons along the stream corridor than he had seen farther south. He had even startled a small group of mule deer out of the bottoms shortly after leaving the vicinity of the dugout. Perhaps the apparent increase in fauna north of the Smoky Hill River, he conjectured, was due to the fact that most of the buffalo hunters had concentrated themselves around Dodge City, a major shipping hub for hides and meat.

As he was traversing a windswept hogback above the creek, a disagreeable stench caught Collins' attention. The dog was visibly sniffing the air as if seeking out the provenance. She jumped off the horse, giving Ulysses a start, and ran toward a ravine that bisected the ridgeline ahead. Collins dismounted and tethered the horse and mules to a scrubby cottonwood tree nearby. He pulled his Colt revolver and followed the dog toward the gully. Walking its edge a short distance, Collins came upon a strange tableau. The shriveled corpse of an Indian was, against reason, standing upright in the bottom of the coulee and emanating a foul odor in the afternoon sun. The remnants of a breechclout fluttered in the breeze. As he drew closer, C.W. could see that a thick tree branch had been whittled and inserted into the body's rectum and jammed into the earth so as to keep the cadaver erect. The head exhibited evidence of having been scalped.

Feeling his gorge rise at the brutality of the scene, he holstered his Colt and turned away, calling to his dog, who had been warily circling the desiccated remains. The deed had been violently inhumane and macabre. His heart went out to the lonely soul left to suffer this contemptuous fate. To Collins, it was more evidence that white people could moralize *ad infinitum* on the savagery of Indian peoples while remaining unambiguously blind to the appalling behavior specific to European ancestry and history. He departed the area swiftly and did not look back.

18

The burned and collapsed sod house squatted north-west of the creek, bracketed by abandoned corral fences and a corn field left scorched and unharvested from the previous summer. Collins assumed this was probably a homestead attacked by the fleeing Cheyenne in the preceding October. The location was situated in a shallow valley between the middle and south forks of Sappa Creek. It was one of the more hospitable regions he had encountered in Kansas, but evidence of an obvious tragedy cast a pall over the scene.

He rode around the ruined farm and found a small cemetery, recent enough to have originated during the depredations of last autumn. There were three crude markers with names scratched into the wood. C.W. did not care to get close enough to read them. It was enough to see that there had been losses on both sides, even though these people assuredly should not have been encouraged to claim land that was the ancestral range of several plains tribes. Acrimony and conflict were bound to result. It was his understanding from Assistant Surgeon Finley that Indian raids had remained intermittent in Kansas throughout the '70s, although the government was not eager to acknowledge this inopportune detail.

As he sat his horse surveying the valley, partially blanketed by a skiff of snow, he heard a horse whinny behind him. Collins twisted in the saddle and saw a rider coming up on him. He lay his hand on the butt of his revolver and turned the gelding. The man rode a tall bay stud horse and appeared, from his clothing, wooly chaps and lariat, to be a cowman. His hat and face were weather-beaten. Collins relaxed and waited for the fellow to speak, prepared for swift action if required.

"Hidy," the man said, pulling up his horse a short distance away.

"Hello."

"My name is Cyrus Grimes. I run my cows through here. You related to these folks?" he asked, nodding toward the ruined sod house.

"No. Just riding through and happened to notice it. Whose place was this?"

"Family called Blecha. Bohemians that came in a couple of years ago. Had a nice place here before the 'poor lo' did for them last fall."

" 'Poor Lo?' What does that mean?"

Grimes gave a derisive sneer. "Lo the poor Indian. Those bloody minded Cheyennes sent the family packing. Where you from?"

Molly jerked her nose at Grimes' horse, trying to bite him. Collins pulled her lead and took another dally on his saddle horn. Gal jumped down to reconnoiter the corn field.

"Around. No problem with me riding over your grazing range is there?"

"No problem," the man answered. "I am on the hunt for a lost bull."

"Was this the only homestead that was attacked?" C.W. had learned many years ago that behaving in an ignorant fashion often led to a superior drift of information.

"Hell no. There were folks besieged and viciously murdered all over Decatur and Rawlins counties...here on the forks of the Sappa, up on the Beaver Creek and over on Prairie Dog Creek. Over thirty people were killed and a good number of women and children were out-raged. Terrible," Grimes said, shaking his head. "Just terrible."

"Did you witness any of it?"

"Just the burying. I was over to Kirwin to purchase a new team of heavy horses and otherwise might have been killed with the rest of them. Friend of mine, Edward Miskelley, was shot off his horse. He was working for the Doweling Brothers Stock Company, moving cows over to winter pasture." Grimes looked at Collins as if he should know who they were.

"Never heard of them," he said, shrugging.

"You sure are not from around here," the cowman said, taking off his hat and scratching the back of his head, covered in a shock of greasy steel gray hair. "There is no way to describe the woeful loss of life and the dreadful job of hunting for bodies and getting them all buried," he went on, tugging his hat back down and shifting in the saddle. "The state of some of the women and children was a sight to see. Many of them people gave up their homesteads and left. One woman could no longer support her family with her man dead and she just gave away her children."

The dog came sprinting out of the corn stalks in a dead run, hot on the trail of a rabbit. The cottontail bounded into the ruins of a chicken coop and Gal whimpered as she scratched at the pile of charred lumber. C.W. whistled to get her attention and she came over to him. He slapped his thigh and she leapt up so he could catch her and put her in front of him on his horse. Grimes' bay spooked a little.

"Easy," Grimes told the horse, pulling lightly on the reins. "That is some dog. You trained her good."

"Not really," Collins said, grinning. "She rather trains herself. I only found her a few days ago."

Grimes raised his eyebrows. "That is something, for

sure. You want to keep her? I could use a smart dog."

"I had better keep her with me. She is attached now."

"I can see that," he said, nodding. "Well, fella, I had better get out and find that bull I mislaid. Hope none of those Bohunks stole him. They get mighty hungry out here and lots of them do not have any idea about farming."

"They rustle cattle?"

"Sure. The cattle outfits been lynching a couple nesters every year since they started coming out."

"Yet you felt sympathy for them after the Indian raids?"

"Well sure," Grimes said, squinting at Collins as if he was regarding an imbecile. "They might be cow thieves, but they are white."

"I see," Collins said. "Well, good luck finding your bull."

"Right," the man said, eyeing Collins charily. "Be seeing you."

Grimes turned his big bay and headed on down toward the middle fork of the Sappa, raising a hand briefly over his head in farewell without looking back. Collins rode off to the northeast, following the creek toward Oberlin. Along the way, he noticed a few abandoned dugouts and other sod houses, some showing signs of destruction from fire or marauding, while others looked as if they had been simply abandoned. Farther along, he seemed to be riding across a great expanse of blackened earth, visible under banks of snow, apparent signs of another extensive prairie fire.

It seemed to Collins that the Homestead Act was at the heart of the destruction of Indian cultures out west, in addition to the violence endured by disenfranchised settlers, especially immigrants. Both groups were the pawns of industrialists looking toward expanding economic opportunities on the shoulders of manifest destiny. The homesteaders shoved the Indians aside while demanding protection from the army and ultimately took the brunt of Indian rage at loss of life and land. This then allowed the government to pass more laws forcing tribes onto smaller and smaller tracts of reservations while making room for more railroads, access to mineral wealth, timber, agricultural ventures and nascent towns.

Eventually, Collins came upon a small cluster of buildings near the creek. He rode in among them and found a false front structure with a rough sign that read "Hardware" and a larger building with no designation. A couple of clapboard houses and three sod huts completed the hamlet. It was the middle of the afternoon, but the place was strangely deserted. A robust, florid faced man came out of the hardware store as Collins rode past.

"Hello there," he called.

C.W. pulled up his gelding. "Good afternoon," he responded, giving a nod of his head.

"Welcome to our humble town of St. John."

"St. John? Named after the Kansas governor, I take it."

The man beamed. "Indeed, friend, indeed. My name is Edward Knowles. My friends and I founded this burg. Sadly, it seems we must needs abandon it."

Ulysses began pawing the ground impatiently. Collins gave a tug on the reins. "Abandon it?" he asked. "Is this due to the recent Indian raids?"

"No. Happily we were spared. The devastation was truly biblical. No we are moving our town to the location of Oberlin. Having chosen this location for its commodious setting, it seems all our imagined future greatness has been eclipsed by the other townsite."

"I see." Collins was impatient to move on, but his new acquaintance was garrulous and pleased to have an ear.

"Get down, get down," Knowles said, beckoning him with great gestures of his hand. "I can make coffee."

Before C.W. could refuse, a strapping man in a large black hat came riding up on a piebald chestnut-colored horse. He looked Collins and his animals over, seeming especially interested in Gal sitting complacently on the saddle.

"Greetings Flanigan," Knowles said heartily. "Or should I say sheriff?"

"James is fine as always, Edward," the rider answered in a pronounced Irish brogue.

"Flanigan is our new sheriff," Knowles told Collins.

"This here is…sorry mister, I never caught your name."

"Collins. Charles Wolfe Collins."

The sheriff trained his oddly penetrating green eyes on C.W. "Wolfe you say? As in Wolfe Tone?"

"Yes. *Is buaine bladh ná saoghal.* I carry the name with pride."

"Aye," Flanigan said, nodding. "He was a brave man and his fame should endure."

The man Knowles was nearly undone by having been shut out of the discourse. "Come now, why not get down and have some refreshment."

Flanigan's horse shook itself suddenly. Joey, the mule, moved away as if threatened and the dog gave a soft bark.

"Thank you, no," Collins said. "I must keep riding for Oberlin."

"I am heading back to Oberlin," Flanigan said. "I can ride along."

"Where have you been?" Knowles asked, attempting to hold them in conversation.

"Over to the Rohan place. They are still imagining Indians and I had to go out to reassure them."

"Well who can blame them? Hudson and Smith were killed right near there."

"That may be," the sheriff said, shrugging. "But these false alarms are keeping me on the move. Folks need to calm down."

Collins' animals were becoming more restive. "Well, I

have to be going," he said.

"Too right," Flanigan agreed, kicking up his horse and moving off. "See you around, Edward."

Turning his gelding and giving a pull on Molly's lead rope, Collins followed after the sheriff. "Goodbye for now," he told Knowles over his shoulder.

The two men rode in amiable silence for a while. The sky began clouding up and the wind began to gain in strength. Gal snuggled in closer. Flanigan kept looking over at her.

"You know this dog?" Collins finally asked.

"No. Just curious about her. Never seen a dog what rides a horse. Knew one once that could drive a team."

"Now that is some blarney," C.W. said, grinning.

"No, god's truth. Big hound. You put the lines in his mouth and he could drive a six-up if he had a mind."

Collins laughed heartily. "Never will I believe it. You feed this rubbish to everyone?"

Flanigan gave him an impish glance. "When I can get away with it."

KANSAS LAND OFFICE

19

The afternoon was fast becoming colder, with a chill wind kicking up from the north and occasional snow flurries. C.W. found Flanigan to be open and forthcoming in response to his inquiries. He seemed to be a guileless man, but with a manner that suggested a deadly undercurrent. All the same, he was entertaining and full of information.

"So let me see," Flanigan was saying. "There were the Laings what took the worst of it. Mister Laing and three sons were killed, the wife and daughters outraged, the homestead destroyed. Mrs. Laing has since relocated to Ontario to live with her brother. Poor woman will never be right again."

"About how many settlers were killed in the raids?" C.W. wanted to hear Flanigan's count and see if it tallied with that of Grimes.

"I heard different numbers, but somewhere around thirty all told, I guess. This is if you include the folks killed up on Beaver Creek and over on Prairie Dog." A gust of wind assaulted them and he paused a moment before continuing. "I helped with some of the burying. It was a dreadful sight, what was done, but I worked for many a year on the Union Pacific as gang boss for grade work. The talk I heard among the men and the blood-curdling stories of assaults on Indians, women and all, caused me to temper my judgement. With all the atrocities and forfeiture those people must have suffered and the unbearable conditions down at Darlington Agency, I truly do not know what I might be capable of. I just do not know."

"How about scalping and mutilations?" Collins asked.

"None. Just destruction and killings. And, of course, theft of food and livestock. But it was fairly extensive."

"You believe some of it was inspired by revenge?"

Flanigan nodded. "I would say so. But they did no more than an Irish republican would do to English farms if given half a chance."

It began to snow in earnest. They rode into a thick grove of trees along the creek and found temporary shelter.

"Perhaps it will ease off in a little while," the sheriff said.

"Perhaps. The animals need to blow a moment in any event." Collins took some jerked meat from his saddlebags and handed a piece to his companion.

"Ta."

Collins brushed snow from the dog and rubbed her ear. "What do you think about the outrages? I am a mite perplexed by the disparity between the Indians being determined to escape, but nevertheless taking the time to violate women."

"I mulled that particular point over meself," Flanigan said, chewing on a shred of meat. "I cannot answer to that."

The weather eased a little and they rode out into the open again. Joey suddenly brayed loudly and a donkey answered from a pen near a dugout on the creek bank.

"That feller could wake the dead," Flanigan observed.

"No doubt," C.W. said, chuckling.

It had ceased snowing entirely when they rode into Oberlin. The town was a small collection of sod, log and clapboard buildings, lined out along a road of frozen ruts and manure. They rode up to the livery stable where a husky young man came out of the barn to meet them.

"Hey sheriff," the boy said. "Find any redskins?"

"Nary a one," Flanigan said, dismounting and loosening his cinch.

Collins lowered the dog to the ground and followed suit. He secured his animals to a nearby rail.

"This is Mr. Collins, Scotty," the sheriff said. "Can you take care of him?"

"Sure can. Put them all up?"

"I would appreciate it. Do you have a pen where they can be together?"

"Out the back, with a shelter and feed bunk. Mr. Atkins will insist you pay double for the big mule, though."

"I will agree to that."

The three of them unloaded and unsaddled the livestock and Collins stowed his gear in an empty stall in the barn. He suspended the food pannier from a rafter and retrieved his carpet bag. Scotty filled the feed bunk for his animals, while Collins rubbed them down with old sacks. The sheriff's gelding occupied the next pen over, where Flanigan fussed over his horse with bits of sugar and fond attention.

H. A. Atkins, the proprietor, walked into the barn as they were leaving. "Good evening, Flanigan," he said. "That your dog?"

Gal was close behind Collins, as usual. "She is mine," he said.

"Do not want dogs here." Atkins was a wiry small man with a nasal voice and an insolent bearing.

"She goes where I go," C.W. said coldly. "I will pay for the privilege," he added.

"Two bits extra a day then," Atkins said.

"He has a draft mule," Scotty informed his boss dutifully.

"That will be another two bits a day. On top of the

usual daily rate for board and feed, of course."

"Jesus, mary and joseph, Atkins," Flanigan said in his best brogue. "Do you want the man to pay for the air he breathes as well?"

Atkins snorted. "A man has to make a living, sheriff. And I do not like dogs." He turned to leave. "Come with me Scotty," he said, grabbing the bulky arm of the stable hand and yanking him. The boy followed along docilely enough, but Collins noted a spark of resentment in his washed out blue eyes.

"Disagreeable fellow," C.W. said, as he and Flanigan walked down the frozen track toward the hotel.

"No lie. But what can we do? Treats the boy poorly too."

The evening was coming on and the temperature was falling. No one was about as they made their way to what appeared to be a newly built two-story building. "Oberlin House Hotel" was rudely painted in big letters on a sign attached to the front. They stepped into the warmth of a sparsely furnished parlor and Gal slipped inside before Collins could stop her. The room was occupied by a couple of gentlemen playing checkers and a man behind a makeshift front desk who was working studiously in a ledger book.

"Good evening, Rodehaver," Flanigan called. "Balance the books yet?"

The man looked up and broke into a big smile. "Well, Flanigan. You arrest somebody, did you?"

"Oh sure. This here is John Wesley Hardin, newly escaped from prison."

"Pleased to meet you, Mr. Hardin. Need a room?" Rodehaver asked, hooking his thumbs in the arm holes of an elaborate brocade waistcoat. "Or are you bunking at the jail?"

"I would prefer a room here, if it is all the same to you," C.W. answered, smiling. "And the name is Charles Collins."

"I can attest to the fact that he is harmless," Flanigan told the man. "And would you be allowing his dog as a special favor to me? The animal is exceedingly clever and performs all manner of feats of intelligence."

"That so?" Rodehaver asked.

"Oh aye."

Collins signed the register book. "Please do not lend credence to any of his statements. But I would be in your debt if the dog can stay. She is well-mannered."

Rodehaver shrugged. "We are an out of the way establishment and often have dogs. We even had a pet badger stay here once. Just not in the beanery. Folks might object. Here is your key...room four on the second floor."

Collins climbed the steps to his room, with the dog waiting at the foot of the stairs, and placed his bag on the single bed. When he returned to the lobby, Flanigan was gone.

The proprietor noticed him looking around. "Flanigan said to meet him for supper."

Gal followed Collins to the open door of the restaurant, just off the hotel lobby. He pressed her to the floor and told her to stay, then went into the room to find the sheriff. He was seated near a window at one of the five tables that occupied the cramped space. A small prim-looking woman in a highneck dress was filling his cup with coffee.

"Mr. Collins, come and join me."

Walking over, C.W. removed his hat and nodded at the woman.

"This is Mrs. Rodehaver. She is the finest cook in the county."

"Oh now," the woman said, blushing. "You exaggerate."

Collins took a chair. "Good evening," he said. "I will have some of that coffee, if I may."

"Of course. I will fetch another cup." Mrs. Rodehaver seemed flustered as she retreated into the kitchen.

"Well now," Flanigan said, again giving free rein to his Irish accent. "It seems you have quite an effect on the ladies."

"Oh sure. Especially dogs and horses."

The woman arrived with a coffee cup and a bowl of sugar. She appeared to have regained her composure. "I will be right back," she said and returned shortly with a china coffee pot that she set on the table. "I can refill this when needed. Now then, we have only the two meals. Buffalo steak with fried potatoes or beans with ham hocks. Apple crisp for dessert."

"I will have the steak," C.W. told her.

"I as well," Flanigan said.

"Very good. It will be out soon." The woman departed, after clearing a neighboring table.

Collins looked around. Three men were seated at a table across the room and looked to be cattlemen according to their attire. They ate without engaging in conversation.

"*Ceart go leor*," said Flanigan, rubbing his hands together perfunctorily. "It is about time that you told me why you have been so entirely inquisitive about the Indian raids of last fall."

"Oh that," C.W. said, with a slight smile. "I wondered that you had not asked previously."

"I am a patient man. But I eventually get around to business."

" 'Though patience be a tired mare, yet she will plod.' "

"True enough. Now cease your obfuscation and kindly proceed in answering my question." Flanigan took a large sip of coffee and smacked his lips in satisfaction.

Filling his cup from the pot, Collins said, "I am employed by the Pinkerton Agency, sent to investigate the raids here in Kansas."

The sheriff put his cup back in its saucer slowly and stared coldly at him. "The Pinkertons? The Pinkertons you say? You, an Irishman...and after what McParland did to the Mollies?"

Collins took a deep breath and sighed. "Yes, I know. It seems a contradiction, but I possess certain skills and I work for the agency on occasion. When I am short of funds, for instance, such as now." He paused and smoothed his moustache pensively. "You are the sheriff and therefore the local 'peeler.' Is that not also a contradiction?"

A grin slowly spread over Flanigan's face. "Well now," he said. "You have me there, true enough."

"I am undoubtedly a burr under Allan Pinkerton's saddle. We knew each other in the late rebellion and he is obliged to employ me for certain jobs, such as this one." Collins disliked lying to the man, but he had no choice.

Mrs. Rodehaver arrived bearing two large plates of food. She set them down on the table and poured more coffee for both men. "Anything else, gentlemen?" she asked.

"We are finer than frog hair at the moment, my darling girl," Flanigan told her with a superfluity of Irish charm.

The woman simply shook her head and walked away. They ate for a while in silence. The table occupied by the cattlemen cleared out and they had the place to themselves.

"Alright, boyo," Flanigan finally said. "Let us hear more of what intelligence you are seeking in regard to the recent depredations."

Swallowing a mouthful of potatoes, Collins said, "I merely require a thorough overview of the events. You have provided much already."

A diminutive middle-aged man entered the dining room. He was dressed in a rumpled suit of clothing of an older style and wore gold-rimmed spectacles. On his head, he sported a dilapidated Tyrolean hat.

"Hey Doc," Flanigan called. "Come join us."

The man walked over to the table. "Good evening, Sheriff," he said with a distinctly eastern accent.

"Doc, this is Charles Collins. Mr. Collins...meet Dr. Bariteau, the only doctor hereabouts. He also sells potions and poisons out of the local apothecary shop."

"Pleased to meet you, Mr. Collins." The doctor pulled up a chair.

Mrs. Rodehaver came over and took his order. "You gentlemen need anything else?" she asked Flanigan and Collins. "Ready for dessert?"

"Why, I was born ready," Flanigan said, winking at her.

"Oh, shoo, you pest," she said, but walked away smiling.

Flanigan poured coffee for the doctor. "Mr. Collins here is asking about the raids of last autumn," he said.

"Frightful," the doctor said. "So many people killed."

"The doctor here attended most of them. "Did you also attend the women who were outraged?" Collins asked.

The doctor appeared discomfited. "No, no...I am not qualified for that."

"Forgive his forthrightness," Flanigan said to the doctor. "He is an operative with the Pinkertons."

"Oh...oh I see," Bariteau said, removing his glasses and wiping them with a handkerchief.

Collins finished his meal, sincerely wishing that the steak had not been broiled so conscientiously. Mrs. Rodehaver arrived bearing dishes of apple crisp along with beans and ham hocks for Dr. Bariteau. She served everyone, cleared some plates and once more departed.

"I would marry that woman if she would only leave old Rodehaver," Flanigan said, taking a large forkful of crisp and shoving it into his mouth.

"You are always a funny man," the doctor told him. "Too funny for a sheriff."

"So they say," the big Irishman said, taking another bite of dessert.

DEPREDATIONS

20

The three men sat over coffee for long hours as Collins attempted to piece together a comprehensive framework of events that occurred during the Cheyenne raids on local homesteads. It seemed that some homesteaders had disregarded warnings, such as the Humphreys. Their son had alerted them to potential danger from the Cheyenne people on the run from the military personnel hunting them, but stayed anyway. The father had been killed and the son wounded. Several of the settlers had no previous experience with Indians and were caught off guard, while others thought they had all been domesticated and were merely friendly beggars. It seemed that the people who did not panic and fought back were mostly spared, offering more evidence that the impetus for the raids was the desperate need for horses and supplies. Further indication of this was the fact that none of the white bodies had been scalped or mutilated, just as Flanigan had told him and the doctor verified.

There was no doubt that the Cheyenne raiders had moved like locusts across the land, with refugees finding shelter at a ranch belonging to a family called Keifer and subsequently in Oberlin. Mrs. Keifer, according to Flanigan, fought off the Cheyenne warriors with only four rounds of ammunition for a Winchester repeater. A drover, who had happened by for breakfast and stayed to help, used a .22 caliber pistol to shoot an Indian through a window. Between the two of them, they discouraged sustained attacks on the dugout. Eventually, several survivors found their way there. As the warriors pillaged through the countryside, they took what they could and destroyed the rest, including cattle, pigs and sheep, houses, wagons and furnishings. The Indians had set fire to many of the dwellings and outbuildings.

Dr. Bariteau, a bit pedantic but obviously compassionate, related his experiences of treating the wounded. He had provided medical attention to survivors as they straggled into Oberlin. Captain Allen's dry goods store, the first of its kind in Oberlin, became a hospital and shelter. The doctor saw to various injuries, such as an arrow lodged in a woman's back, exposure to the elements, burns, emotional strain and physical deprivation. Many of the homesteaders had felt it necessary to hide for several days before making their way into Oberlin. Some of the victims with more serious wounds could not be saved. The little log schoolhouse had been used as a morgue. Residents took turns as sentries and rifle pits were dug in the event that the Indians would make an attack on the town.

Incited by anger and grief, homesteaders and cattlemen banned together into informal posses to hunt down and engage the Cheyenne raiders. Most of the men ended up helping bury the dead or assisting unfortunate families they found along the way. A few days after the attacks, a group of men came upon an old Cheyenne man, woman and boy hiding in brush along Beaver Creek. The woman and boy escaped, but the old Indian was chased down and killed. A cattleman scalped the body and the trophy was still on display at Allen's store. Another antiquated Indian was found near Beaver Creek by a different posse and was beaten to death in honor of one of the white victims of the depredations. A young Cheyenne boy found wounded, a full six weeks after the raids, had been brutally dispatched and scalped. Collins figured that the corpse he had discovered standing near the Sappa Creek must have been the handiwork of similar retribution.

Tragically, shortly after the depredations and killings, a prairie fire raged through the homesteads around Oberlin. This was sufficient to force a greater number of families to abandon their homesteads and depart the region. Many of them had been made destitute and found it necessary to live with relatives. Other settlers on Prairie Dog Creek and Beaver Creek had also suffered gravely at the hands of Cheyenne raiders. Several of the farms there were likewise abandoned.

"I doubt if we will see a great many new homesteaders arriving to the area this year or next," Flanigan said. "Word has got out and even though the Cheyennes are long gone, folks are apprehensive and convinced they will be attacked again at any moment."

Mrs. Rodehaver came to the table. "Gentlemen, I require that you leave. I have much to do yet before retiring."

They stood up and prepared to depart. Both the doctor and Flanigan had rooms in the hotel. The sheriff had a small ranch outside of town, he explained, but often was forced to stay in Oberlin.

"Most matters that require my consideration occur in town," he explained.

Gal was still waiting patiently just outside the dining room. She wagged her stumpy tail when Collins came into view and took up her position behind him. They all climbed the stairs to the second floor together, bidding each other a good night and promising to meet for breakfast. Inside his room, C.W. lit an oil lamp and sat on the bed to remove his boots. He fed the dog scraps he had saved from the meal and found himself to be weary and dejected, brought low by the stories of devastation wrought by mutual hatred and misunderstanding. He seriously doubted that the future held much promise for either the remaining Cheyenne apostates or surviving homesteader families.

As he was preparing for sleep, Collins reviewed the information provided to him by the doctor. There had been many gunshot wounds, but the man had definitely not examined the women nor confirmed any of the supposed assaults. It seemed that a few of the women and girls had been kept hostage for a period of time and were later released upon the prairie, but Collins now suspected that the tales of rapine were probably conjured out of the persistent and lurid tales associated with women captives. It was all the usual justification for annihilating Indians as wonton barbarians. He was aware that quite a few of the women who had been captured by Indian tribes over the years later insisted unwaveringly that they had not been ravished. None of his experience with Indian peoples caused him to believe that their moral code would allow for such behavior, especially given the respected status of women within the tribal systems that he had observed.

The ruination of people and property, however, he could easily accept as authentic. Whether it was among his own Irish villagers, inmates of Andersonville, women ensnared in violent marriages or beleaguered Indian peoples he had known, he had observed that sustained indignities, treachery and misery could engender unforeseen conduct. Collins thought that the utter destruction wrought upon the residents of northwestern Kansas could only be explained as the consequence of virulent wrath; born of injustice, betrayal, abject suffering and bitter loss. As Flanigan had avowed, given such gravities, he certainly could not adequately predict his own response.

Slipping into the bedding of frayed quilts and woolen blankets, he burrowed deep. There was no stove in the room and, even though some warmth rose from the first floor kitchen range and parlor stove, it had become quite chilly as the night progressed. Gal jumped onto the bed and nestled herself into the small of his back. Although comfortable, Collins found he could not fall asleep. Echoes of previous atrocities haunted him, as they were wont to do when he was faced with new and equivalent carnage. Granted, he thought, his sympathy lay more with the Indians than with wretched nesters, tossed up upon the prairie like jetsam and seeking some condition of existence that offered more than their former drudgeries. Still, he had witnessed plenty of butchery and bloody corpses in his time and the doctor had been fairly explicit regarding the deplorable condition of the victims.

Rolling onto his back, Collins stroked Gal's ear and recalled favorite passages of Shakespeare in order to obliterate the distressing memories that kept rising unbidden. In the wee hours of the morning, he fell asleep at last.

PRAIRIE FIRE

21

Over a hearty breakfast the following morning, Flanigan, Collins and Dr. Bariteau settled back into a discussion of the Indian raids. Mrs. Rodehaver was again on duty and quite attentive. Unable to ignore their conversation, she finally paused to add her assessment of the events.

"These are the same brutes who are pampered by our government on the choicest food, furnished the best clothing and supplied with the very best repeating rifles that are manufactured. Being so equipped and mounted on fast ponies and being good shots, small wonder it has proved disastrous to the citizens of this state."

Startled by this effusive and unsolicited outburst, Collins gazed at her coldly and said nothing. Flanigan fidgeted a bit and the doctor repetitively wiped at a dab of egg yolk on his plate with a crust of bread.

"Well, that is what I believe, right enough," she added. "And I am not the only soul here in Oberlin who adheres to such an opinion."

The woman bustled off to the kitchen and the three men were silent a moment.

"There are strong feelings, right enough," Flanigan finally said. "No mystery as to why."

"No indeed," Dr. Bariteau agreed.

"It is astounding, however, to find people who have such a skewed notion of the government's treatment of Indians," C.W. said. "I cannot account for it."

"*Dall súil i geúil dhuine cile,*" Flanigan said.

"What are you saying?" Dr. Bariteau asked.

Collins smiled. "He is saying that an eye is blind in another man's corner," he told the doctor. "I, myself, would say that hatred causes such blindness."

"True enough," the sheriff said. "But these people have suffered greatly and had little enough compassion for the red man to begin with."

"I will not argue with that," Collins said. He took a sip of coffee and made certain that Mrs. Rodehaver was out of earshot. "On another tack, I was curious about the claims of the warriors stealing money. I believe the doctor told me that Mrs. Westphalen was shot with an arrow because she would not give up her money?"

"That is correct," Bariteau said.

"And you, Sheriff, mentioned others who reported sums of cash money stolen?"

"True," Flanigan said, nodding. He ate a last morsel of bacon and belched loudly.

"I frankly have never heard of Indians stealing money," C.W. said, ignoring his fellow diner's lack of decorum. "In fact, I have heard several humorous tales regarding the Indian's complete disregard for currency and have, myself, witnessed their indifference. It does not feature."

"All I am able to recount is that a Captain Wedemeyer of the 16th Cavalry came through at the end of October and took a tally of losses suffered by the homesteaders. Many of them reported the theft of money."

"Well, given my doubts resulting from a sound acquaintance with human nature, could it be possible there was an eye toward exaggerated remunerations?"

"It is not unlikely...but, again, these people have suffered. Perhaps they feel it is owed," Flanigan told him.

"It may be that the savages have learned about money," Dr. Bariteau posited.

"Perhaps." Collins slipped some leavings into his

pocket for the dog. "I should wander down and check on my livestock," he said.

"Will you be staying for the exhibition this evening?" the doctor asked.

"Exhibition?"

Flanigan grunted loudly. "A traveling spiritualist is making her way through these parts. She claims to be in touch with the victims of last fall's misfortunes."

"I have heard she is quite astounding," Bariteau said, excitedly. "She is a disciple of Cora Scott Richmond in Chicago. Certainly you have heard of Mrs. Richmond?"

"I believe I have heard mention of her, but do not give credence to such matters," Collins told him.

"Nevertheless," the sheriff said, "I will have to be present so as to ascertain whether there is fraud or dissembling involved in the proceedings. You might find it enlightening in that regard."

" 'Whose tongue soe'er speaks false, not truly speaks; who speaks not truly, lies.' I cannot abide those who prey upon misfortune."

"Then you may be able to assist in ferreting out deceptions. You are, after all, a Pinkerton man." Flanigan said, employing a disparaging tone.

"I suppose I could stay another day."

Mrs. Rodehaver returned to remove empty dishes and ask if they desired anything further. She was markedly cooler in manner than before.

"No thank you, fair lady," Flanigan replied in his charming tenor. "It has been a sumptuous feast and no mistaking."

The woman softened a tad in spite of herself. "Well I am glad you enjoyed your meal."

The men left the dining room and Collins looked for his dog. She was under a nearby chair and bounded out to meet him.

"Very well, gentlemen, I am going to the livery stable,"

Collins told his companions. "I have enjoyed our conversations."

The doctor shook his hand vigorously. "I hope I will see you this evening. It should prove to be quite stimulating." He strode briskly into the cold morning, headed, no doubt, to his office and drugstore housed in a nearby sod structure.

"I have a small matter I must look into," the sheriff said. "Might I expect to see you later, then?"

"I imagine so," C.W. told him.

"Most acceptable. Until later, Mr. Collins."

"*Slán,* Mr. Flanigan."

Collins strolled leisurely down to the stables with Gal following behind. He had made up his mind that interviewing individual victims of the raids would not be necessary. Exhorting survivors to relive their tragedies could do nothing to add to his wealth of knowledge at this juncture and he was admittedly loath to subject himself to detailed accounts of their anguish, especially given his thoroughgoing imagination. He also did not wish to mislead any of them into thinking he could assist in the reimbursement of their losses.

Scotty was mucking out a stall in the barn, his breath making foggy billows as he labored.

"Good morning," Collins said.

"Mornin'. Already fed your stock." The stocky boy leaned on his pitchfork a moment.

"Thank you. I wanted to stop in, but not because I doubt your care of them."

Scotty bent down and attempted to coax the dog to come to him. She ducked behind Collins with her ears back.

"Sorry. She is shy of strangers."

"Ain't we all?" the youth said and returned to his work.

Outside in the pen, he found his mules at the hay

bunk while Ulysses was busy cleaning up some spilled oats on the ground. He greeted all of them individually, looking them over to ensure their soundness and general welfare. He had learned long ago that being attentive to his animals prevented missing an injury or problem that could later impact their overall health. His gelding came over and almost knocked him off his feet with a shove of his nose. Collins scratched the horse's forehead and rubbed his eyes.

Gal gave a short bark and he looked up to see Atkins. He was just inside the door of the barn scrutinizing the scene.

"Told you. No dogs."

"I am paying for the privilege."

The man sniffed loudly. "You leaving?"

"Not yet."

Atkins turned on his heel and disappeared into the barn. Collins gave a final pat to his animals and went back through the barn to leave from the front onto the main thoroughfare. He found Scotty and Atkins speaking to a large man sitting on a spring wagon drawn by a pair of fine black Percherons. The fellow displayed a thick beard that extended down to the middle of his chest.

"Good day, friend," the man said to Collins. "I do not believe we have met." He climbed down from the wagon seat, with more agility than Collins would have expected from his size, and held out a hand.

"Good morning," Collins said, shaking his hand.

"I am David Banta."

"Charles Collins."

"This here is a preacher," Atkins said. "He is a Baptist. I myself am a Methodist. We do not believe in drowning people to save their souls."

Banta gave Scotty instructions as to his team and wagon. He seemed to ignore Atkins' discourteous manner. "There is room for all in God's world," he finally remarked.

The livery owner retreated to his office inside the stables. Banta and Collins stood together a moment and watched while Scotty unhitched the team and ground drove them around the side of the barn.

"Nice boy," the preacher said. "Too bad he has to work for Atkins."

"He has to?"

"He and his father, John Wright, were out here looking for a place to homestead. They were separated in the raids of last October and the man is still missing. Sheriff Flanigan found a body last December in a brake of brushwood down along the north fork of the Sappa that might have been him, but the boy was not certain. The mother is dead and he has no other relatives."

"Were you here during the attacks?" Collins asked, taking out his pipe and packing it with tobacco.

"I was over east in Slab City with a dying man. Fell from a horse and was dragged some distance. Came back in the midst of folks stumbling into town, wounded and mortally afraid."

Drawing on his pipe energetically, Collins put a match to it. The sun was poking through a blanket of thin clouds, sending soft shafts of light to illuminate patches of rooftops. The wind began to make itself known.

"It must have been tragic," C.W. said, issuing puffs of smoke from his pipe into the rising breeze.

"It was frightful." Banta took a leather satchel from the back of the wagon. "Well...Mr. Collins was it? I am pleased to meet you. Perhaps I will see you later?"

"Perhaps. Had you heard of the spiritualist exhibition slated for this evening?"

The man stroked his impressive beard. "I had," he said acridly. "Were you planning to attend?"

"Only as an impartial observer."

"Pure poppycock," the preacher said as he strode away.

Collins was not certain whether Banta was referring to the event or his plans to attend.

I WILL CIVILIZE THEM

22

Mrs. Sarah Hudson sat across from the spiritualist, a young woman named Miss Emma Crowley, her eyes closed. Mrs. Hudson had the care-worn face and coarse hands that Collins had observed on many emigrant women of the plains. Miss Crowley's fingers were pale and delicate and the widow's hand appeared rough and uncouth in their grasp. The medium had explained to the group of people, gathered in the hotel parlor, that she would summon a spirit to speak through her and who could send messages from the dearly departed to their bereaved loved ones. Incongruously, Miss Crowley claimed this spirit was that of an Arab girl from the 13th century, named Amara. While Sheriff Flanigan and C.W. were quite amused by the apparent charlatanism, most of the crowd, with a few exceptions, appeared to be enthralled by the proceedings. Collins was surprised to see the Baptist preacher was in attendance.

In the dimly lit room, illuminated by three candles, Miss Crowley was praying softly for a healing white light to fill the widow woman as they awaited the arrival of Amara. Suddenly the girl gasped loudly, throwing her head back and appearing to swoon. When she raised her head again and spoke, it was in a high child's voice with a spurious foreign accent. Collins and Flanigan turned to grin at each other.

"Our loved ones never truly leave us," the voice said. "Mr. John Hudson is here with me...he is sorry you are left alone, but he is at peace. He says he is sorry about the mules."

Mrs. Hudson broke into wailing, pulling her hand away and burying her face in her shawl. "We lost the mules," she cried. "Them red devils stole our mules. Oh John...poor John..."

"You see," Dr. Bariteau said, excitedly. "How could she know about the mules?"

Flanigan leaned close to Collins. "Astounding that a man of science could be so easily deluded," he said softly.

Miss Crowley seemed to come back to herself. "Oh my goodness." She looked about dazedly. "You must not carry on so. You frighten poor Amara and she cannot reach me then."

Mrs. Hudson was still weeping profusely. Mrs. Rodehaver came over and took charge of her. They retreated together into the dining room.

"This is rather entertaining at that," Collins told the sheriff.

The gentleman who appeared to be the girl spiritist's manager spoke to the audience. "Please limit your remarks and support Miss Emma in her communications with the other side. This is quite taxing and we must lend her our strength and faith and limit our histrionics."

"Is there another one here who wishes to speak to their loved one?" Miss Crowley asked breathlessly.

An older woman came forth and sat across from the medium. The manager stepped over to collect a dollar from her. She reluctantly handed him a coin after which he moved back into the shadows.

"My name is Abernathy," the woman said. "Mary Abernathy. I lost my dear husband, Moses, in an attack by those murderin' injuns."

"Do you wish to speak to him?"

"Can I? I mean is it really possible?"

"Give me your hand. I will try to have Amara find him."

Again the girl rocked her head back then lifted it up after a long moment. The little girl voice said, "Moses is close by. But he is shy and not ready to speak. He wishes me to tell you that he will be at your side. Look ever upwards, and just try your best day by day, and that will lead you here in the end…right up to this glorious world."

"Why, my Moses would never say such a thing," the widow said disdainfully, squinting at the girl across from her. "And I will be goddamned if he was ever shy."

Flanigan gleefully elbowed Collins hard in the side.

"We are a thousand times more joyous than when on earth," the voice said. "The world is nothing, and all that is in it is only a make-believe. This is the real life where we can express ourselves to the fullest, where love prevails and where all sorrows flee away."

"Well that may be so, but those of us down here still have to make do. Can he tell me where in hell he hid our cash money?"

"He says do not be concerned. All will be well."

"Well this is a bunch of hogwash," Mrs. Abernathy said loudly, pulling her hand away. "The old man never could answer a straight goddamn question." She got up from the chair and abruptly exited the building. She let loose with a few choice curse words as she left.

Flanigan was laughing quite audibly. Collins attempted to stifle his mirth, but was incapable.

"Come, come, dear friends," the medium's handler was saying. "Please be respectful."

Emma Crowley seemed distressed by the general merriment that had erupted in the room. "The spirit may not want to discuss what is of interest to you. Once a person crosses over, what was important during their earthly life may not be important to them anymore." Her speech was back to normal and she was twisting a handkerchief abstractedly.

Mr. Rodehaver lit some of the parlor lamps and Collins could see the girl's face was flushed and damp. Her companion came to her rescue and, lifting her to her feet, guided her up the stairs and into a room. Dr. Bariteau was shaking his head in dismay.

"This is too bad. Too, too bad. I was so interested in hearing more. After all, she knew about the mules."

This statement inspired another bout of laughter from Flanigan. The doctor gave him a reproachful glance and made his way out of the hotel. Collins and the sheriff went into the dining room and sat at a table.

"I believe the poor girl requires more schooling if she is to be plausible," Collins said.

"This was better than the medicine show I saw over near Denver last year. They had a midget that juggled with his feet."

Mrs. Rodehaver brought coffee, having apparently settled Mrs. Hudson somewhere and resumed her serving duties. David Banta walked into the room and came over to their table.

"May I join you?"

Flanigan waved him welcome. "Did you admire the show?" he asked the preacher.

" 'Show' is the right of it," Banta said, taking a seat. "I thought it cruel to deceive those unfortunate women."

"I do not think Mrs. Abernathy was deceived," Collins said, smiling.

"Perhaps not, but the entire exhibition was shameful."

"I do wonder what ol' Abernathy did with the money," Flanigan said.

David Banta was not amused. "He probably drank it up, knowing him."

Collins finished his coffee, placed a dime on the table and stood. "I am for bed and will be leaving early in the morning. I have enjoyed meeting you both."

Flanigan came to his feet to shake his hand. *"Go raibh an ghaoth go brách ag do chúl,"* he said, by way of farewell.

"Go raibh céad maith agat," C.W. told him, gripping his hand a moment. He turned and left the dining room.

————∾◆∾————

23

Riding northwest from Oberlin, Collins realized he could see more and more cattle roaming the countryside. According to Flanigan, cattle drives came up the Texas Trail, passing nine miles west of the town, to Ogallala and the Union Pacific Railroad. This had led to the development of ranching along the route and a few large outfits ran their stock upon great expanses of prairie into southern Nebraska, especially along the Republican River and the South Platte. With a shipping destination nearby, the locally raised beef tended to weigh more when sold. Other herds were wintered over and then driven on to Montana Territory or the gold fields of the Black Hills the next season. He came upon the trail and decided to follow it to Beaver Creek and on into Nebraska.

Collins had heard of Ogallala. Thousands of head of cattle passed seasonally through its stockyards and it had a reputation for violence that rivaled Dodge City. Saloons and brothels prospered in service to the gangs of drovers that arrived with money to spend and the town attracted every type of gambler, sharper and huckster while the yearly boom lasted. Gunfights and fistfights were common, but local residents were willing to endure disruptions for the sake of formidable monetary recompence. There had even been a famous train robbery in the vicinity a couple of years before. All that mattered to him was that would surely be a telegraph office in the town and he desperately needed to send a telegram to

Schurz with an update. He also intended to send another message that was equally imperative.

The landscape was once again bleak and uninspiring. The wide swath of cattle trail remained denuded of vegetation from the previous season and drifts of snow punctuated myriad clumps of buffalo grass and sagebrush along the perimeter. It was raw with windchill and Collins wore his bearskin coat, wrapping Gal in its folds where she perched on the saddle. Ulysses and the mules blew clouds of vapor while they trudged along and ice coated their muzzles and whiskers. C.W's mind wandered as he rode, contemplating the overwhelming disparities that existed between Indian cultures and those of western Europe.

It seemed to him that the Indian people he had spent time with possessed a boundless respect and affection for the land itself. They did not speak of owning land and expressed confusion when whites claimed to own it, especially during treaty negotiations. He had observed a fervent devotion for their surroundings and sacred places that he had never witnessed in white settlers, especially farmers. Another divergence could be found in spiritual beliefs. The Indian afterlife, from what he had learned, was a continuation of this life in an idealized construct. It occurred to Collins that this must mean Indians had developed an existence that was consummately gratifying and, therefore, they desired the same intrinsic state of being to endure after death.

The Christian afterlife, by contrast and in its most simplistic manifestation, was a reward for good or bad acts. The deceased were sent to heaven or hell for eternity, after being judged by divine entities. Whether a departed soul was directed to one destination or the other, the incarnation of each bore no similarity to human life on earth, even though descriptions of either termini might vary according to dogma and denominations.

What this must mean, Collins reflected, was that Catholics and Protestants were none too fond of life on earth, probably because European and American societies were abusively hierarchical and founded mostly on acquisition. Ironically, he thought smiling, these civilizations had already created a very palpable version of hell in the present world and the balance of humanity was being forced to live in it by way of governmental bureaucracies and colonization.

A prairie chicken exploded from behind a snow drift as Ulysses sank a hoof through the crust. The horse lunged sideways, throwing Gal from the saddle and almost unseating Collins, then crow-hopped a few times until C.W. regained his equilibrium, dropped Molly's lead rope, and pulled slack from the reins to yank the gelding's head up. The animal stood quivering while Collins dismounted and stepped over to reassure him. He looked around for the dog, but she was not in sight. The mules stood a few feet away, seemingly unperturbed, and Joey was rubbing his forehead on Molly's breeching. She thumped him lightly with a rear hoof.

Collins gathered up Molly's rope and led the mules over to Ulysses. He tightened the cinch and swung up, keeping the reins taut and speaking soothingly to the horse. The dog came trotting over from somewhere, but he let her travel on the ground while the gelding calmed down. C.W. chided himself for not remaining sufficiently attentive in unfamiliar territory, especially when the remorseless wind was making his poor horse nervy. After a mile or so, he reined in and slapped his thigh, signaling to Gal she could launch herself up so he could catch her. Ulysses tossed his head, but stood quietly enough while the dog adopted her customary position, momentarily chewing at an ice ball on her chest.

In a short while, their course brought them to the brink of Beaver Creek. Collins judged it to be late morning. He dismounted, loosened the cinches and reconnoitered. Gal ran down the bank on a mission of her own. The stream was frozen, so he slipped a small hand axe from his packs and chopped a large hole to allow the animals to drink. The ice was not thick and broke easily. While the horse and mules took turns at the water, Collins pulled out the map and compass to confirm his bearings. He had come upon Beaver Creek about the time he had calculated and he figured he could make it to the Republican River before nightfall.

After readjusting all the saddles, relieving himself and filling his pockets with hardtack and chunks of turkey meat, Collins climbed into the saddle and called for Gal. She bounded out from a clump of willows and leapt to scrabble up his thigh onto his lap. He rubbed her head and slipped her a piece of meat, then lightly pressed his heels to move Ulysses downstream, looking for a place to cross. He presently came to an open clearing where the creek widened and they crossed without difficulty. He judged that the location was probably the ford used by cattle herds, the banks being low and rounded.

As they traveled northward, the land did not alter in its monotony, mostly featureless except for the occasional swell or shallow coulee. Once in a while he sighted a herd of antelope, bunches of cattle or a sod homestead off in the distance. The cold gusts of wind kept Collins from nodding in sleep from ennui, pummeling him and his animals like a persistent fist. He sang songs and talked to his horse and dog and further pondered the incongruity between white and Indian cultures, while remaining alert to the environs. The afternoon passed slowly and he was mortally jaded by the time he came to the banks of the Republican River in the early evening. The waterway bore a light skin of friable ice and was unexpectedly low.

Riding west along the floodplain, Collins found a sheltered horseshoe bend with easy access to water and a deep pool. The area on the south side of the stream also offered thick brush for cover and some wizened grass for the animals. He dismounted and stood a moment, letting the blood settle back into his legs. While the dog explored their surroundings, he swiftly unsaddled the stock, set up camp and gathered firewood. As he labored, he tried to recall how the Republican River had acquired its name. He remembered it had to do with French trappers, back in the late 16th century, who referred to the Pawnees as republicans and the river as *Fourche des Republiques*. Just why the trappers called the Pawnee people republicans was anyone's guess. Perhaps, he thought, because they possessed a tribal government absent of monarchy.

Furious barking brought Collins out of his reverie. He was kneeling by the fire ring, feeding wood to the flames, and his rifle was leaning against the pile of saddles by the tent. He came to his feet as Gal flew past and took a position behind him, baring her teeth and snarling. With a hand on the butt of his revolver, C.W. awaited the approach of whatever entity was crashing toward the camp through dense growth off to the southwest. In short order, a tall dapple grey horse emerged from the vegetation carrying a thickset man in cattleman's garb. The fellow wore a silverbelly hat and a beard reminiscent of the showman, Buffalo Bill. It did not endear the stranger to him, as he held Bill Cody in low regard.

"Evening," the man said.

Collins put a hand to his dog to calm her. "Hello."

"My name is William Street. I have been up to Ogallala and was headed for the Holstine-McCoy Ranch on the forks of the Beaver, but am running out of light. I have camped at this very spot more than once and now you have it."

"I do indeed," Collins said.

"Room for me?"

"There is room if you picket your horse out a ways."

Street led his mare some distance downstream, unsaddled and tethered her to a stout tree. He returned carrying saddlebags, a bedroll and a bulging flour sack. C.W. had coffee brewing and was frying up the rest of the ham donated by Private Corky Brown. He pushed two large potatoes into the coals on the edge of the fire. Gal lay near the tent and maintained a persistent low growling.

"Your dog is none too friendly," Street said, dropping his bedroll and saddlebags near the fire.

"Nope." Collins was not feeling overly sociable himself.

The man dug around in the flour sack and pulled out a paper package. "This here is some corn bread," he said. "Mrs. Sheidly, up on the Big Springs, always sends some with me, knowing my taste for it. Good with coffee," he added, eyeing the coffeepot.

Pulling the extra tin cup from a pannier, Collins tossed it to his unwelcome guest.

Street filled the cup and sat on his bedroll. "Headed to Ogallala?"

"Yes."

"Nice mules," Street said, thumbing toward where Molly and Joey stood side by side, nose to tail. Ulysses was searching for the occasional dried leaf in a brake of dogwood trees. "That one mule is quite a size." He paused, plainly ill at ease. "This is good coffee."

Collins was not particularly inspired toward civility, but relented. "There will be enough ham and potatoes, if you care to join me. Would go nicely with the corn bread."

"Thanks. Might I have your name?"

"Charles Collins."

"Well, Mr. Collins, I am grateful for your fire and victuals. Did not plan on sleeping rough."

As they ate, the man embarked on a story about the depredations of the previous October and his part in the events. Apparently, he had just returned from a cattle drive, beginning in San Antonio and ending in Ogallala. Having a small ranch near Oberlin, he was headed home when he heard of the raids at a friend's ranch near the town of Atwood. He was talked into riding back north with some of the men so as to pursue and punish the Indians. While stopping over at the Circle O Ranch, on the Republican River several miles to the east of C.W.'s camp, one of Major Mauck's orderlies arrived to employ a man to carry dispatches to the telegraph station. He was selected, mostly against his will, to make the ride to Ogallala. The man recited too many details about horses, mud and false Indian alarms, but Street finally carried his account to the telegraph office. He had ridden almost 140 miles without sleep.

"I sent the dispatches and made camp on the edge of town. I then was woken about ten that night by the operator and held up at the telegraph office for hours," he said. "Newspapers and army officers sent message after message requesting information. My most important interview was with Major Thornburgh at Fort Sidney. He wanted to know where I thought the Cheyennes would cross the South Platte. The major had troops and supplies at the ready."

Street poured more coffee, stuffed a big bite of ham in his mouth and washed it down. He wiped his face with a coat sleeve. "Thornburgh asked me to scout on south of town the next morning and let him know the location of the Indians. He would have an engine steamed up and ready to pull out in a matter of thirty minutes. The troopers were to disembark at the nearest station so as to stop the Indians at the river."

Collins finished his meal, fed the dog with leftovers and took out his pipe. "It is difficult to believe the Indians would come so near a town."

"Well let me tell you…I went out early the next morning to reconnoiter. I climbed the railroad windmill and spotted them about two miles east down the Platte. I rode straight back to the telegraph office and sent the news to Major Thornburgh. In no time at all, his reply came stating he was on his way with instructions for me to follow the Indians to see which direction they took after crossing and where they might cross the North Platte. I got another fellow to ride with me and we watched as the group crossed the river, but were forced to retreat when several of the warriors began shooting at us."

While he smoked, Collins studied the man. He seemed genuine enough, though somewhat longwinded. He supposed the man was telling the truth, but one could never be certain. Street pulled out a pouch of tobacco and rolling papers. He built a smoke and lit it with a smoldering branch from the fire.

"Back in Ogallala, I joined up with a party of cowboys set to embark on a scouting expedition. We rode northeast of the river toward the North Platte and came upon a small bunch of warriors butchering a beef. We came around to their flank and opened fire, but the horses did not like us for that and our shots went wild. When the Indians reached the river, they settled in behind a bank and made it pretty warm. We headed back for town and found that Major Thornburgh had arrived. I reported to him and he expressed his desire for me to accompany him on the pursuit north. I told him I had never been north of the North Platte River, but he told me a man that could make a ride such as I had would be worth having along."

Stretching and knocking the ashes from his pipe, Collins came to his feet. He was fatigued and somewhat weary of his companion, but he did wish to hear the final result of the man's involvement. "Did you finally engage the Indians north of the river?" he asked, tossing a last limb of cottonwood onto the fire, sending a shower of sparks into the gloom.

Street coughed and spit into the flames. "They scattered into small bands and melted into the sand hills. It was tough going with short rations and water and Thornburgh's command missed them altogether, even though we had been joined by a couple of good old buffalo hunters who knew the country. We finally united up with a Major Carlton on the Niobrara. We rode on into Camp Robinson and us scouts were all sent home by way of the stage to Sidney. I heard the Indians lately broke out of Camp Robinson and are now all dead."

"I heard that as well."

The man stood up. "They killed a lot of folks down on the Sappa and Beaver and outraged several women and girls," he said gathering up his bedroll to lay it out. "Should of stayed down at Fort Reno, no matter their reason for sneaking off. There is no more room in this country for the red men and no more toleration for their barbarity."

Without another word, Collins walked into the darkness to check on his livestock. There was nothing to say.

OGALLALA

24

The country north of the Republican River was marked by hills and coulees and scattered trees, in sharp contrast to the terrain south of the river. This soon flattened out again and Collins found himself once more riding through uninspired landscape, barren of interest or variation. He continued to follow the Texas Trail, aiming for Frenchman's Fork, about twenty miles to the northwest. Beyond this, according to William Street, the trail would follow Stinking Water Creek almost to the South Platte. Street alleged that the name of the creek came from an incident wherein several buffalo became mired in bog along the stream and were trampled by the rest of the herd, their corpses creating a terrible stench. He had impressed upon Collins that the water was clear and sweet, but remained treacherous with boggy ground along its perimeter.

Street had ridden out of camp after having coffee and sharing the last of the cornbread. His mare was a trifle tall for him and slightly cold-backed and he had some difficulty getting mounted. C.W. could not adequately determine the reason why the man aggravated him, but he was not sorry to see his back. He supposed it was the man's cockalorum, an attribute he never favored. And, of course, his apparent attempt at emulating William Cody.

Around noon he struck Frenchman's Fork. The banks were thick with brush except where the trail cut through, making a ford that was wide and so shallow, that he was forced to take his animals upstream a short distance to allow them to drink. There was ice along the edges of the stream, but open water in the middle of the rivulet. He did not bother to dismount and Gal seemed disinclined to jump into the creek from his saddle. Making his way back to the ford, they skirted a low hill and rode through a deep gully that topped out on a bench. From there, the track dropped down to the confluence of two streams. Collins remembered Street telling him he would come to the forks of the Stinking Water Creek if he kept to the trail.

His chosen route followed the northbound fork past some modest buildings, a small horse herd and bunches of cattle with tails set against the cold wind. Collins rode on by, wanting to cover as much territory as possible and not eager to encounter more strangers. He passed the ranch without incident and was able to travel quite a distance before dusk overtook him and he was obliged to make camp. Despite the persistent yipping of coyotes nearby, Collins slept well and set out again early the next morning.

The next two days blended together as he followed the trail along the Stinking Water across land that was indistinguishable from one mile to the next. The terrain was broken by coulees and low buttes to the east of the creek, but was mostly open and featureless to the west. The Stinking Water ran itself out on the second day and C.W. shared his own dwindling supply of water with his animals. Finally, the track dropped into a ravine and followed it down to the valley along the river. By the time he had reached the banks of the South Platte River, the animals were in sore need of rest and water. Collins made camp in a secluded grove of trees southwest of Ogallala, about a mile from where the trail met the river. Snow was beginning to fall as he settled in for the night.

The next morning, he woke to a few inches of snow.

He built a fire with the aid of some paraffin and leisurely made coffee. After a meal of the last of the antelope meat and bread, he washed the dishes, grained his horse and mules and picketed them securely. Collins stowed his packsaddles and the rest of his gear in the tent, suspended the food pannier from a lofty tree branch and saddled Ulysses, slipping his rifle into the scabbard. With Gal in front of him, he followed the river to the ford that led into town. He was hoping for a bath and a shave, but more than that, it was imperative he send telegrams. He also needed to purchase more provisions.

There was not a single soul in evidence as he approached a small collection of buildings, set with their backs to the river. The first structures he came to on the road into Ogallala were twin false front buildings sheltered by narrow porches and amply declaring multiple commodities for sale, by way of precise lettering on the clapboard of the second stories. These establishments were situated perpendicular to the street that lay along the fronts of the other buildings. Collins peered through the large windows as he rode past, but nary a person was manifest. He turned into the snowy lane that extended a short distance and surveyed the remainder of the village. From the dearth of hoof prints in the pristine white blanket, he was clearly the first to travel there that morning.

To his left lay the railroad and just across the tracks he could see a livery stable and a squat stone building that appeared to be the local jail. The only other buildings across the way were two rather nicely built frame houses and what appeared to be the Union Pacific depot. To his right, he noted another provisioner, closed for the winter as per a sign tacked to the door, and a good-sized saloon, also with a clear statement of closure attached to the entry. The first signs of tenancy he observed was the bundled form of a man propped against the front wall of the "Cowboy's Rest Saloon," so proclaimed by immense lettering across the front of the edifice. It was a damp and cold roost and C.W. could only guess that the fellow had been too inebriated to journey homeward the evening before.

He made his way to the end of the road, passing two more structures, individually a small purveyor of shoes and boots and a low log building that was unmarked regarding its purpose. The next building was designated as the Ogallala House and smoke rising from a stovepipe gave him hope he might actually discover a person with whom to converse. He reined in at the hitching rail and dismounted. Gal chose to remain balanced on the saddle and out of the snow. Ulysses had grown so accustomed to her, he turned his head to touch noses with the dog in a sociable manner.

Stamping his boots on the wooden flooring of the porch, he knocked on the door, then finding it unfastened, stepped into the warm interior. The furnishings were primitive, according to the standards of larger towns, but the walls were covered in a cheerful paper and adorned with several chromophotographs of mountain scenery as well as a large buffalo robe. Several pieces of furniture filled the space and the middle of the room was occupied by an ornate Crown Jewel heating stove. Collins stood by the stove a moment, enjoying the heat. He heard a door open. He turned to see a buxom woman with voluminous locks of dark brown hair piled on her head. She had a pleasant round face, flushed from some type of exertion, and she was wiping her hands on an apron.

"My goodness, where did you spring from?" she asked, breathlessly.

"I did not mean to startle you," Collins said, removing his hat. "I am camped near the river and you are the first person I have found this morning."

"We are mostly deserted in the winter, as you can see. My name is Martha Rooney. My husband and I run this establishment. Did you want to stay?"

C.W. gave a slight bow. "Pleasure to meet you, Mrs. Rooney. My name is Charles Collins. I do not wish a room, but some information would be very welcome."

"Well of course, Mr. Collins. Did you care to step into the dining room and have some coffee?" she asked, smoothing back a loose strand of hair self-consciously. "Mr. Rooney is chopping wood out the back. I can fetch him."

"Please do not trouble yourself. I am only eager to find the telegraph office. I did not detect it as I rode into town."

"Oh no, you would not have seen it. The office is a mile to the west near the stockyards. Mr. Searle will be on duty as the westbound train is due just before noon."

"Does the train stop at the depot here in Ogallala?"

"Not unless there is a passenger and that is rare this time of year. The Number 5 will have taken on water and coal at North Platte and will run right on through here shortly."

"Any hope of purchasing a few supplies in town?"

"Oh yes. Aufdengarten's store is at the end of Railroad Street. You would have passed it I think. He will be around there somewhere, now he has given up ranching."

"Is there a tonsorial parlor or," he paused, "a bath house that might be open?"

Mrs. Rooney blushed and shook her head. "No, no I am sorry. Everyone just makes do in the winter. The saloon down the way might accommodate you for the bath."

"I will be taking my leave, then. I have shed some snow melt on your floor," Collins said, looking down at his boots. "I apologize."

The woman blushed again. "That is no bother."

Smiling and nodding a farewell, Collins donned his

hat and headed for the door.

"Come by for a meal later, if you have a mind to," Mrs. Rooney called to him as he opened the door. "We always have plenty and Mr. Rooney would be glad of the company."

"I just may do that, thank you," he said, stepping onto the porch.

Outside, he saw that Gal was curled up on the seat of his saddle, nose tucked in under her hind leg. He checked his cinch and swung up, settling her onto his lap. As he turned to ride west toward the stockyards, a light snow began falling. The large flakes resembled downy feathers. The deciduous trees along the route took on an ethereal aspect, dusted in white with every branch made distinct by the contrast of light and dark.

Passing by the dual storefronts on the end of town once more, Collins saw that someone had built a fire and smoke billowed from one of the stovepipes. He would stop by later after sending his telegrams. He supposed that Aufdengarten was a Germanic name and so, here again, was another Prussian. Truly, he thought, it might be said that there were as many Irish immigrants in America as German, but since they were generally looked down upon as papists, they did not have the political leverage that Anglo-Saxons possessed, nor were they as acceptable.

Riding along the railroad tracks, he was suddenly aware of a rhythmic chugging noise coming from behind him. It was becoming more noticeable and Collins realized it must be the Number 5 on its way westward. Knowing that Ulysses had little experience with steam engines, he rode some distance away from the railroad grade and pulled up to wait for the train to pass. It went by at a good pace, pouring clouds of steam from its stack. His gelding danced around, not particularly pleased by the iron beast, but Collins patted his neck and told him all would be well. The train slipped by, hauling a good many freight cars, all bound for Julesburg, Cheyenne and points beyond.

The telegraph office was just to the north of a railroad siding leading to the stockyards. The pens were empty and deserted and the top rails were garnished in white fluffy powder. Collins rode up to the front of the building and dismounted. This time, Gal jumped down and followed him. She slipped inside as he closed the door behind him. The interior of the office was almost as chilly as the exterior. The small stove in the corner did not seem to hold a fire and the man seated at a table with the telegraph apparatus was bundled in a heavy woolen coat and fingerless gloves and wore a shawl tied over his bowler hat. He turned abruptly at the sound of Collins' arrival, holding a copy of the *Columbus Journal* that he had been reading.

"May I help you?" he asked, glancing up at Collins placidly.

"My name is C.W. Collins. I desire your services."

The telegrapher sat up and lay his paper aside. "That can be arranged. Your dog is not going to piss on something is he?"

"She will not."

"Very well then. My name is Edward Searle. You wanted to send a telegram?"

"I did. The first is to Herr Burschenschaft at the Willard Hotel in Washington D.C. Here, I will write it out." Collins found a telegram blank on a desk nearby. The operator handed him a pencil.

"What kind of name is that?" Searle asked.

"Collins?" C.W. asked, thinking the man was a bit of a wag.

"Burken...whatever."

"It is Prussian, I believe. I have it spelled out here," he said, indicating the blank on which he was composing his message.

He informed Schurz of his location, a few details of the depredations, mentioned the Captain Wedemeyer report and the seeming ineptitude of the military in not having thwarted the Cheyennes' progress north through Kansas and most of Nebraska. He also communicated his intention to search for Dull Knife and Little Wolf. He did not wish to include an excess of detail as Mr. Searle would undoubtedly be curious about the import. He handed the communication to Searle and began to fill out another blank. The man perused the form, then proceeded to tap the key.

Smoothing out another blank, C.W. addressed the next communique to Superintendent James Morrow Walsh of the North-West Mounted Police at Cypress Hills, Saskatchewan. In it, he requested information regarding an Indian woman by the name of Arbuckles who might be residing with Sitting Bull's band, currently positioned near Fort Walsh. When Searle had completed sending the first message, Collins gave him the next one.

"This might cost a pretty penny," the telegrapher told him, laying the paper on the table in front of him.

"It will be worth it and more," Collins said, smiling to himself.

25

Snow was still falling when Collins exited the telegraph office. As expected, Searle had attempted to draw him out as to his business and the actual identity of Burschenschaft. The wily fellow endeavored to detain him through various means, but Collins extricated himself and left shortly after paying for his telegrams. The messages had been expensive, but he had brought ample funds with him along with several bank notes sewn into the lining of his frock coat. He would not have to request additional funds from Schurz for quite some time.

Gal trotted behind Ulysses as he headed back toward the Aufdengarten store, making furrows in the deepening powder with her compact body. On arrival, he secured Ulysses to a porch post and told his dog to stay. Stepping onto the wooden walkway perpendicular to the door, he glanced through a window and saw a diminutive man working behind a counter, calibrating a set of scales. He found the door unbolted and stepped in. The store's climate was considerably warmer than had been that of the telegraph office.

"Hello there," the shopkeeper greeted him. "A might wintry today."

"Quite wintry," Collins said, mildly surprised that the man did not have a German accent. "Are you Mr. Aufdengarten?"

"Oh no...oh indeed not. I am his clerk."

"My name is Collins. I need to stock up on a few

items if you are open for business.”

“Oh indeed, indeed,” said the fastidious little clerk. “I am George Miller and I will do my utmost to serve you.”

“May I have a slip of paper and pencil?”

“Absolutely, indeed.” The clerk placed a notebook and pencil on the counter.

Pausing to think, Collins wrote a small list of goods he required, especially meat. He noticed a box of Spratt’s Dog and Puppy Cakes on a shelf off to the side.

“Are those dog cakes of any use?” he asked, indicating the box with a finger.

“Oh yes, yes indeed, I believe so. A fine English gentleman had us order them for his dogs. He was out here last summer to see about purchasing a ranch. A lovely gentleman...oh yes indeed.”

“I see. Well you may add two boxes to my supplies, if you will.” Collins finished writing his list and handed the notebook back to Miller.

The clerk put C.W.’s purchases together and split the load between two burlap sacks at his request. He paid the clerk and thanked him.

“Oh you are quite welcome. Indeed so welcome. Be careful, mind.”

Stepping out onto the porch, he saw that the snow was falling harder now and the wind was picking up. Gal waited under the cover of the porch roof until he had tied the sacks of goods behind his saddle, swept the seat clear of snow and mounted up. She jumped up into his arms and they headed back toward the river, Ulysses plowing through growing drifts built along clumps of brush. The ground under the snow was sticky mud and made for dodgy navigation. Collins pulled his hat down and put up the fur collar on his coat against the stiff westerly breeze. It seemed to him the temperature was falling swiftly.

The road was barely visible as he headed toward the

river crossing. He rode down into the flood plain and the gelding traversed the stiffening mire of the ford. Through the near whiteout, he could make out a shape on the far bank. Cautiously, he drew nearer and saw it was a Studebaker wagon crabbed sideways in slushy muck, the lone draft mule struggling in its traces. A figure was at its head, attempting to calm the animal and get it to alter its course. The mule was in a turmoil of agitation and plainly would not heed any effort to mollify it nor cease its lunging. Collins kept clear of the skirmish and dismounted by a dead cottonwood, tying his horse to a branch and impressing upon Gal to stay in the saddle.

Moving toward the wagon over treacherous footing, C.W. called out so as to not startle the individual at the mule's head. He came closer and saw the personage was bundled in an old union cavalry overcoat and a wool balaclava. Peeking out of the voluminous garments was a pale face of delicate but stern beauty. The woman appeared alarmed at Collins' approach and stepped back, stumbling and almost falling backwards on the haphazard terrain of the river bank. He caught her shoulder and held her steady until she regained her equilibrium. Gal jumped down and began barking loudly and the mule balked and turned uphill, pulling itself and the wagon free of the quagmire and disappearing into the white veil above them.

"No!" the woman exclaimed and floundered up the incline in the direction of her rig.

Collins followed her with the dog on his heels, excited by all the commotion. He gained the top of the riverbank and found the woman standing several yards away. She was stock still beside her wagon, contemplating a slender tree wedged firmly between the wagon box and left rear wheel. The mule appeared to have quietened down and was chewing on a cottonwood sapling. The woman looked up when he came near.

"Should we back your mule up and find out whether the wheel can be freed?" he asked.

Her dark eyes flashed. "Where did you come from, anyway?" she asked tartly. "Your dog is the cause of all this."

"In truth, you were quite entrenched when we came upon you," he responded. "My dog is the reason your mule pulled free," he said, grinning.

Her face relaxed and she smiled back. "Perhaps. At any account, I could use your assistance now. I will get Jack to go backward if you can see to the wheel. And for godssake, keep your dog out of the way."

They extricated the wagon in short order and found neither the wheel nor the axle had been damaged. The snow had let up and the sun poked out between ragged clouds. Collins judged it must have been around mid-afternoon.

"Thank you," the woman said, holding out a mittened hand to shake. "My name is Annie Guthrie. I have a homestead a few miles southwest of here on a bend of the South Platte. I was headed to Aufdengarten's for supplies."

"I am Charles Collins. I have a camp near here and am traveling north to Fort Robinson. If you care to accompany me, I will make coffee and some food. I just resupplied at the store." He hesitated a moment. "Unless, of course, your husband would take umbrage."

The woman gazed at him blankly. "Husband?"

"You...you said there was a homestead. Did I mistake you?"

Annie Guthrie raised an eyebrow, an arched black line against her smooth forehead. Color had returned to her cheeks. "It is my homestead. There is no husband. The claim was filed in my sister's and my name, but Margaret died last year and now there is only me."

Judging himself a perfect fool, Collins shrugged and smiled wryly. "My apologies. I should not have presumed."

Jack brayed impatiently. In the distance he was answered by Joey.

"What is that now?" Miss Guthrie asked, on her guard again.

"One of mine, no doubt. Come, let me offer you the hospitality of my camp. It is quite comfortable."

"Very well. I am cold right through and could use a fire." She laid the lines up on the wagon seat and climbed on. "Lead the way."

Collins scrambled back down to his horse with Gal behind him. Ulysses had broken the branch to which he had been secured and was at a short distance away, occupied with scavenging for grass beneath the snow. Retrieving his sodden reins, he swung into the saddle and they struggled up the slick bank to where the woman waited. He rode alongside the river, keeping to the main road he had taken earlier in the day. Guthrie followed, slapping her lines and telling her mule to get along. The dog ranged far afield, captivated by scents beyond human ken.

They came to his camp and he could see that all was secure. The woman drove her mule and wagon off into a small adjacent clearing. She expertly unhitched the animal, tied up the lines and led him down to open water to drink. C.W. unfastened the burlap sacks and placed them near his tent, unsaddled his horse and rubbed him down with a saddle blanket. He hobbled Joey and Ulysses and turned them loose to drink and forage. Once Molly was released from the picket rope, she ambled to a glade upstream and began pawing snow from tufts of dried grasses.

Collins gathered more wood and, finding there were no coals left from the morning, used more paraffin to start a fire. He filled the coffeepot with water, put it on the flames and ground beans. Miss Guthrie tethered her mule to the wagon and fed him some grain from an old dishpan she had stowed under the seat. When the mule had finished his ration, she came to the fire. Collins offered her his folding chair.

"This is a comfortable camp," she said, accepting the seat and glancing around.

"I have been forced to rough it too many times," he told her. "This time, I outfitted myself in Chicago and Dodge City."

She observed him curiously. "Outfitted yourself for what?"

"I am on assignment for the Pinkerton Agency," he said, hoping she would not be too inquisitive so that he would not be forced to embellish.

"The Pinkertons..." she said, thoughtfully. "They are not always on the side of right, are they?"

Pouring coffee grounds into the pot, Collins shook his head. "No. But when they are not, I do not accept employment."

"Do you always know?"

He could see this woman was not only comely, but sagacious as well. "Perhaps not. But I have been known to resign on occasion," he said with a grin.

Retrieving one of the sacks filled with supplies, he pulled out a loaf of bread and cut thick slices with his new skinning knife. Placing the bread by the fire to toast, he went over to take down the food pannier and bring out a tin of jam he had purchased in Dodge City. Annie Guthrie sat and talked quietly to Gal, who had arrived in camp and was circling the woman.

"You do not care for dogs?" he asked as he returned from the tent with cups.

"On the contrary, I am very fond of dogs. I have five at home, all different shapes and sizes. I just do not care for them when they come out of nowhere with strange men."

Collins poured coffee and handed her a cup. "Strange men? Now surely, I am not so strange."

She lifted one side of her mouth humorously and ac-

172

cepted the cup, clasping it gingerly in her mittens. "We shall see. One never can judge too soon."

"And what strange land do lone women homesteaders hail from?" Collins asked, spreading jam on toast and giving her a slice.

Miss Guthrie regarded him sardonically. "The land of independence and adventure. There are many wom-en who choose to not have husbands and babies...and therefore do not let their lives slip by in unending toil." She sipped her coffee and took a bite of toast. "Tasty," she said.

"Do you not toil on your homestead?" he asked and added wood to the fire.

"Of course. But everything is in my name and, profit or loss, I take the responsibility. There is no drunkard spending a year's worth of my hard labor on a one night spree."

Gal finally approached the woman and she offered the dog a small piece of toast. Accepting it guardedly, Gal ran a few feet away to devour her treat.

"Not a high regard for men, I take it?"

She held out her cup for a refill. He obliged and poured her more coffee. Gal crept near the woman and lay down. Miss Guthrie lightly smoothed the wet hair on the dog's head.

"Not a low regard either. But I have seen the worst of them and not many of the best."

Fully cognizant of the multiple shortcomings of his fellow men, he said, " 'I am a man more sinned against than sinning.' "

"Easy enough to say," she responded, tipping her head saucily.

"Perhaps, but true all the same."

"And what of you?" she asked.

"No wife...never a wife." He finished his toast and wiped crumbs from his moustache.

"Not a high regard for women, I take it?" she asked acerbically.

"Oh now," he said, training his sapphire blue eyes on her and flashing his most charming smile. "I have the highest regard for women. The highest regard, indeed."

26

He was drinking coffee by the fire before daybreak when she came out of the tent. She was wrapped in her overcoat, her hair was disheveled and there was a slight rash on her chin.

"I should have shaved first," C.W. said, rubbing his face.

"No matter," she said, blushing.

Pouring a cup of coffee, he passed it to her and touched her hand for a moment. "You are lovely," he said.

Annie Guthrie's face turned crimson. "I am a crusty old maid. You must not dissemble."

"I assume, then, that you have no looking glass in your sod hut. How did you come to be out here, anyway?"

She sipped her coffee, the cup cradled in two work-hardened hands. "I was a schoolteacher in Salina, Kansas. It was flat, wearisome country filled with flat, wearisome people."

Collins sliced strips of bacon and laid them in a skillet. He cut up potatoes and added them to the pan. The dog lay nearby, watching him intently. "So that is where you are from?" he asked the woman.

She shivered and moved closer to the fire, pulling the capacious military overcoat tighter around her. "I was raised by my older sister in Maine and thought to seek adventure out west. I only found desolation. Margaret eventually joined me in Salina and we both agreed that there had to be a more agreeable survival. I came up here and looked around and we filed our claim." She paused and stared into the flames. "Consumption took her and now I am alone."

Handing her a plate of bacon and fried potatoes, he said, "And are you more content as a lady granger than teaching school in Salina?"

"Yes. Much more content." Miss Guthrie ate a piece of bacon. "I love side meat. I have not had any in quite a while."

"What do you grow on your homestead?"

She licked her fingers and took a sip of coffee. "I have a modest garden, of course. Some chickens, a milch cow and a few geese. Mostly I run a small herd of cattle. When I need extra income, I teach reading and writing. I also sell eggs and cheese and jam. Wild fruit grows in the breaks along the river."

"Do you worry about Indians?"

"No. I have never seen any except dipsomaniacs and wretched mendicants. When the Cheyenne came through last October, they were far to the east. Besides," she added in a quiet voice, "I have learned to accept whatever comes."

"And what of the big cattlemen? Do they object to your small scale operation?"

"The herd law protects my rights and Sheriff Bradley is honorable enough to enforce it... when guaranteed not to infringe upon the interests of those who back him politically. I keep my head down."

Finishing his breakfast, C.W. stood up and stretched his legs. He found the box of dog cakes he had purchased. Taking one from the package, he held it out to the dog. She took it and ran behind the tent.

"I can do the dishes," Miss Guthrie said.

Coming back to the fire, Collins shook his head. "I will do them in a while." He sat back down on the chunk of deadfall he had been using as a seat, leaving the chair for Miss Guthrie.

She ate the last of her meal and handed him her plate. "Thank you." She picked up a stick and poked at the fire. "You are Irish, I believe," she said after a moment.

"Gan amhras."

"Does that mean yes?" she asked.

"Surely."

Jack the mule brayed loudly from where he was picketed.

"I must get back to my place," Miss Guthrie said, standing. "My cow wants milking."

He helped her harness the mule and hitch him to the wagon. Molly wandered over to observe the proceedings.

"I must go," she said awkwardly when all was completed. Her head was bowed and she would not meet his eyes.

Placing a hand beneath her chin, he lifted her face and bent to kiss her lips. "It has been a pleasure," he told her and stroked her dark hair.

She looked into his eyes enquiringly. "Will I see you again?"

"No," he said, shaking his head. "But I will not forget you."

He thought she might give in to tears, but instead she shrugged and smiled wistfully. "Nor I you," she said and climbed onto the wagon seat. Taking up the lines, she released the brake and spoke to Jack, the mule. The animal leaned into the harness and Miss Guthrie rolled out of camp without another word. As she was about to pass out of sight around a bend in the road, she raised a hand and waved without looking back.

Slightly melancholic now the woman had departed, Collins busied himself taking care of the dishes and cleaning up camp and preparing to return to the telegraph office. He grained his stock and fed the dog another cake. Stowing his gear in the tent and again suspending the food in a tree, he caught Ulysses and picketed the mules. In a short while, he was ready to head back to Ogallala.

The sun had come out and the day had warmed considerably, turning the snow to soft mush. His gelding made his way judiciously through deepening muddy sludge and it took some time to travel the distance back to town. The telegrapher was once again sitting in an unheated office when Collins walked through the door.

"How are you?" Mr. Searle asked, when he looked up from what appeared to be the same newspaper.

"Well, thank you. I have come to discover whether there have been replies to my telegrams."

Searle put the newspaper aside and stood up to hand him two slips of paper, folded in halves. "You have received replies to both."

The first was from Secretary of the Interior Schurz.

> Washington DC Feb 3 1879
> To C.W. Collins Ogallala Neb
> Require more information regarding
> military culpability
> Inquiry initiated as of Jan 25 Fort Robinson
> Recv'd Wedemeyer report
> Dull Knife not imperative Find Little Wolf
> Prevent armed conflict if possible
> Herr Burschenschaft

The success of this last directive was contingent on the reply to his second telegram. He opened it and read.

> Fort Walsh Sask Canada Feb 3 1879
> To C.W. Collins Ogallala Neb USA
> Arbuckles affirm
> Arrive junction White River and Chadron Crk
> Approx Feb 19
> JM Walsh
> Sup NWMP

This was excellent news, indeed. Collins felt heartened and bid Searle farewell in a jovial manner. The telegrapher once more determined to postpone his departure, but to no avail. Outside, it seemed considerably warmer than within. He wondered briefly why the man eschewed a fire in his stove, but did not dwell on the question. Instead, he mounted up and headed in the direction of the Ogallala House, intending to enjoy a meal cooked by Mrs. Rooney. Perhaps he could also gather information pertinent to military incompetence during the previous October.

In front of the hotel, C.W. lowered Gal to the muddy street and dismounted. There were a few horses tethered to the rail and a buckboard with a team of hardy looking blue roans stood on the north side of the building. The dog followed him onto the porch, but he told her to stay and she lay down near the door. He entered the lobby and heard voices in an adjacent room. He went to investigate and found a small dining room wherein sat several men, gathered at two of the tables. Their attire professed occupations associated with cattle, except for a couple of fellows whose clothing signified them as town dwellers. The tables were covered in dishes and the remnants of a meal.

Mrs. Rooney came out of the kitchen and noticed him. "Oh hello Mr. Collins. So glad to see you. Do come in and meet everyone."

The group of men, whose conversation had been interrupted by the woman's salutation, looked over at Collins. He nodded to the assembly.

"Sit down, Mr. Collins," Mrs. Rooney said, indicating a nearby table.

C.W. removed his hat and coat and placed them on a chair, then sat down at the table.

"This is my husband, Sam," she told him, gesturing toward a red-headed man in city duds. "And this is Mr. Aufdengarten, who owns the store, Mr. Tom Moore, ramrod for the Bosler brothers, and these are some of his herders."

"Hello," Collins said.

The men all muttered a greeting in one form or other.

"I will fetch some coffee," Mrs. Rooney said and left the room.

"What brings you to these parts?" asked Tom Moore, the Bosler foreman.

"I am gathering intelligence regarding the Cheyenne Indian breakout of last October."

"Who for?"

"A client."

"A client?" Aufdengarten asked in a negligible German accent. "Are you a lawyer?"

Mrs. Rooney returned with a large graniteware coffeepot. She placed a cup in front of Collins and filled it, then topped off the other men's cups. "Mr. Collins," she said, turning to face him. "I have chicken and dumplings today, with stewed tomatoes on the side and bread pudding for dessert."

"I will have everything except the bread pudding, thank you."

The woman nodded and went into the kitchen, leaving the coffeepot on a trivet near her husband. Collins sipped his coffee, then came to the realization that the occupants of the other tables were gazing at him, apparently awaiting an answer to the Prussian's question.

"No, I am not a lawyer. I am a Pinkerton operative."

The group seemed to relax as a whole, as if a lawyer was something much worse than a Pinkerton detective and more capable of inspiring concern.

"Poor time of year to be traveling," Moore said. "You horseback?"

"I am. I have a good outfit."

"What did you wish to learn around here?" Aufdengarten asked.

"I am most interested in military operations. Was

it your impression that the commanding officers had a firm grasp of the situation?"

Tom Moore regarded him cynically. "Major Thornburgh was out of his depth entirely. He is an eastern fella and new to our neck of the woods."

"Sent here from Fort Steele by way of West Point," one of Moore's men said. "Fresh as a newborn colt and no savvy of the land, 'specially them sand hills. Troublesome country."

Mrs. Rooney arrived with C.W.'s food, effectively pausing the discussion momentarily. She poured more coffee and cleared plates from the other tables.

"Anything else whatsoever?" she asked. Not having received an affirmative, she again exited the room.

Hungry now, Collins took a couple of bites of chicken. He glanced over at Moore to encourage him to continue his narrative.

"Indians crossed the railroad near Alkali Station, about twelve miles east of here," Moore continued. "Thornburgh had a small detachment of mounted infantry and two companies of cavalry. Deputy Hughes and I were among some of the locals who accompanied the command. We arrived at the North Platte around dusk and most of his supply wagons got stuck fast in the middle. Only an ambulance and two commissary wagons made it across. He decided to push on and leave all but the ambulance behind. They gave us cold bacon and hardtack for four days' rations."

Swallowing a mouthful of food, Collins asked, "Was he on his own?"

"General Merritt was to head east from Fort Laramie and Colonel Carlton down from Camp Robinson," Aufdengarten told him. "Captain Mauck was pursuing from the southwest."

Mr. Rooney finally spoke up. "We later learned that Mauck did not pursue the Indians much past Sidney, calling it quits there in spite of a posse of good Nebraska men along for the ride. He had been chasing them redskins since the Arkansas and had bungled the entire affair."

Moore rolled a smoke thoughtfully. He took a match from a breast pocket and struck it on the heel of a boot. Taking a deep pull on the tobacco, he exhaled and said, "Thornburgh was on his own as far as the military was concerned. He had a few good boys with him that tried their damnedest to advise him. The major had no ears and the Indians out foxed him. They kept gathering up wild cattle and running them across their trail, then split up and scattered all to high heaven."

Another of the cow hands broke in. "We pulled out on the second day, seeing how he was barkin' at a knot. Those soldier boys almost died up there in those god-damn hills."

"What of Merritt and Carlton?" Collins asked, directing his question to Moore.

"Merritt set up patrols along the Big Horns, in case the Cheyennes went that way. Carlton met up with Thornburgh near the Running Water. The major's troops were lucky they did, being out of food and water as they were.

"Mauck did catch an old injun," Rooney suddenly said. "Some of the troopers brought him back to us and we took good care of him."

"Care?" Collins asked, fairly certain as to the man's meaning.

"Some of our citizens dispatched him after having a little entertainment," Aufdengarten told him dispassionately.

Moore, the foreman, appeared to be mildly revolted, but quickly altered his expression. "When you go to war," he said softly, "every man you meet is an enemy."

27

Emphatically dissuaded by the men at the hotel from attempting to cross the sand hills along the route taken by Major Thornburgh, Collins broke camp the next day and struck out along the old Oregon Trail. Following the North Platte River meant he and his animals would always have water. From Clarke's Bridge, about ninety miles up the river, he could head north along the Sidney and Black Hills Trail. Tom Moore had warned him that water would be a greater concern along this northerly route and to make plans accordingly. Red Willow Creek, Blue Water Creek and Point of Rocks stage stations would be the only opportunities for replenishing his supply until he reached the Niobrara River. Moore also warned that provender for his livestock would be equally dodgy, due to all the freight trains that traveled the road, no matter the weather or conditions.

It took him three days of dedicated traveling to get to Clarke's Bridge and the Sidney and Black Hills Trail. Given the time of year, there was limited activity along the old emigrant road. Collins kept to himself and camped in isolated areas. Evidence of almost forty years of wayfarers, and thousands of wagons passing through, left a swath of barren ground, tree stumps, discarded and decaying household goods and an abundance of animal skeletons and crudely marked graves. He had heard that cholera, dysentery, scurvy and accidents claimed the lives of a considerable proportion of the men, women and children who ventured west. Indian attacks had been the least of their worries, despite dime novel hysteria to the contrary.

Riding past a modest group of buildings on the south side of the river, on the morning of the fourth day out of Ogallala, C.W. came to a wooden barrier at the entrance of a rather astounding engineering feat known as Clarke's Bridge. It was solidly built of wood and spanned a wide section of the North Platte. Apparently quite sturdy, considering that it supported heavy freight traffic to the Black Hills mining district, it was guarded by a few soldiers lounging in front of a neighboring building. He halted Ulysses in front of the barricade and waited for someone to emerge from the toll shack.

"Why you need two mules, when one is a giant?" asked a private who was leaning against the corner of the structure.

Collins disregarded the question. A pale blonde young man walked out of the door and inspected his outfit.

"Two dollars to cross," he said blandly.

Reaching into his frock coat, he pulled two coins from an inside pocket and handed them over. Gal growled as the man reached up to take the money.

"Careful there, Dilworth, that there dog might be rabid," one of the troopers said.

The toll agent jerked his hand back. "Just pitch it to me, mister," he said, causing the soldiers to laugh heartily.

Collins tossed him the fee and Dilworth, now with a face the color of raw mutton, raised the bar to allow him to pass. Ulysses balked at the sound of his hooves on the wooden planking, but Collins spanked his rear lightly with the end of a rein and he moved along, with Molly and Joey coming up behind him. It was a narrow bridge and he was relieved to have it all to himself, unsure as to his gelding's reaction to an encounter with a freight wagon pulled by several yoke of oxen. The crossing seemed unending and C.W estimated the span to be well over one thousand feet. About halfway, there was an uninteresting little island occupied by a lone tree with a solitary raven perched atop. At the end of the bridge, there sat a two-story blockhouse, manned with a few more patently apathetic soldiers. He gave them a cursory nod as he rode past.

The morning progressed uneventfully and he arrived to the Red Willow station around midday. It was a one-story soddy with a pitched roof and corral and lean-to nearby. Several horses occupied the pens and smoke rose from a crude stone chimney, showing the station to be inhabited and in operation. Collins rode up to a hitching post, told Gal to get down and dismounted. The dog was now in excellent health and could run for long distances on her own, but she continued to express an interest in riding with him and he indulged her.

After securing his animals, easing the cinches and directing Gal to stay put, Collins started for the door and was met by a hale, bandy-legged man who fairly exploded out of the building.

"Hello there," he said merrily, through lavish moustaches. "Just in time for dinner, my man. Just in time. Come. Let us get your stock situated then I can show you where to bed down." The man made for the horse's reins wrapped around a rail.

"Hold up," Collins said, "I am continuing my journey yet today."

"You are not staying over?"

"No. I plan to make for the Blue Water station."

The jovial fellow's countenance altered to reflect alarm. "Across the badlands and almost twenty miles distant?"

"I was under the impression that we are on the very margins of the sand hills."

"True, true," the station man said, nodding. "But the route is traitorous and changeful, 'specially if you got no background with it."

"Well," C.W. said, smiling, "I am prepared to make a dry camp, if needs must. But at the moment, I could use a meal and some feed for my animals."

"Sure deal."

The station keeper directed him to lead his stock to a small pen off the lean-to. He looped the reins and lead ropes around their necks while his new companion pitched hay into a crude feed bunk. A full water tub was in the corner, and with his horse and mules set for the time being, Collins followed his host back to the sod building. Gal stayed in the pen near Molly.

"Name's Rayford Thacker," the man told him as they walked.

"I am Charles Collins."

"Come in, come in now, Mr. Collins," Thacker said, holding the door. His former ebullience was returning.

Inside, it was quite warm and smelled of food. A pig iron pot steamed on a sizable cookstove that stood in the middle of the room. Thacker sat him down at a table and poured coffee and spooned up bowls of beans replete with chunks of venison. He ate without speaking, while Thacker told one story after another about bandits and robberies, horse thieves and Shakespearean actors. It seemed apparent to Collins that this fellow was used to holding court before stagecoach passengers, many of them new to the west. He found him passingly entertaining at that. After two helpings of food, C.W. was amply full and leaned back from the table.

"Mind my pipe?" he asked.

"Aw hell no, not a bit. Will have one myself, if you can spare the tobacco. Been out for a couple of days."

Thacker embarked on yet another tale while they smoked amicably. In short order, however, Collins told him he must move along down the trail and rose to depart.

"Sure I cannot incite you to stay?" Thacker asked.

"No, but thank you."

"Daily mud wagon...stagecoach...will be coming through shortly. Lots of interesting folks to meet."

Shaking his head, Collins said, "I really must keep going." He placed a silver dollar on the table and ignored the man's protests.

Outside, the day had clouded up and turned cooler. They walked to the corral and Thacker helped him fill canteens and tighten cinches and lead the animals out to the road. The dog came out from behind the lean-to and C.W. allowed her to jump up and scramble onto the saddle with him.

"Damn dog rides," Thacker observed.

"She does indeed. Thank you again for your hospital-ity, Mr. Thacker."

"Watch the trail. It splits up into several branches from spring roads and sifting sand and be sure to stick with the one that is clearest," the station man cautioned. "And be sure to keep an eye out for rock piles that mark the way. Without these rocks you will go amiss."

"I will, thank you."

"Weather looks to be turning," Thacker said, looking up at the darkening sky.

Waving to the man and taking his leave, C.W. felt less confident than he had, but the trail was quite evident for the moment and the weather was holding and he was equipped for most contingencies. He had ridden for a couple of hours, remarking each cairn along the way as he moved into the margins of sand hills country, when the sound of galloping hooves could be heard behind him. He pulled his animals a goodly distance off the road and soon a stagecoach, moving at breakneck speed hauled by a six-horse hitch, appeared around a bend. The conveyance was bright red, albeit mud-spattered, with canary yellow wheels and leather curtains blocking the windows. "Gilmer and Salisbury Stages" was painted in gold letters just under the roofline and he counted no less than five men clinging to the top railings.

The driver gave an offhand nod and the stage passed, bouncing and rocking haphazardly on the uneven ground, and soon disappeared from view. Collins could only think that his mode of travel was far preferable, even if solitary. Voyaging alone might be more perilous, but given the frequency of stage holdups, according to Thacker, he considered himself to be in good stead. He avoided stage travel for the most part, regardless, as it crammed him into company with people he did not care to know. Gold, however, was a powerful magnet for human greed and discomfort was, apparently, the price for admission. Mining boom towns had always seemed to him to be cesspools of noxious rabble willing to endure any physical mortification in anticipation of easy riches.

As he well knew, chance often put paid to aims and purposes. Another hour had not passed before the wind came howling down from the north, bringing driving snow that accumulated at an alarming rate. He snugged down his hat and began straightaway to search for a sheltered place near the road, knowing he could easily lose his way as the blizzard grew in strength. In the lee of the tallest hillock he could find with alacrity, he halted his animals. Slightly sheltered from the pernicious wind, he tied Ulysses to Molly's breast collar, unsaddled him and unloaded the mules. Leaving the packsaddles on the mules, he kept Joey tethered to Molly as well, knowing she was the most steady of the three. He secured her to the heaviest pannier to prevent her from unintended drifting and she turned her rump to the storm and lowered her head resignedly. Joey and Ulysses lined out beside her.

Clumsy in the bitter cold and barely able to see, Collins laid out the tent and dragged his bedroll inside the recalcitrant tarpaulin, while putting his weight upon it to keep it from blowing away like an unfurling sail. He crawled into the writhing shroud and rolled out the cumbersome bedding, all the while struggling against what seemed to be a malevolent and invisible foe. Placing the heavy bedroll on one half of the tent, he was able to keep it pinned until he could drag his saddle in to put more weight on the cloth. Bringing both sides together under the bulky bedroll and saddle, he created a sheath under which he could shelter. Calling the dog, he squirmed into the bedding fully clothed and pulled Gal in with him. Resigned to his fate, he lay silently in his cocoon of flailing canvas as the day disintegrated into a glacial perdition.

BLIZZARD

28

He awoke in a panic. There was a weight bearing down on his chest and he could not breathe. Fighting his way toward the end of the tent sheeting nearest to his head, Collins dug through a snowdrift that had built itself against his profile and crawled clear of the mound to inhale chilled and oddly tranquil air of early evening. He turned to make an escape for his dog and got to his feet to look for his horse and mules. They stood stolidly nearby, Ulysses and Joey tethered to Molly as before. They were coated white with snow like ghosts in the bluish light of a fading sun. His panniers were buried, but for the most part all was in order and he knew they had had a fortunate deliverance, especially because the storm had been transitory.

Digging his supplies from their snowy cache, his first priority was to grain the animals. He poured a generous portion of oats on the snow for each one. From another bundle, he pulled out cheese, bread and jerked meat for himself and dog cakes for Gal. He knew that a fire, even one of buffalo or cow chips, would be an impossibility now that everything was amply buried. Regrettably, his tent would have to remain collapsed for want of any stick or branch to use as a prop. Anticipating a cheerless camp with small comfort, Collins set to work shoveling an open area with a tin plate, organizing his kit, clearing snow off the tent canvas, shaking out his bedroll and setting up his chair and table so he could have a dry place to perch.

As the sun disappeared below the horizon, Collins crawled back into the crumpled tent, this time setting his saddle on end as a buttress against the heavy material weighing him down. Calling the dog, he slipped inside the bedding, too restless to sleep and frustrated at another delay. To distract his mind, he spoke aloud all the lines he could recall from the Chorus at the beginning of The Life of King Henry the Fifth. Gal listened with alert ears as if to catch the meaning. It was utterly dark when he finally slept.

The next day dawned cloudless and glistening. Eager to be on his way, C.W. packed up his meager camp, loaded the mules and saddled his horse in short order. He was on the road by early morning, vigilantly seeking out piles of rocks that marked the Sidney and Black Hills Trail. A couple of times, he was forced to dismount and wipe cairns clean of snow to make sure they were indeed markers for the trail. It was still fairly early, nevertheless, when he came in sight of the Blue Water stage station. He was much relieved to find he had remained on course.

Stopping only briefly to purchase a bite of hay and some grain for his horse and mules and swallow some hot coffee, he was back on the trail after no more than an hour. The station tender was an odd, overtly religious man of few words who had been considerably uninterested in Collins' affairs. The trail was now quite distinct due to the tracks left by the stagecoach that had passed him the day before. He had learned from the laconic Blue Water man that the stagecoach had laid over at the station for the extent of the blizzard and then left in the predawn.

Traveling at a considerable pace, despite unreliable footing in places, C.W. and his animals covered the distance to the Point of Rocks station by the middle of the afternoon. An older man and woman by the name of Thompson ran the station, which was a long and narrow log and rockwork building. Having learned his lesson and wanting to rest his horse and mules, Collins requested to pitch camp among the sparse trees behind the station. The couple were welcoming and invited him to dine that evening. While he was settling his animals and organizing his camp, a small shotgun freight outfit pulled in. It consisted of two sturdy wagons, pulled by four-up teams of draft mules and hauling machinery of some type. The freighters watered their mules, stretched their legs and moved on, making for the Niobrara River.

The evening passed pleasantly enough, although supper consisted of sourdough pancakes and bacon. The Thompsons were simple people without much education, so conversation was limited to weather, local gossip and general inanities. C.W. turned in early and slept well. The next morning, he and his animals were rested and prepared to continue their journey. He bid farewell to the Point of Rocks way station and set out for the Niobrara River, as the sun rose into a brilliant blue sky.

It was around noon by the time he reached the valley of the Niobrara. As the Thompsons had informed him, the trail led to a ranch owned by a fellow named Hughes, then across the river to the Running Water stage station. There were two large freight trains, drawn by several yoke of multi-colored oxen, stopped over in the station yard. The wagons were plainly headed back to Sidney, as they appeared to be empty. Men and animals milled about in chaos as the bovines were being watered and fed. A small store near the station appeared to be offering a supply of whiskey, as evidenced by the empty bottles littering the ground and the teamsters' conduct and colorful verbosity. Unaccountably, one of the company appeared to be a woman.

Vegetation was scarce along the river and he was no

longer interested in any type of social intercourse, especially with inebriated bull whackers, so he pushed on toward the White River. The trail climbed into steeper country of scattered yellow pine and sandstone bluffs, then lost altitude again and opened onto gentler terrain covered in thick knee-high grasses among patches of dirty snow. It was nearly dark when he came upon the watercourse, where he found the area trampled and stripped. He reconnoitered and, a short distance east of the heavily used road, he found a campsite in some trees with fodder for his livestock and plenty of wood for a fire. He made camp with the idea of settling in for a couple of days to rest up his mules and gelding. Sitting by a roaring blaze and smoking his pipe, Collins was more comfortable and content than he had been since his camp on the South Platte. Thoughts of Miss Guthrie made him smile.

The fire was dying down and he had finished his pipe and the last of the coffee, when a voice called from the darkness. He fetched the Winchester from where it rested against a nearby tree, sat down again and laid it across his lap. Gal leaned against his leg and growled low. He put a hand on her head and she stopped. In a moment, a compact man bundled in a buffalo coat came out of the shadows into the halo of firelight. He carried a Spencer carbine cradled in the crook of an arm and Collins noted that he wore beaded moccasins and buckskin leggings.

"Was about to make camp when I saw your fire," the man said. "Name's Benjamin Clark."

"The scout," Collins said flatly.

"Right. The scout." He rubbed an ear. "My horses are in the trees over there. Mind if I bring them in and bunk down here?"

"Not at all."

The man hesitated. "I have some companions as

well...A Cheyenne squaw and her son. Any objections?"
"No."
Clark returned, leading two horses and followed by a small Indian woman and a slim teenage boy. Their clothing and moccasins were in tatters and they were wrapped in threadbare woolen blankets. Collins stood and motioned them toward the fire where they knelt and leaned into the warmth. He refilled the coffeepot with water and grounds and placed it on a flat hearth stone. The scout tethered his animals, unloading the packs on the one and unsaddling the other. The dog moved timidly toward the boy and when he reached out a tentative hand, she cautiously sniffed his fingers. He stroked her softly while the woman watched passively. Both of the captives seemed bereft of everything but despair.

Stepping over to his packs, C.W. pulled out the venison haunch he had purchased from the Thompsons at Point of Rocks. He handed the meat and his Green River knife over to the woman and indicated that she should take both, then built up the fire.
"I have army issue Indian rations for them," Clark said as he walked up to the fire.
"What in the hell is that?"
"Canned beans, coffee and hard tack."
The woman sat motionless, watching Clark, holding the knife in one hand and the meat in the other. Clark nodded to her and she began to slice pieces off the deer loin. She then handed the knife to the boy and said something in her own language. He got up and went toward the river.
"What is the story here?" Collins asked, returning to his seat on the folding chair.
The scout sat down on the ground near the fire. "I was summoned by Miles up at Fort Keogh to fetch these two and bring them to Camp Robinson and from there back down to Darlington Agency. Some drovers found

them over on the Snake last October."

The boy returned with a sturdy willow branch and sat down to sharpen one end. When he had finished, the woman hardened the point in the fire, then skewered pieces of venison on the stick and held them in the flames.

"They had got left behind when their ponies wore out and kept traveling north on foot as best they could, trying to catch up, but lost the trail. They was taken over to Fort Keogh by a couple of soldier boys since nobody had an inkling where their people had got to and the troopers over at Robinson and Sheridan was all excited over hunting the missing Cheyennes. Mostly neglected, as you can see." Clark shrugged. "Then I got orders to report to Miles and escort them over to Camp Robinson so's the military nabobs could ask them some questions."

"For the military inquiry?"

The scout nodded. "Scared the bejeezus out of them… thought they would be killed or worse. Word has already got 'round of the slaughter up near Hat Creek."

The woman pulled a slice of meat from the end of the stick and leaned over to give it to Clark. He juggled it between his hands, blowing on it until it had cooled enough to eat.

Repacking his pipe and crossing his legs, Collins studied the man. "You were with the Kansas Sixth," he said.

"I was," he answered when he had swallowed a bite.

Collins paused then said, "We knew each other in Westport during Price's raid into Missouri. You were scouting for Blunt."

"Your name?"

"Charles Wolfe Collins."

Clark eyed him a moment. "Captain C. W. Collins… you did your own breed of scouting, as I recall."

"You might say that," Collins said with the trace of a smile.

"Behind enemy lines," Clark added ironically.

"Undoubtedly."

"Friend of the bastard Pinkerton."

"Decidedly not."

The scout finished his meat without another word. The woman and boy were still roasting and eating the rest of the venison. The dog sat watching the proceedings with great interest. Collins smoked quietly. He had heard that Clark was close to Phil Sheridan as well as Crook. He had also heard that the man had been with Miles in Montana Territory, when he had been hunting Sitting Bull. Yet the scout was married to a Southern Cheyenne woman and had several children with her.

"You have, then, heard of the final conflict between the Cheyenne and 3rd Cavalry on January 22nd?" C.W. finally asked.

Clark nodded. "Hard to understand why they would not just let them go. It was only a small band of mostly women and children left and the winter snows would probably have done all of them in." He took a chew off a plug of tobacco and moved it into his cheek with a finger. "Could have at least given them a chance. Guess the boys in charge could not allow them to get loose and encourage other Indians to take off from the reservations."

"What did you find out about the inquiry taking place at Fort Robinson?"

"Not much. All closed mouths up there. A major out of Fort Laramie is in charge. Prob'ly just a maneuver to wash the dirt off. Over now, in any event."

"Over?" Collins asked with dismay. "When did it adjourn?"

"A couple of days ago."

"Bollocks!"

"Did you have dealings with them?"

"I had hoped to observe the proceedings," Collins said, shaking his head.

"Too late, I guess."

Retrieving his two cups and modest supply of sugar

from his packs, Collins poured coffee. "Sugar?" he asked.

"Naw. Rot the rest of my teeth out."

Collins handed him a cup. "Would you ask them if they would like some coffee and sugar."

"No need. Look at them."

The woman and boy were showing great interest in the coffee and small sack of sugar. Collins handed both over to the woman. She poured an impressive measure of sweetener into the beverage and sipped at it with relish. She gave the boy his share and he finished it in one single gulp. C.W. refilled the cup and the process was repeated.

"What are their names?" Collins asked.

"The woman is *Méenévoestá'e* ...Feathered Dress Woman. The boy is called *Hóma'óhtsē'hóhtse*... which means Afraid of Beavers."

The two were alert to the sound of their appellations. Collins gave them a smile and poured more coffee.

"Do they want to go back south?" Collins asked.

Clark gave him a thoroughly derisive glance. "What do you think? After their struggles to come this far? Her man was killed on Punished Woman Fork."

"Then why not allow them their freedom?"

Looking at the fire, the scout said, "Miles would skin me. Ever have dealings with him?"

"Yes."

"Then you might have an idea."

"I do."

29

When C.W. came out of his tent in the early morning, Clark was nowhere in sight. The woman and boy were still bundled in the saddle blankets and extra bedding Collins had arranged for them. He went to check his livestock and gather more wood. When he returned, Afraid of Beavers had the fire going and his mother was folding the blankets. Collins filled the coffeepot and put it on to boil. Ben Clark returned with an armload of dry branches and threw them down on the pile by the hearth ring.

"A might chilly," was all he said.

"The coffee will be ready soon."

Clark hunkered down by the flames and warmed his hands. "Least it will be getting warmer the farther south we get."

Gal emerged from some brush carrying a hare. She took it over near the pile of packsaddles and panniers and began to eviscerate the carcass.

"Got some bacon," Clark added.

"I have a loaf of bread."

Feathered Dress Woman toasted bread on a forked branch while the bacon fried. They shared the two cups for coffee, the mother and son partaking of the rest of Collins' sugar.

"Apparently the soldiers did not give you warm clothing for these people along with the 'Indian rations,' " C.W. observed.

The scout gave a short bark of humorless laughter.

"I was surprised to learn that neither the drovers or the troopers had done worse than leave them half-naked. Worked them like dogs at Fort Keogh, but nothing worse."

"I can spare those extra blankets."

"Damn good of you. The post provisioner refused to sell me aught for these people. A genuine, dyed in the wool shitbag."

"I am baffled how you can be in such good graces with the military and, more particularly, Sheridan," Collins said, looking at him quizzically. "Especially when you know what is happening to the plains tribes and your wife's people."

"Man's got to live. Have been able to undermine some of the idiot maneuvers of my superiors. Learned it under Blunt and some others you can guess at."

"I can guess."

"Not much point in denying that old ways for the Indians are dying and I might as well be in the middle of it to lend a hand."

Now that he understood the man more, Collins warmed to him. "It is often worthwhile to position yourself as best you can in order to be of some assistance. Especially in an untenable situation. I, myself, have made the odd attempt," he added wryly.

"Given the squabbling between the military and Indian Bureau and the grandiose egos of some of the soldier boys, I do the best I can. My woman, *Ma'ō'éstse,* is a strong believer in my honor and I do not wish to disappoint her."

" 'If I lose my honor, I lose myself.' "

"True enough."

Afraid of Beavers was rolling around on the ground with Gal, playing tug-of-war with a corner of his blanket. His mother was kneeling nearby holding a hand over her mouth, shyly concealing her mirth at their antics. Collins was heartened to see them lighter of spirit.

"You are normally posted at Fort Reno, are you not?" he asked the scout.

"I am."

"Were you in residence while the Northern Cheyenne were there?"

"For a period of time."

"Were the conditions really so terrible for them?"

"I was sent north around April, but before I left, I witnessed a good many issues of rations. They never received what had been promised and were starving. The fall hunt was an utter failure and many of them were sick and dying. They were forced to sell most of their robes and skins just for enough food to get by. One of the head men, 'Hog,' came to me before I left and made it plain they wanted to return north."

"So they had legitimate justifications for leaving?"

Clark shrugged. "You tell me. What would you do if you were starving and dying in the benevolent care of the U.S. government?"

"The reservation system is in sorry need of overhaul, there is no doubt."

The man laughed derisively. "You are assuming the goal is to not kill them all off. Indians have become a problem that the boys in Washington would like to have solved in the most practical manner."

Pouring more coffee for Clark and himself, Collins asked, "Perhaps I am being imprudent, but what is the truth of the Washita? I heard you were there at the battle."

The scout smoothed his moustache down a couple of times and sighed. "I was. Not so easy to talk about."

"Well then..."

"No...I will tell you. I can tell you. I wish to god I had not been a part of it. Right off those two chuckleheads, Custer and Myers, were mostly engaged in killing ponies, women and children. It was a god-awful slaughter. Though perhaps I should not have, I had warned them of larger camps to the east. In spite of this, Elliott went tearing ass along the river with a handful of men and ran smack into Cheyenne and Arapahoe warriors coming from the other encampments. Custer never bothered to look for him, but took some captives and used them as cover to get the hell out of there. His report to Sheridan was pure bullshit and Captain Benteen never forgave him."

"Is it true he took a Cheyenne girl for himself?"

"Raped that poor child near to death during the winter of '68. Think his brother had a go at her too."

Clark spoke to *Méenévoestá'e* in her language. She answered with palpable choler. "She remembers well how the girl was ruined for other men," he told Collins.

C.W. shook his head sadly. "There are simply no adequate words for such deeds. And yet they are woven into the fabric of human history."

"Well, I am not much for that strain of scholarly thinking," Clark said, "but I shed nary a tear when I heard of the man's destruction."

" 'False of heart, light of ear, bloody of hand.' "

"You sure have some good words," the scout said admiringly.

"They are not my words. They belong to William Shakespeare."

"Never could read a line of that. Sounds good when you speak it though."

The Cheyenne boy had left camp while they were talking. He returned with several trout wrapped in his blanket. He laid them on the ground and his mother looked at Collins and said the word "*motáhke*," making a cutting motion with her hand. He handed her his knife and she began cleaning the fish.

"You are trustful," Clark said. "You have spent time with Indians,"

"I have."

"What are you doing here Collins? What in the hell are you about?"

"I am not really at liberty to say, but suffice it to tell you I am not working against the Cheyenne people nor for the military."

"No skin off my ass, but this is a mighty strange meeting and no mistake."

"I will grant you that."

Getting up to stretch his legs, Collins walked over to his packs and took out the last of the dog cakes. Gal ate them up quickly, but he decided they were rather silly, especially in light of the dog's ability to hunt. He noticed the woman leaving camp with the sharpened stick from the night before. He went to check on Ulysses and the mules. Molly was napping in the weak late morning sun, her lower lip relaxed and trembling like an old man's. Ulysses and Joey were cropping dried grama and switchgrass in a narrow meadow along the river bank. He was pleased to give them more time to regain their strength and put on some weight.

Clark was napping on a buffalo robe near the fire when Collins returned to camp. Feathered Dress Woman was kneeling beside a small pile of soil-encrusted tubers, forcefully rubbing each one clean with a scrap of cloth. She used his knife to peel them and then placed them in a pot of steaming water suspended over the fire. She saw him examining the roots.

"*Mo'kóhtá'éne,*" she said, gesturing at them with her lower lip.

He did not try to repeat the word, but nodded. He went to get his rifle from inside his tent and saw her watching him intently when he walked past. Collins smiled and mimicked horns above his head to show her he intended to look for antelope. A light of understanding came into her eyes and, with the hint of a smile, returned to her work.

Climbing out of the river bottom, C.W. was able to more thoroughly survey the surrounding countryside. He ascended a small hillock and took in the expanse of grasslands bounded by timbered sandstone escarpments. The grey and naked trees along the White River wound through the valley like a wooly caterpillar, extending out of sight in both directions. The untrammeled beauty of the landscape gave him a greater understanding of the profound motivations that drove the Northern Cheyenne to risk everything to return to their home country. For a moment he found it difficult to swallow.

Movement, near the timbered ridges to the south, caught his attention. He watched as a ponderous freight train emerged from the sandstone breaks and made its way down the Sidney and Black Hills Trail toward the White River. Collins counted six yoke of oxen for each three trail wagons. As the train drew closer, he could hear the gaudy oaths and loud cracks of bullwhips skillfully employed by the teamsters. The mud-encrusted wagons seemed to tower over man and beast, double-boxed with five-foot-diameter rear wheels, and packed high with goods covered by sheaths of canvas. As the freight train came into full view, C.W. tallied twenty-six teams and bull whackers. The preponderance of goods being transported was stupendous and underscored the sheer number of people now inhabiting the Black Hills gold fields. They passed by within a quarter mile of him and seemed to take a laborious eternity to make the journey down to the ford across the river.

Moving away quietly through dingy skiffs of snow and tall grasses, he did not perceive a single antelope or deer, probably due to the cacophonous passage of the freighters. In the open country southeast of the river, however, Collins came upon a flock of wild turkeys. He shot a large hen and shouldered his kill to make his way back. The winter sun had almost disappeared behind the low ridges to the west as he neared camp and he could see a fire flickering through the bare cottonwood trees. He found himself pleased that Clark and his companions had joined him. *Bi'onn an rath i mbun na ronna,* he thought to himself. There is luck in sharing.

WASHITA

30

"Headed over to Camp Rob then?" Clark asked, picking a fishbone out of his mouth.

Looking up from his plate of trout and what Clark had told him were mashed prairie turnips, Collins said, "I plan to. I am obliged to reconnoiter."

"Reconnoiter what exactly?" the man asked dryly.

"As Cicero wrote, 'I prefer silent prudence to loquacious folly.' It is best I tell you nothing."

"Who in hell is Cicero?" Clark asked, scowling at Collins.

"A Roman scholar. I do not mean to be chary, but I am currently employed by someone who wishes to remain anonymous. On my honor, I cannot violate his trust."

Clark studied him a moment, then nodded. "I can savvy that."

Feathered Dress Woman offered them another trout. She had roasted the fish over the fire on the now ubiquitous sharpened willow branch she seemed to use for all purposes.

"This woman is a good cook," Clark said. "I have no idea how she found *mo'kóhtá'éne* this time of year. They usually dig them in June when the plant has flowers on it." He paused, then said, "I would take her as a second wife but the soldier boys would have a conniption."

Nodding his thanks, C.W. accepted one of the trout. Gal sat nearby, watching him attentively. The boy threw her the tails and heads from his fish and she picked at them delicately, holding the bits between her front paws and discarding the bony parts.

"What will happen to them at Darlington?" Collins asked.

"Not sure. They will receive some sort of annuities. Without a man to speak for them it will be hard."

Collins turned to look Clark square in the face with forceful gravity. "Let them go," he said quietly. "Say they escaped."

Clark was about to take a sip of coffee. He lowered the cup and frowned, returning Collins' gaze intently. "It will mean trouble," he finally said.

"Perhaps, but not much. Is there somewhere they can go?"

He nodded slowly. "They could go to the new Red Cloud Agency on Pine Ridge. They could blend in and the folks up there would care for them."

"Then do it. You must do it. Ask Feathered Dress Woman what she thinks of this."

Clark spoke to the woman in her language. She answered at length. Afraid of Beavers appeared excited by the conversation, his eyes bright and watchful.

"She says she has relatives with Red Cloud. She says she would rather die than return south," the scout told Collins.

Feathered Dress Woman touched C.W.'s arm lightly and repeatedly, saying, *"Néá'eše... Néá'eše."*

"She is thanking you," Clark said. "I told her it was your idea."

"Damned nice of you," Collins said, grinning.

The sun had gone down and the twilight was growing cold. Collins put more wood on the fire and put more water and grounds in the coffeepot while the woman spoke at length to her son. C.W. went out to check on his horse and mules before it grew completely dark. They were standing together quietly in a sheltered hollow not far away. The dog had followed him and Ulysses put his nose down to sniff at her. She licked his muzzle. The horse jerked his head up and perked his ears at the sound of an owl hooting in a tree downriver. Collins scratched the gelding's jaw and then went over to pat Molly and Joey and speak to them soothingly.

Back at the fire, Clark and the woman were speaking and Afraid of Beavers was putting in a word here and there. It was all very animated and Collins enjoyed the sound of the Cheyenne language. He took out his pipe and smoked while the discussion continued and he waited for the coffee to boil. He filled the two cups when it was ready and went to his packs for a tin of jam, now the sugar was all gone. Feathered Dress Woman happily spooned jam into a cup of coffee and she and her son shared it with relish.

"Now that is a sweet tooth," Clark said, wrinkling his nose.

"What have you been saying to them?" C.W. asked.

"Telling them they cannot say a word about me letting them go and how to get up to Pine Ridge without running into some of the bastard civilians around here. I heard some of them bottom-feeders scalped and mutilated the bodies of Cheyennes the morning after they broke out."

Collins stared at him. "How could that have happened?"

"Ask the soldier boys over at the fort. Ask the post adjutant, Lieutenant Cummings. I heard he saw some of it."

"Is it possible for them to arrive safely to the agency?" Collins asked, not wanting to think about this new information. "Should I go with them and look out for them?"

Clark spoke to the woman. She shook her head and smiled openly at Collins.

"She says they know this country. They know how to keep hidden."

They sat quietly until the fire died down, then Feathered Dress Woman and Afraid of Beavers wrapped themselves in blankets and curled up by the glowing coals.

"May I assume that the survivors are again domiciled at Fort Robinson?" C.W. asked after a while.

"They are gone. Red Cloud requested they be placed in his care. There were about sixty of them, nearly all women and children, and the most wretched collection of mortals you have ever seen. Whatever crimes were committed in Kansas were paid back in full by the abject suffering of the survivors." Clark spit expressively. "Seven of the men and their families were held back and are scheduled to be transported to Fort Leavenworth for trial. I believe they have already left for Sidney."

"Trial? For the depredations in Kansas?"

Clark nodded. "Wild Hog did himself harm in an attempt at suicide. He understandably does not trust white justice." He tossed the remainder of his coffee on the coals. "They are all afraid of being sent to prison in Florida." He sighed expressively. "The Northern Cheyenne people will endure, but they have been sorely tested."

Collins knocked the ashes from his pipe, bid Clark goodnight and went to his tent. He was asleep almost instantly, in spite of the pervasive sorrow that plagued him.

In the early morning, Gal woke him with muted yipping, her ears alert to a sound nearby. He extracted himself from the warm bedroll and stepped out with rifle in hand. Clark was warming his hands over the fire, already lit and inviting. Collins donned his bearskin coat and went over, leaning the rifle on his packs.

"Morning. Got the coffeepot filled with water if you want to get to grinding," Clark said.

Looking around, C.W. saw no evidence of his Cheyenne guests. "Where are they?" he asked.

The scout glanced up at him. "Gone," he told him and looked down uneasily, rubbing at a stain of grease on his knee.

"When? I wanted to send them with some food."

"They took the turkey and helped themselves to some

bread and jam." Clark came to his feet and made an appeasing gesture with his hands. "Now do not get peeved. Indians have a different idea of ownership."

"I am not peeved. They are welcome to all of it."

"You are a particular sort of fellow, there is no doubt," the man said and hunkered down again by the fire.

Retrieving the mill and the beans, Collins sat down and ground coffee. With the pot on to boil, he fetched the remaining venison and the last of his potatoes to fry for breakfast. When the meal was over, he scrubbed all the dishes in the river and tidied the camp. He would remain at the site while visiting the fort, since it was in close proximity. He went to catch up his horse and when he slipped the head stall on Ulysses, he noticed a tiny silver bell braided into the horse's forelock. When he brought the gelding into camp to saddle him, he pointed the ornament out to Clark.

"That was *Méenévoestá'e.* It was the last little possession she had left."

Collins stood silently for a moment. "Do you think they will make it?" he asked finally.

"They will."

When all was prepared and the animals were saddled and packed, the men parted company. Clark was headed south back to Indian Territory and Fort Reno.

"I hope Miles does not rain too much calumny upon your head," Collins told the scout.

Clark shrugged. "He is clear up on the Tongue. With any luck, I can stay out of his reach until he simmers down."

Swinging into the saddle, C.W said, "It was a genuine pleasure, Benjamin. May the wind be always at your back."

"*Nêstaévâhósevóomâtse,*" Clark said, also mounting up. "I will see you again." He snagged the lead rope of his packhorse, gave C.W. an offhanded salute and rode out of camp.

Collins headed westward along the south bank of the river while the scout made for the Sidney and Black Hills Trail. He called Gal and had her jump onto Ulysses before he crossed a sturdy bridge that spanned the stream. The day was overcast and dreary and his spirits were depressed, thinking about Feathered Dress Woman and Afraid of Beavers and Woodchuck and all the other Cheyenne people whose future was uncertain. He angled out of the river bottom toward Camp Robinson, wondering how he could get a telegram sent to Schurz without tipping his hand to the military personnel. He did not expect to learn much, in any event.

31

He rode into the lower end of the parade grounds and pulled in Ulysses to survey the surroundings. To his left was a barracks building with broken windows and what appeared to be a multitude of bullet holes in the rough-cut siding. Just to the north was a smaller building with a flag flying on a pole in front. He nudged his gelding forward and dismounted near the structure. He heard the bugle call for stable duty and saw groups of soldiers headed for the stables southwest of the parade grounds. Gal stayed on the saddle as he ducked under the low porch roof and knocked on the door.

"Yes," came a voice from inside.

Opening the door and stepping in, Collins stood just inside and waited for his eyes to adjust.

"Can I help you?" asked the second lieutenant behind a desk in the rear of the building.

"Are you Lieutenant Cummings, the post adjutant?"

"I am."

"My name is Charles Wolfe Collins. I am a Pinkerton operative and would ask a few minutes of your time."

The middle-aged man eyed him suspiciously and scratched the back of his neck. "Well, I really am not sure I can be forthcoming. In what regard?"

"Firstly, may I sit down?" Collins asked, gesturing at a chair.

The soldier nodded and he seated himself.

"In what regard?" the lieutenant asked again, in a

slightly belligerent manner.

"In regards to the defilement of Cheyenne bodies on January 9 and 10 by civilians. I believe you were a witness to this?"

Cummings appeared discomfited. "This is a military matter. I really cannot speak to this without..."

The lieutenant was interrupted by the door opening abruptly. A stocky older man with major's insignia on his immaculate uniform entered the building. "James, I require a clean memorandum book," he began saying then noticed Collins, who had come to his feet and was observing the man amusedly.

"Good god...Captain Collins," the major exclaimed, gaping. "This really is a stunner."

"Not a captain any longer, Andrew."

They shook hands. "This is an old acquaintance," Major Evans told the adjutant. "We have known each other since before the late rebellion." Sitting down, the major motioned for Collins to follow suit. "Why are you here, Charles? It seems a peculiar place to find you."

"I still accept occasional employment from Allan. Just now, I am investigating the Cheyenne debacle here on the post."

Evans shook his head and sighed. "A disaster. The army is already receiving general condemnation on that account." He turned to speak to the adjutant. "Can we get some coffee?"

The lieutenant stepped into an adjoining room and returned with cups, which he filled from a coffeepot on the woodstove in a corner of his office.

"Ta," Collins said, accepting a cup.

"I was ordered into the field by Crook back in January. Had my damn horse shot out from underneath me," Major Evans said and blew on his coffee to cool it.

"I understand there was a recent inquiry into events?"

Evans set his cup on the edge of the desk. "There

was. I was placed in charge of the proceedings." The major took out a cigar case and offered a maduro to Collins. They smoked and sipped their coffee wordlessly for a moment, then Evans asked, "You have a client, then?"

"I do. One who desires to remain anonymous."

"Where are you staying?"

"I am camped on the river east of here. I am quite comfortable."

"You must come to my quarters. I do not have elaborate accommodations, but we can make shift."

"I would be delighted." Collins could hear the fatigue call being sounded. "Do you currently have duties to attend to?"

"No. I am still conducting informal interviews with some of the soldiers in regard to last January, at the clandestine behest of General Crook, but there is nothing pressing."

"Might we walk and converse, then?"

"Most certainly." The major finished his coffee and set the cup back on the adjutant's desk. "Come, I will give you a tour." He took C.W.'s cup from him and set it down as well. "James," he said, turning to the adjutant, "send someone to find me if required. I will be somewhere on the post."

"Yes sir," the lieutenant said and gave a passing salute.

When they had stepped outside the building, Collins asked, "Where do you have Señorita Juana hidden away? Somewhere over in Wyoming Territory, perhaps?"

"Oh come now, Charles," Evans said, his face flushing crimson. "Will you never let me live it down? That episode ended years ago."

"Do you remain unmarried?"

Collins walked over to ease the cinch on Ulysses. The dog had jumped down and was lying in the sun on the southside of the building. He told her to stay and Major Evans and he began to stroll across the parade grounds toward the row of officers' quarters. Various troopers were passing by en route to their assigned duties. "Yes, I remain unmarried. There is, however, a grass widow back in Elkton whom I find intriguing. And you?"

"I am not fit for marriage." Collins turned to look back at the barracks, adjutant's office and the guardhouse that stood just to the north. "Did I hear correctly that Crazy Horse died here?"

"Right over there. Stabbed in front of the guardhouse. I know there were pivotal men in the military who breathed a sigh of relief at his demise, but the man was actually quite young. I was always rather fascinated by him." They had arrived in front of one of the officers' quarters. "Shall we go in and speak further in private? I do not believe you are truly interested in touring stables or army barracks."

"Thank you, Andrew. I find it quite opportune to come upon you here. I require information that would not be otherwise forthcoming."

Evans looked at him askance with a hint of unease. Collins tossed his cigar stub on the ground and they stepped onto the porch and went into a door of the duplex adobe dwelling. A heating stove warmed the front parlor and they removed their coats. Evans draped the garments on a table off to the side and placed his campaign hat on top.

"I am decidedly not settled in here," he told C.W., taking a seat in a worn leather arm chair. "I am due back to Fort Laramie and will be departing tomorrow. It really is only by chance you found me. I was supposed to have returned three days ago, but I wanted to interview a few more individuals."

Collins sat on a ladder back chair near a window. "When precisely did you come here?"

"I arrived in the field with two companies of men from Fort Laramie and assumed command of the search for the Cheyenne prisoners on January 19. General Crook sent me here as there was dissatisfaction with Captain Wessells' abilities. Crook then ordered me to preside over the inquiry proceedings."

"After hearing all the testimony, what is your opinion of the entire debacle?"

"Bungled from start to finish...might I offer you a short brandy?"

Collins shook his head. "Bungled from the capture last October until the escape? Or bungled from the moment the Cheyenne ran away from Darlington Agency?"

Evans walked into an adjoining room and returned with a glass half-filled with brown liquid and a cup of tepid coffee for C.W. and resumed his seat. "In my considered opinion, misconducted from start to finish." He took a sip of brandy. "I simply cannot believe that a ragtag bunch of Indians could lead the U.S. Army on a haphazard pursuit across three states without a surfeit of strategic blunders and poor leadership. My god, they had old people and little children and were singularly able to avoid capture in spite of several commands in the field."

"Can you relate a summary of events that took place here as delineated by the inquiry?" Collins set the cup of coffee on the nearby windowsill.

Pausing with the glass of brandy near his mouth, Evans studied Collins. "Who is your client, Charles?" he asked quietly, yet firmly.

C.W. removed his hat and ran his fingers through his hair thoughtfully. "How well may I trust you?"

"As well as ever. I simply will not answer any further questions without knowing."

"You place me in an awkward position. I have given my word to not reveal my client's identity and yet my directive is to gather as much intelligence as possible."

The major shrugged and finished his brandy, clearly

unwilling to say aught else.

Sighing, Collins said, "Very well, but I am trusting you with my reputation for discretion, my future employment and my personal integrity. Please do not compromise what I am about to tell you."

"We have known each other for a great many years. If you recall, I have never violated your confidence, even under duress."

Nodding, Collins stood up, put his hat on the table with the coats and walked over to look out a window at the parade grounds. He saw that the dog was now waiting for him on the porch just outside the door. "I am in the employ of Secretary Schurz. He does not desire that the Indian Bureau should be transferred to the authority of the War Department and hopes to use the events surrounding the military failures in regard to the Northern Cheyenne apostasy to ensure this does not occur. I believe General Sherman and he are at loggerheads over this matter." He turned to look at his friend.

Major Evans stared at him in disbelief. "I thought you were Grant's man," he finally said. "Knowing this, why would Schurz seek you out?"

"It is of little consequence. Can you provide me with the intelligence I require?"

The man got up to pour himself more brandy, then returned to his chair. "No doubt Secretary Schurz has been made privy to many of the events. The most damning incidents are the inability of the military to apprehend the Indians prior to the depredations in Kansas, the failure to capture Little Wolf and his band, the treatment of the Cheyenne prisoners here and the indiscriminate slaughter of women and children after their escape from the barracks. The officers all gave testimony that they strove to avoid killing women and children, but they were ordering the use of artillery. Forty rounds or more on one occasion, for godssake."

"Is it your opinion that there may have been alternative recourse?"

"Did the dignity of the government truly require the forcible removal of these people back to the Indian Territory prior to a full investigation into the merit of their complaints? That a violent outbreak of some sort must occur should have been apparent to everyone who considered the temper of the Indians."

"Was Captain Wessells incompetent, in your opinion?"

"Between us, absolutely, but I will not officially damn the man. I will say he is an individual not long on vision. His decision to withhold food and water until the Indians would agree to go south was catastrophic. And, in spite of his many protestations, his deficiency of initiative, a lack of firm authority over the men in his command and his dearth of foresight led to carnage, the loss of brave soldiers and the slaughter of women and children. I believe if Major Carlton had been in command, many of the disastrous occurrences would have been avoided. I also believe if the man had not been wounded, he would be destined for a court of inquiry."

"I understand that some of the Indians had carbines and revolvers."

Evans nodded. "True. Apparently, they were not adequately searched when imprisoned last October and secreted their arms under the floorboards of the barracks and upon the persons of women and children."

"What of the rumors that some of the bodies were mutilated?"

"How in the hell did you hear about that?" Evans asked with discomposure.

"Well?" Collins sat back down on the chair.

The major drank most of the brandy in his glass. "According to Lieutenant Cummings, post adjutant, he found several bodies that had been scalped." Evans looked down at the floor and continued in a low voice.

"Some of the women had been defiled and were left indecently exposed...it was unclear whether they had been violated before or after...well...dying. According to Cummings and several other officers, civilians were observed in the vicinity and the inference was that they had committed these barbarities." He lifted his head to stare at Collins. "Now we are even. If you breathe one word that I provided this information to a civilian, my career will be at an end."

"You are secure in my prudence, Andrew." He paused. "I cannot help but think the slaughter here is evocative of Camp Grant."

Evans regarded him sadly. "Those were my thoughts. My thoughts precisely."

Collins again came to his feet and went to the window. When he had regained a modicum of equanimity, he said, " 'The evil that men do lives after them.' "

"Shakespeare?"

"Shakespeare."

32

After partaking of a noon meal provided by the wife of one of the officers, Collins and Evans again occupied the parlor of the quarters. The major made a fresh pot of coffee and built up the fire. The day was becoming colder. Gal was allowed to come in and lie by the stove and Ulysses had been secured to a rail in front of the building and provided with a nosebag of corn.

"Would it be possible for me to speak to one of the soldiers who were in the field? Someone who was there at the final conflict?" Collins asked.

"It is possible." Major Evans had poured a generous amount of brandy into his coffee and the effects of his protracted imbibing were beginning to show, despite the ample meal he had just eaten. "I would not, however, believe it to be expedient, given the identity of your employer."

"Is there no one with whom I may speak? Perhaps I could present myself as a newspaperman?"

The major seemed to rouse himself at the idea. "Yes... by god, yes. There is a sergeant who would most probably be amenable. A moment." He went to the door and stepped onto the porch. He called to a trooper walking across the parade grounds and gave him instructions to find Sergeant Johnson and send him over. He closed the door and returned to his chair. "The man is garrulous and a natural storyteller," he told Collins.

"Thank you, Andrew. This may prove rather beneficial."

Collins got up to pour himself more coffee and made a point of refilling Evans' cup to the brim. He knew well the man was fond of drink and he did not wish him to become inebriated. There was a knock on the door and he went over to open it. A non-commissioned officer with a bushy handlebar moustache and sandy hair stepped into the room. He saluted the major and removed his hat.

"You wished to see me, sir?"

"Sit down, Sergeant." Evans said, motioning him to a tattered ottoman across the room.

"Thank you, sir," the man said and took a seat.

The major nodded in Collins' direction. "This gentleman is Mr. Collins. He is a newspaper correspondent and desires to ask you a few questions regarding the last fight with the Cheyennes on the 22nd. You were present, were you not?"

"I was. I can give him a good accounting." The man appeared to be quite eager.

"Very well," said Evans. "Proceed."

"Let me see..." Johnson turned his hat around and around in his hands pensively. "After Major Evans had his horse shot from under him...sorry sir..."

Evans waved his hand, dismissing his apology. "Go on, Sergeant."

"After that, the major's command guarded the bluffs where the Indians had been skulking, thinking maybe the Indians were still holed up there, but Captain Wessells and a couple of scouts cut the trail where the Indians had come out of the bluffs and crossed the valley to the east. About fifteen miles from Bluff Station they had entrenched in a ravine on Indian Creek. One of the scouts, Woman's Dress, was wounded and a soldier was killed. Captain Wessells went back to collect his command and direct them to surround the gully. The four troops were undermanned, an average of twenty to thirty men to a troop, owing to various reasons. Anyways, they closed up on the position and began firing. They continued to fire into the rifle pit for two and one-half hours."

Collins raised a hand to interrupt. "You called it a ravine before, but just now you called it a rifle pit?"

"Yes sir. The Indians had dug in and piled dirt and brush and later, we found they had hollowed out a place in the side for the children."

"I see. Pray, continue."

Johnson rubbed his nose, then said, "Alrighty...well after offering them the chance for surrender more than once, Captain Wessells was wounded above the eye. In the end we must have poured over 200 rounds into that ravine and the screams had quieted some. Of a sudden, we heard what must've been war songs and three Indians jumped out of the hole and threw themselves into the ranks of the soldiers. One of them had no weapon at all and one had a knife. The other had an old six shooter. I do not think it was even loaded. They were all killed double quick. The last one to keep up a fight was an old woman with a carbine. One of the soldiers finally shot her in the hand and the carbine was knocked out. When she was taken out and put on the ground on her back, Lieutenant Chase stooped over her and tried to change her position so as to ease her suffering. She reached out and took his hand and spit in his face. Just goes to show how those Indians was thinking. She had been shot in the back of the head and died that night." The sergeant looked over at Collins. "Hey...should you be taking notes or something?"

"I will remember everything," C.W. told him, thinking to himself that he would rather not remember any of it. "How many survivors were there?"

"There were ten live people taken out of that hole, all women and children, but two died soon after. We pulled all the dead out and laid them side by side to count them. Later we buried them there, according to Major Evans' orders."

"What of Dull Knife?"

"He is believed dead."

Major Evans had been silent throughout the sergeant's narrative. He stood up and put more wood in the stove. Gal growled faintly and came over to lie beside Collins.

"Is that what you needed, Mr. Collins?" Evans asked.

"Yes, I believe that is sufficient. Thank you, Sergeant Johnson."

"That will be all," the major told the man, sitting down again. "You may return to your duties."

"Yes sir," Johnson said, coming to his feet, placing his hat on his head and saluting. He went briskly out the door and closed it behind him.

"As we agreed earlier," Evans said, "far too reminiscent of Camp Grant...far too reminiscent. Only this time the soldiers were as culpable as the civilians. One hundred and fifty prisoners were brought here and approximately one half were killed. Unconscionable." He adjusted his position in the chair and assumed a more formal manner. "Presumably, Secretary Schurz will receive the transcript of the inquiry proceedings from the War Department. That should provide him with the testimony and any further intelligence he may require. We questioned some of the Cheyenne survivors first. It is all in there."

"I have enough for now."

"Then I would suggest you take yourself away from the post as soon as possible. I do not wish to seem inhospitable, but I would hazard a guess that Sergeant Johnson is spreading the word of your presence as a newspaper correspondent at this very moment. It could become awkward for you. Lieutenant Simpson is currently the post commander and he is scrupulous in his adherence to military protocol."

Collins nodded. "I understand your meaning. Tell me, Andrew, do you trust the telegrapher here? Do you believe I am able to send a confidential telegram to Washington?"

"Unquestionably not. I will get you some paper and a pencil and you can write it out. I will send it when I am back at Fort Laramie. Will that be acceptable?"

"Perfectly."

Evans went to open a satchel resting upon a small rolltop desk in the back of the parlor. He took out a graphite pencil and a notepad and stepped over to give them to C.W. He wrote out the message and handed it to Evans.

> To Herr Burschenschaft
> Willard Hotel Washington DC
> Have further intelligence to relate
> Sensitive but will keep
> Military appears blameworthy
> Dull Knife presumed dead
> Will now proceed search of Little Wolf
> CWCollins

"You will have to add the date and all," he told the major, handing him the pad and pencil.

"Of course." The major perused the communication. "It is more than possible I will never see you again. Does Schurz really expect you to seek out Little Wolf?"

"He does."

"Well, good luck to you," Evans said, shaking his head dubiously.

Collins stood and donned his coat and hat. "Andrew, it has been excellent to meet with you again," he said, putting out a hand to shake. "And I am most grateful for your candor and assistance."

The major shrugged. "I care not whether the Indian Bureau remains under the auspices of the Department of the Interior or under the War Department. It is plain that the army blundered in this instance, regardless. The truth will be known."

"Farewell, then. Be careful as you go."

"You as well, Charles. Do not be reckless."

Collins went out the door with his dog following. He removed the nosebag from his horse, draped it over the rail and tightened his cinch. He mounted up and angled southeast out of the fort, back toward the river, thinking that he was probably following the very route taken by those desperate people on a freezing cold night, not long ago.

33

When he found her near the camp, Molly walked up to C.W. and leaned her forehead against his chest. She held it there for a moment and he slipped his arms about her neck in an embrace. Joey and Ulysses were blowing in one another's nostrils with pricked ears, as if they had not been compatriots that very morning. Gal began to run around barking and Collins knelt down and roughed her up in play. She took off bounding through the surrounding shrubbery, making laps around the clearing where they were gathered and occasionally rushing past him just out of reach. He was laughing and making grabs for her when, of a sudden, he heard the snapping of brush behind him. He came to his feet and rested his hand on his revolver.

"Easy friend," a tall, rangy man told him, coming into the clearing and holding his hands up in a placating gesture. He was leading an old gaunt chestnut mare, her hair dull and matted. The horse shied when he raised his hands, a sign, thought C.W., that he beat the poor animal. The stranger had a black, heavily waxed moustache with tightly twisted ends and a flat-brimmed hat with a tall rounded crown. Collins perceived an artfulness about him.

"What can I do for you?"

"Why not a jot, my friend, not a jot. I was merely on my way to the fort and heard the dog. My name is J.W. Dear. I used to be agency trader here. Still run a store down the way."

Collins began to walk back toward his camp a few yards away. He wanted to take a swift inventory of his possessions. The dog preceded him, edging along warily and keeping a watchful eye. "I expect you need to keep moving," he told the intruder. "Dusk is coming on."

"The saloon and my pals will keep," Dear said, following along and leading his spavined horse behind him. "Just curious who you are, friend. You got some nice livestock."

Seeing that his belongings were intact, C.W. relaxed and turned to face his unwanted guest. "What do you want here?"

"Why nothing...nothing at all."

Dear was scrutinizing his gear appraisingly, as if judging the collective worth of his property. It was then Collins noticed an odd ornament on the man's hat. "What is that?" he asked, slightly ill.

"What?" Dear asked, distractedly, maintaining his perusal of the goods around the camp.

"The article tied to your hatband."

The man looked at him and smirked unpleasantly. "Oh you perceived that, did you?" He removed his hat and toyed with the object. "This here is the scalp of a dead Cheyenne squaw. Not just any scalp, mind...here take a look."

He attempted to hand the hat over to C.W. for closer inspection. He refused to accept it, crossing his arms and narrowing his eyes in suspicion.

"What do you mean?" Collins asked in a soft voice.

"Oh I mean pretty special. This here is the scalp from her petticoat lane." Dear's leering grin broadened. "She was already wounded and I dispatched her, since them troopers had their hands full elsewhere. Shot her in the head...then I took me a little trophy so's I could remember."

A prolonged silence settled between the two men.

Dear was caressing the scalp as a child fondles a kitten.

"Gura féis ic faelaib do chorp," Collins finally said, almost inaudibly.

"Pardon me?" Dear asked agreeably, cocking his head as if straining to hear. He put his hat back on.

Collins stepped over to the pile of panniers and saddles and leisurely retrieved his Winchester repeater saying, "May your body be eaten by wolves." He cocked the hammer and raised the gun menacingly. "Hit the fucking trail."

"Now see here, friend..." the trader began to say.

Striding closer and brandishing the rifle to point him out of camp, C.W. sicced the dog on the man. Gal grasped his meaning and made a feint toward Dear, snarling.

"Hey for chrissakes!" he yelled and swung into the saddle. "I could bring back some of the boys and learn you something," he said through set teeth.

Collins called the dog back so as to not injure the decrepit mare. "That would be an impressive miscalculation," he said evenly, aiming the carbine directly at the man.

Dear dug his heels into the mare's rawboned sides and yanked at the reins to turn her out of the river bottom and onto flat ground that opened to the south. Collins was sorely tempted to shoot him out of the saddle, if only to spare the animal. He sighed deeply and began to gather wood for the fire. If the man made good his threat and returned, he thought, then perhaps he would have the opportunity to shoot him after all. He sincerely welcomed the prospect.

The encounter with Dear only exacerbated the angst he had been experiencing since the interview with Sergeant Johnson. Once more his thoughts returned to Camp Grant in Arizona Territory. He had been in the territory on a commission for President Grant when half a dozen lowborn brutes of the first order, calling themselves a "committee of public safety," enlisted around a hundred Papagos and fifty Mexicans and rode to Camp Grant from Tucson. Arriving just before daybreak, they shot, clubbed and mutilated defenseless Apache women and children and carried off almost thirty infants to be sold as slaves. He had been in the vicinity and knew the commander assigned to Camp Grant, Lieutenant Royal Whitman. When rumors of the butchery had circulated, he went to see if he could lend assistance.

He had found Whitman in such an aggrieved state, he barely recognized him. When Collins had spoken to Acting Assistant Surgeon Brierley, he was informed that the wounded had had their heads bashed in with stones, some of the women had been ravished prior to being shot and an infant of two months had been found with bullet wounds and one leg nearly hacked off. The entire encampment had been burned and there had been no survivors other than one woman who was so egregiously injured, she would be paralyzed for life. A burial detail was engaged in interring the bloodied and dismembered corpses and C.W. had been thunderstruck by this formidable evidence of unrestrained antipathy.

The culprits and their supporters publicly justified the attack as retribution for raids committed by other Apache bands on white settlers. Whitman, due to his efforts to seek justice for the people who had relied upon him for protection, became one of the most vilified individuals in Arizona Territory, accused of drunkenness and lechery with Apache women. General Crook chose to appease the good citizens of Tucson and was about to relieve Whitman of duty when the several telegrams Collins had sent to President Grant had borne fruit and the lieutenant was retained as commander of Camp Grant. Nevertheless, Crook and Whitman had become adversaries over the lieutenant's insistence that the offenders be severely punished. Ultimately, as a result of renewed depredations committed by aggrieved Apache warriors and changes in military policy, Whitman had been court-martialed and found guilty of "conduct unbecoming to an officer and a gentleman." The perpetrators of the massacre were tried and found innocent after only nineteen minutes of deliberation by a Tucson jury. C.W. had eventually surmised that the actual motivations for the slaughter had had to do with Tucson residents fearing that peace with growing numbers of Apaches, achieved by Whitman at Camp Grant, would have the potential to remove lucrative military contracts and trade. Nothing like bloody violence to guarantee continued occupancy of the U.S. Army.

While Collins sat by the cold hearth ring, revisiting past tragedies, the sun had disappeared behind the sandstone buttes to the west. He roused himself and built a fire, then grained his animals, gave Gal a stale loaf of bread and heated a can of beans for himself. He had intended to resupply at the post and would need to hunt for fresh meat again soon, but now greatly desired to escape the proximity of Fort Robinson and the pall cast upon the environs by recent iniquities. He would make for the confluence of Chadron Creek and White River, where game was sure to be more plentiful at a distance from the Sidney and Black Hills Trail. In due course, he planned to pass through Camp Sheridan and would be able to purchase additional goods at the sutler's store there.

After a restless night, C.W. made a pot of coffee and began packing up camp in early dawn. He caught the horse and mules, saddled them and proceeded to arrange his loads. While securing the packs on Joey, the mule turned to shove him repeatedly with his nose. Collins halted his exertions and took a moment to pat the mule's head and scratch inside his long ears, causing the animal to close its eyes in contentment. He smiled and found his mood somewhat amended. He paused to take a deep breath and admire the natural beauty of the surroundings, reminded that simple pleasures are balm for abstract vexation.

After a final appraisal of the packs and tightening of cinches, he mounted up and called the dog. He headed out of the river bottom to the open grasslands southward, following the stream's course to the east. The day was clear and bright with nary a breath of wind. Collins enjoyed being back in the saddle on sweeping grasslands and Gal was exuberantly leaping here and there, sniffing and examining the ground with fervor. He wondered idly how long he would have to wait for the rendezvous on Chadron Creek and whether his friend had been altered in any way.

After a while, he drew closer to a distinctive landform to the southeast. Benjamin Clark had spoken of the history regarding the location, known as Crow Butte; the site of a famous old battle between the Sioux and Crow. According to the scout, the Sioux had besieged their enemies atop the butte, cutting off their only escape route. The Crow had supposedly escaped by killing a horse and using the hide to make a rope, leaving an old man to keep the fires tended and the Sioux distracted. Collins had not found the story credible, especially given that the Indians had supposedly used the makeshift halyard to lower all their horses from the precipice.

Around noonday, C.W. detected a small herd of mule deer among some trees along a narrow creek that cut across his path. He eased down from the gelding and wrapped his reins around a sapling, slipping his rifle out of its boot and pushing the dog to the ground as a signal to stay. Making his way quietly, he drew near the creatures and knelt to take steady aim at a plump doe. He dropped her with one shot, scattering the rest of the deer and sending them bounding across the open land beyond.

Hunkering down beside the doe, Collins deftly rolled the carcass upon its back and hooked the hind leg behind his knee. He pulled out the Green River knife and slit the belly from rectum to sternum, afterward splitting the rib cage and severing the windpipe to remove the offal in an intact bundle. The dog immediately began to forage in the pile for tidbits. As C.W. was not overly fond of sweetbreads or organ meat, he allowed her to consume her fill. He beheaded the deer, quartered it and used extra pigging strings to add the meat to Molly's and Joey's packs. Ulysses was made restless by the odor of blood, but settled down when Collins mounted up and they proceeded on their way. The dog followed with a crimson muzzle, toting along what appeared to be the liver and a portion of intestine that resembled a glistening serpent.

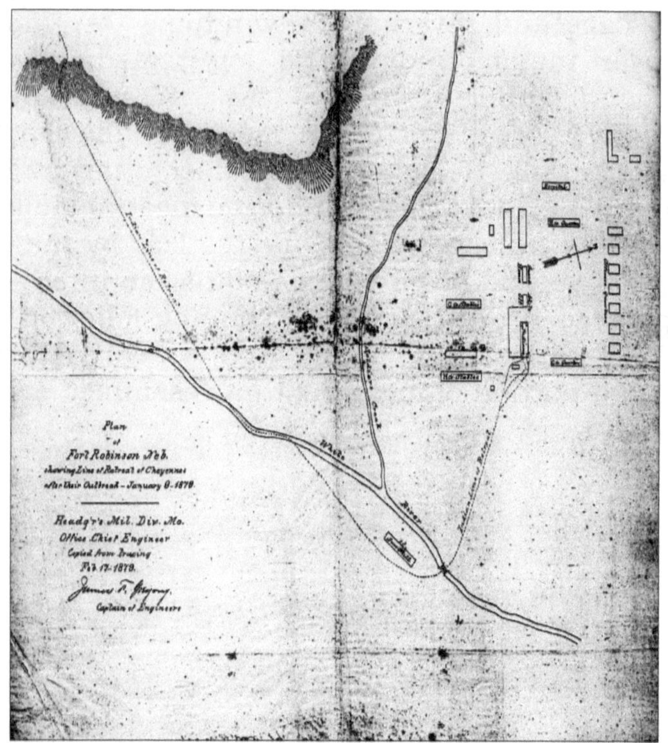

FORT ROBINSON

34

By early evening, Collins had his camp set up near the confluence of the White River and Chadron Creek, as specified in the telegram from Fort Walsh. He suspended the deer quarters high in a tree, then gathered a goodly supply of firewood. He thought perhaps he would have to wait a few days, but had no precise notion how much time was required to travel from Cypress Hills in Saskatchewan to his present location, despite the telegram having specified February 19 as the date of rendezvous. Given that he had received the communication from Fort Walsh only a fortnight previously, he felt certain he had not missed the meeting. He chafed at having to expend what might be a matter of days waiting for his friend, but he was at an impasse without assistance.

Over the following two days, C.W. struggled with boredom at the enforced delay and the prosaic nature of the landscape. He napped, read Shakespeare, explored the area and hunted, procuring another deer and two turkeys. He built a drying rack and tried his hand at jerking meat for the trail and attempted to construct a bow, using a willow branch and sinew from the deer carcass. Meanwhile, his mules and horse grew stouter on the ample forage in the vicinity and Gal satiated herself on entrails and the local population of rabbits and grouse.

In the predawn of the third day, he awoke with a start at the adamant growling of his dog. He felt pressure from her small body as she backed against him away from some perceived threat. Reaching for the Colt under the bedroll, he sat up with the revolver at the ready, searching the near darkness for potential danger.

"I could have slit your throat while you slept," came a voice from inside the tent.

"I would make certain to shoot you before I died," he answered.

Reaching for the lantern, Collins struck a match and the interior of the shelter was illuminated. He smiled broadly at the person kneeling just inside the opening and stroked the dog's head to reassure the animal.

"Háu mithákhola," the woman said with a crooked grin, pulling the scar near her mouth tight.

Collins fought down the urge to throw his arms about his friend, knowing her reticent ways. Instead, he asked, "Coffee?"

"Coffee."

Wakalyapi built a fire while C.W. dressed. When he emerged from the tent, the coffeepot was sitting on a flat rock near the flames and she was sitting on his chair grinding coffee beans. He walked over and rested a hand on her shoulder. "Thank you. Thank you for coming."

"It is good to find you well," she said quietly, eyes fixed upon the fire.

"And you? Are you well?"

The dog crept closer to sniff at the woman, then bolted when she leaned to deposit the ground coffee into the pot. "I am well."

Wakalyapi stood and walked over to a dun horse that wore her distinctive McClellan saddle. She loosened the cinch and stripped the animal of tack and bundles, turning it loose to graze with Collins' stock. After a prolonged display of blowing, stamping and squealing between the dun mare and Ulysses, observed closely by the mules, the horses regained their equanimity and wandered away.

"You have another dog," she said, returning to the fire and placing a saddle blanket on the ground to sit upon so as to give Collins his chair.

Knowing better than to make a remark about the seating arrangements, Collins said, "Yes. The dog found me many days ago and I fed it. How is Ziyela?"

"That dog is with Kinealy."

"And *Kcanptepte?*"

"Also. At Fort Walsh."

He filled the two cups with coffee and gave one to the Indian woman. Now the sun was rising and he could see her more distinctly, she did not appear to him to be greatly transformed. She wore the cavalry coat with colorful beading he remembered from before and tall moccasins with fur leggings over grey striped wool trousers. Her head was bare and he thought perhaps there was more silver in her hair, but her face remained the same.

"Well, Charles, do you find me very much changed?" she asked, as if reading his thoughts.

"No. Just the same," he said, sitting down. He had nearly forgotten about her perceptive nature and uncanny insight. "And me?"

Wakalyapi scrutinized him a moment. "Old. Used up."

He laughed. "Perhaps. But with a spark of life yet."

Gal came to sit between them as Collins fried deer steaks for breakfast. All he had left for bread was hardtack, but he still had a tin of jam. They ate quietly and Wakalyapi shared a little of her meat with the dog.

"Tell me, Charles," she finally said, setting her plate on the ground and pouring more coffee.

He understood her meaning. "You have heard of the Cheyenne people escaping from the agency down south?" he asked, taking out his pipe and tobacco pouch. "Tobacco?"

She shook her head. "I have heard something. I have heard they were hunted down and mostly killed."

He packed and lit his pipe. "This is true, but another group led by Little Wolf evaded the soldiers. I have been required to find them."

The woman regarded him thoughtfully. "Why?"

"I think mostly to keep them from suffering the same fate as Dull Knife and his band of followers."

"Dull Knife? I had heard from those who come back and forth across the medicine line that Morning Star's strength was failing and the young men were making decisions."

Collins shrugged. "I know nothing of this, only what I have been told by soldiers. Dull Knife and about one hundred and fifty Cheyennes were captured near here last October and imprisoned at Fort Robinson. They broke out last month and were killed or recaptured. Wild Hog and some others have been sent to Kansas for trial. Dull Knife is supposed to be dead."

"Where are the others?"

"Sent to Red Cloud. He requested they be allowed to come."

She produced a small briar pipe and a beaded pouch. He could smell the pungent aroma of the smoking mixture as she filled her pipe. They smoked in silence for a while. "We must go to the Red Cloud Agency on White Clay Creek," she finally told him. "I will be able to find out some things."

"It is essential that I resupply at Camp Sheridan." C.W. said. "I believe it is on the way?"

"It is on the way."

"Are you and your horse in need of rest?"

"I will take this day. We will leave tomorrow."

"I have grain for your mare."

They walked together to bring oats to the horses. Wakalyapi gave small handfuls to the dun, not wanting to bring on colic. She spent some time with Molly, running her hand down the mule's forehead and stroking her ears.

"This is a good mule," she said. "I am happy she left the army."

"Yes, I suppose she is a deserter," he said, smiling. "You have no pack animal this time."

"No. Too slow." She walked over to where Joey stood with Ulysses and reached up to scratch the animal's jaw. "Puny."

"He is not full grown," Collins said.

As they strolled back to camp, Wakalyapi said, "I think you have brought Shakespeare."

"I have brought Shakespeare."

"Good."

ESCAPE

35

"Tell me of Kinealy and the others," Collins said, as they rode across open country headed east toward Camp Sheridan.

"Kelly and Flanagan died of the coughing sickness last winter. That man Connor returned to the *wašíčula ektá,* the whiteman's world. A place called Ottawa, where he said he could vanish."

A large raptor circled overhead. Collins watched it and finally identified the bird as a golden eagle. "The others remain with Sitting Bull?"

"Yes."

He looked over at his companion. "And Kinealy?"

"He hunts and interprets for the *wawóyuspA-šá.* He is a friend with the man Walsh."

High pitched squeaks caught the dog's attention and she went to explore a prairie dog village on a low hillside nearby. The rodents eluded her, diving into the safety of their burrows, emerging to sound the alarm then retreating again below ground. Collins watched amused as Gal darted here and there until she abandoned her quarry in futility and returned to her now accustomed position behind the gelding. He assumed the eagle had the same prey in sight.

"Does he remain with the others?" he asked.

"We have a lodge near them. But *Ithúnkasan* travels often to Fort Walsh. He brought your message from there."

"Who?"

"Kinealy. Kcanptepte has named him after the weasel. This is how he is called now."

Laughing, Collins said, "He truly does resemble a weasel."

They came to a substantial stream. Dismounting, Collins and Wakalyapi loosened the cinches and led the horses and mules to water. He saw that the Winchester repeater he had given her was in a beaded scabbard hanging from her saddle.

"This place was named after a *sihanská* called Bordeaux who bought furs at a house near here," the woman said. "Beckwourth traded with him."

"You have been here before."

"Yes." She played with the small bell still braided into the gelding's forelock. "This is very old...a very old kind."

"Feathered Dress Woman, who was with the scout Clark," C.W. said by way of explanation. "I believe she will be at the Red Cloud Agency by now."

They crossed the stream and continued on their way, traversing lush meadowlands, then coming to another branch of the creek. The sun climbed high above and the temperature warmed unseasonably. The country opened out onto tableland that was rather arid and sandy. C.W. stopped to remove his frock coat. He reached in his saddlebags and handed some jerked meat to Wakalyapi. She took a bite of it and his vanity forced him to await a response.

She studied him with a trace of mirth. "Tastes like *šúnkče.*"

He raised an eyebrow. "That does not sound favorable."

"I am able to eat it."

"Will you tell me the meaning?"

"I will tell you," she said, but stated nothing more.

After a while, the terrain became more broken with dry creek beds and rolling ridges. In the early afternoon, they climbed a steeper stretch of land that had been denuded by logging, then descended into a riparian area. A cluster of buildings and a flagstaff just to the north declared the emplacement of Camp Sheridan. Two distinct jagged sandstone buttes stood above the northwestern boundary of the post as mute sentries.

Calling the dog, Collins slapped his thigh and she jumped up with him on the horse. Wakalyapi looked over but said nothing. They skirted to the east of the preponderance of buildings, making their way toward the structure distinguished by the flagpole. It was a long building with two chimneys, a covered porch and board and batten siding. Two privates idled on the porch, one seated and the other leaning against a rough sawn column. C.W. reined in his gelding by the corner of the building and dismounted, impressing upon Gal to remain in the saddle. He handed the reins and Molly's lead rope to the woman.

"Will you allow me to leave you here for a moment?" he asked.

"Yes."

Stepping onto the porch and nodding to the soldiers, C.W. walked to the door and entered the interior office. In the dimly lit room, he observed white washed walls adorned solely by one faded Colton's map of the Wyoming and Dakota territories and a writing desk, behind which was seated a portly lieutenant of pleasant demeanor. In front of the desk, there were two leather bound campaign chairs.

The adjutant greeted him affably and asked, "How can I be of service?"

"My name is C.W. Collins. I am passing through and wish to resupply at your post trader's establishment. I merely wanted to alert you to my presence; out of courtesy and so as to not raise concern."

The officer nodded amiably, exhibiting no inclination

to rise from his seat. "Your consideration is much appreciated. We get few travelers through here...mostly horse thieves and they generally do not make their visits known in advance."

"Well then, Lieutenant, you may now be assured we are not horse thieves."

"We?"

"I am travelling in the company of a guide and interpreter," Collins told him. "Will you kindly direct me to the post trader?" he asked, not wishing to engage in additional conversation.

"It is the building closest to the creek due west of here," the adjutant said, gesturing with his head toward the back wall.

"Thank you. With your permission, I will go about my way,"

"If you care to billet here for the night, we are able to find you quarters."

"Most gracious," Collins said with his hand on the door latch, "but we must proceed upon our journey."

He exited the building and found the porch abandoned. The two soldiers were, instead, standing proximate to Wakalyapi and his animals, vociferous in harassment. The woman was stolidly ignoring their devilment, gazing impassively at the roof of the building.

"I am telling you," one was saying, "if this is a squaw, I will owe you one full bottle of Old Orchard."

"To hell with that," the other private said, pointing to Gal, cowering upon the gelding's back with teeth bared, "What I want to know is if this dog can really ride that horse. *And* lead a pack string to boot."

Walking toward the men, C.W. said, "You will need to move away now." He pulled his .45 and pressed the end of the barrel to the neck of the nearest trooper.

"Hey, fuck you," he bellowed, jerking aside and turning to face Collins.

The other trooper began to laugh uproariously. "I think you shit yourself, Wiggins."

Slipping the revolver back in its holster, Collins tightened his cinch and swung into the saddle. "Stop behaving the clodpolls," he said, settling the dog in front of him.

"*Wašíčun witkó,*" Wakalyapi said under her breath.

"What?" asked the belligerent Private Wiggins, stepping aggressively toward her. "What was that?"

The other private grabbed his shoulder. "Come on, let it go."

Wiggins pulled loose and attempted to seize the dun's headstall.

C.W. nudged Ulysses forward, intentionally guiding the horse toward Wiggins, sending him off balance and knocking him down. "Do not get to your feet until we have departed," he told the private as he rode past, the mules nearly treading upon the prostrate trooper. "Otherwise I will shoot you and damn the consequences," he added while still within earshot.

Leading the way to the post trader's building, Collins turned to look at Wakalyapi. "I believe I would have relished shooting him," he told her.

She smiled, pressing her fingers against her mouth in a habitual gesture. "It is of no consequence," she said.

The post trader, a sullen man named Cooper, sold them some of the goods they required, but his stockpile was low due to the fact that freight wagons bound for the Red Cloud Agency and Fort Randall had not been through Camp Sheridan of late. Apparently, the new agent McGillycuddy had dismissed the original freighter who brought supplies up the road to the agency and there had not yet been a replacement contracted. With the woman's assistance, Collins loaded the supplies on the mules, readjusting his packs and tightening the rope hitches. They were about to mount up and continue on their journey, when a lanky man in a spotless uniform approached them.

"I am Captain Monahan," he said conversationally. "A couple of soldiers have charged that you threatened to do them harm."

"That is correct," C.W. told him. "I offered to shoot one of them."

The officer was momentarily taken aback. "The reason?"

"They were provoking my guide and annoying my animals...most especially Private Wiggins."

"I see," the captain said meditatively.

"Now we have resupplied and propose to author no supplementary dispute, are we at liberty to depart?"

"Do you wish to lodge a formal complaint against privates Wiggins and Peabody?"

"Not necessary. I am certain that boredom instigated their actions."

Monahan smiled and shook his head. "Our greatest challenges are the remoteness of this post and the dearth of entertainment suffered by our enlisted men. Especially since the Spotted Tail Agency was relocated. I apologize for their behavior."

Wakalyapi mounted up and waited indifferently, silent and composed.

"No apologies required. Thank you, Captain." Collins climbed into the saddle. "At the very least you have a lovely location here. I imagine the hunting to be excellent."

"Quite excellent. If you happen to come through this way again, please be my guest."

"I will undoubtedly do so. Thank you. My name is Charles Collins. It is a pleasure to make your acquaintance." He leaned down and they shook hands.

"And yours as well. Safe travels."

As they rode out of Camp Sheridan toward the road north, Wakalyapi said, "These soldiers have nothing to do. Why are they here?"

"I believe they retain the garrison to watch over the Red Cloud Agency."

She made a rude noise. "Always we are treated as children. Yet it is the *wašíču* who behaves with no manners."

The dog put her nose in a badger den and yelped loudly when the animal appeared suddenly in the mouth of the hole. Gal lunged and feinted at the badger repeatedly, but it snarled and hissed and remained wedged securely in its burrow. The dog finally retreated, trotting unceremoniously up the road as if battle had not been freshly waged.

SUTLER'S STORE

36

They camped on White Clay Creek south of the new Red Cloud Agency, desiring to arrive in the morning. Collins hobbled the horses and situated them on a verdant meadow near the campsite, then brought the mules to join them. When he returned, Wakalyapi had built a hearth ring and was gathering wood. He arranged the camp without bothering to pitch the tent, as the weather remained unusually warm and they were planning a swift departure the next day.

"Were you going to speak with Red Cloud?" C.W. asked, sitting by the fire after they had dined.

"*Wahtéšni kin!*" she exclaimed. "Too long has he been tame. I will speak to others who will know more."

The following morning, they rode into an immense encampment of lodges, extending in all directions on the west side of the creek. Collins had Gal on the horse with him, not wanting her to be savaged by the packs of dogs roaming the vicinage. Horses also wandered freely about the village or were picketed near lodges.

"I will try to find *Phá Thánka*. He will be able to help us speak to any *Šahíyela*, Cheyenne, people," Wakalyapi told him.

They rode slowly through the camp and the woman spoke to people here and there. Occasionally, it seemed to Collins, she was recognized and greeted warmly, but she did not pause to explain their presence. Finally, she found a woman who was evidently crippled, walking with a young girl in front of a lodge. The child helped the woman to lower herself onto a blanket on the ground near a smoldering fire. When Wakalyapi spoke to her, she shook her head, but the girl was able to converse.

"This woman is Moccasin Woman," Wakalyapi told Collins. "The girl says this woman was shot in the leg when they ran away from the soldier prison. Now a distant cousin from the family of her Oglala grandmother is keeping her. They are very poor. Perhaps we are able to share something?"

Dismounting, C.W. rifled through the packs on Joey, extracting a quarter of venison wrapped in burlap and a full tin of crackers he had purchased from the post trader the day before. He handed the items to Wakalyapi who took them to where Moccasin Woman was seated.

"*Néá' eše,*" the woman said, looking shyly at Collins.

He smiled, recognizing the word from Feathered Dress Woman.

Wakalyapi spoke more to the girl, who in turn spoke with Moccasin Woman. After the exchange, she told C.W., "There is a rumor that Morning Star is alive and has arrived here. We should find someone and see about this."

"I trust your judgement."

"There is a man, Rowland. He is married to a *Šahíyela* woman. This woman says he may have seen Morning Star recently."

They rode to the agency buildings where there was a school under construction, a large warehouse for ration goods, a barn, corrals for U.S. Indian Department beeves, the agent's residence and various outbuildings. Not far away, was the home of William Rowland, a one-story log building with a variety of chickens pecking around the front and a brown milch cow in an adjacent pen. An Indian woman in a simple faded cotton dress was sitting on the top step of a rudimentary porch, beading a moccasin. Wakalyapi dismounted and walked over.

She spoke to the woman, who gave a brief response and made a sign with her hands.

"This woman is Cheyenne. I understand only a little of her language but she says her man has gone to see the agent McGillycuddy. We will find him there."

"I do not believe we should let on to the agent what our interests may be."

The woman swung up on her dun mare. "Yes."

They returned to the collection of agency buildings and dismounted near the corrals.

"I will remain here," Wakalyapi said. "Perhaps I will see somebody." She called the dog to her and held her close.

"I promise to return swiftly," C.W. said and headed toward a building that appeared to be a hub of activity.

When he advanced nearer the structure, he heard raised voices and saw there was a gathering of Oglala men surrounding two white men, one slight and quite young with unusual facial hair and the other more weathered and stocky. The older man was signing to the Indians and speaking the occasional word, while the younger man was giving instructions regarding the message. The Oglala men seemed to be speaking all at the same time in an animated fashion. The result was unintelligible cacophony.

Leaning against a wagon off to the side, Collins decided to observe and bide his time. The discussion lasted some little while and finally broke up with the young man retreating into the building and the Indians separating into smaller groups and walking away, apparently discussing the proceedings. The older man stood for a moment shaking his head. Collins walked over to him.

"Are you William Rowland?" he asked.

"I am he," the man said in a deep voice and faint southern accent.

"My name is C.W. Collins. Your wife told us you were here. I would appreciate a private word with you."

The man gave him a doubting glance. "My wife told you?" He shrugged. "Alrighty."

They strolled together to where Wakalyapi waited with the animals. She was kneeling on the ground sketching images in the soil for a small girl. The child ran away as the men drew near. The woman rose to her feet.

"This is Wakalyapi," Collins told Rowland.

He nodded to her in greeting. "Coffee," he said grinning. "They coulda named me similar, much as I crave it. What did you require?"

"We heard that Morning Star had come to you. That he is here," Wakalyapi said.

Rowland lost his mirth and eyed them suspiciously. "Now why would that interest you?" He peered about the immediate area, as if wary of scrutiny.

"We are not agents of harm," Collins reassured him. "We only desire to ask a few questions."

"That may well be, but if Dull Knife is alive, he has good reason to not be found."

"I will be truthful, Mr. Rowland. I have been charged to find Little Wolf. The person who employs me is highly placed and wishes to spare him the nefarious fate of Dull Knife and his people. With help, perhaps I will be able to get to Little Wolf before the soldiers find him."

"I do not believe that *Ó'kôhómôxháahketa* can be found. And I have given my word I would not reveal Morning Star's whereabouts."

"It is of no consequence," Wakalyapi said. "We will go."

Frowning, Collins told Rowland, "I find you honorable, but it is of no use to me."

"I am sorry. Did you care to have a meal with me and my woman?"

"No. But thank you."

They checked their cinches and mounted up.

"Farewell," Collins said to the man as he turned his horse away and gave Molly's lead rope a firm tug to get the mules lined out. He slapped his thigh and the dog joined him on the gelding.

"I am sorry," Rowland called after them.

When they had ridden a short distance, Collins asked, "Where do we go now?"

"We will ride east. There is another village over there."

They rode past a cluster of Sibley bell tents around which loafed a handful of white men. Collins surmised they were hired hands for the agency. A couple of the men stared impolitely, but said nothing. When they had traveled some distance away from the encampment and agency buildings, he let Gal down to run. They shortly came to another creek and stopped to water their animals. There were a few tipis down the way, but no one in evidence.

"This is Wolf Creek. Do you remember?" asked Wakalyapi.

He smiled. "It seems a very long time ago."

"Yes."

" 'Tis in my memory lock'd, And you yourself shall keep the key of it.' "

She looked over at him.

"Hamlet," he told her.

Continuing on their way, they crossed open prairie punctuated with horse herds and small bunches of deer and elk. The day was clear and lovely, with a slight breeze rippling long and golden grasses. A raft of ducks flew over, announcing their passing with raucous calls. The dog chased after the birds as if able to catch them.

"I have been reading Shakespeare," Wakalyapi said after a while. "I have been reading the book you gave to *Ithúnkasan.*"

"And do you find him easier than before?"

She thought a moment. "Only a little. His words are a tangled cord."

"You will find that if you step back a pace from the

words to search for the meaning, the story is made more visible."

"As when searching for game by looking too hard for tracks? It is possible to miss the entire herd."

Collins considered her analogy with approbation. "Precisely."

"And can you give me a saying?"

"From Shakespeare?"

She nodded.

They rode silently for a short distance. At last, he said, " 'With eager feeding food doth choke the feeder.' "

Wakalyapi contemplated this. "As in words, not food."

"Not really what Shakespeare intended, but it suits and you understand my meaning."

"Yes."

The dog came trotting back to them, exhausted from her abortive pursuit. As they progressed upon their way, Collins pondered the incongruity of discussing an English playwright with an unfathomable Indian woman while employed upon a commission from an eminent politician in a remote and dangerous corner of the world.

37

In the early afternoon, they came upon a man who was skinning out a cow elk. A horse and pack mule were tethered to a yellow pine nearby. The dog found the innards a few feet away and began rooting around. Collins rode over.

"Do you want me to call her off?" he asked.

"Naw, I already got the organ meat packed up." He came to his feet. "Name's Ben Claymore," he said. "Used to haul freight for Indian agent Irwin, but the bastard McGillycuddy sent me on my way after he came in." He looked over at the woman. "Your wife?"

"My guide. We heard there was a small encampment up the way."

"Right. Just kinda aim yourself along this creek here and you will find it."

"You no longer haul freight, yet you remain here. Do you mind my curiosity?"

"Naw, got nothing to hide. Work now for T. G. Cogill. He trades with the Indians and operates a place over on Porcupine Creek. Treats me fair and no more fond of McGillycuddy than is good for him. Wait a tick." Claymore knelt and finished skinning the elk. He cut a backstrap from the carcass and offered it to Collins. "You got something to put this in?"

Wakalyapi reached in a bundle hanging from her saddle and pulled out a hank of cloth. She dismounted and handed it to Claymore. He wrapped the meat and gave it to her.

"*Pilámayaya.*"

"Sure, got plenty," the man said, wiping his hands on stained wool trousers.

Mounting up, the woman stowed the package in a buckskin bag and tied it in front of her.

"Thank you for the meat, Mr. Claymore," Collins said. "Now we had better keep traveling."

"Come on up to the Porcupine, get the chance."

They rode north along the creek, holding to a roughly straight route while the stream looped and curved here and there. The dog materialized beside them, her nose dark with dried blood. The terrain became slightly elevated and they followed the stream bed now skirted by timbered ridges. The creek finally opened into a pretty little valley scattered with canvas and hide covered lodges. Plentiful horses grazed between the tipis and along the creek bottom and they could see people engaged in a variety of tasks. Collins halted a moment to call the dog.

"That dog is *wóiha,*" Wakalyapi said. "You are *wóiha.*"

He settled Gal in front of him on the horse and they made their way toward the village. "What does that mean?" C.W. asked. "Or perhaps I do not wish to know," he added pointedly.

"Humorous."

"Yes...Possibly. It is true that many dogs do not ride a horse, but she is more intelligent than most."

A figure emerged from one of the smaller lodges, then walked briskly in their direction. Collins recognized Afraid of Beavers. He was smiling and speaking excitedly in the Cheyenne language. They reined in their horses and Wakalyapi signed to the boy and he signed back.

"You know him," she said.

"Yes," Collins said, smiling broadly at the young man. "He was with Benjamin Clark, the scout, on the White River. His mother should be here too."

Afraid of Beavers reached up to pat the dog. She leapt down and frisked around him playfully, undoubtedly remembering him. The boy beckoned them, with emphatic gestures, toward the lodge where they had first seen him. They dismounted and led their animals. The boy went ahead, calling to someone. Feathered Dress Woman came out of the tipi and some other people began to gather around.

Wakalyapi handed him her reins and slipped away. Collins stood dumbstruck, unsure of what he should do and unable to communicate. Feathered Dress Woman touched his arm lightly and motioned him to come with her. He mimed that he needed to tend to the animals and she spoke at length to her son. The young man came to take the reins and Molly's lead rope away from him. Collins felt it would have been impolite to resist, so he let the boy take the horses and mules, unsure of what would be done with them or his belongings.

The Cheyenne woman touched his arm again and beckoned him into the lodge. The other people wandered away, except for an older man and two women. Feathered Dress Woman motioned for him to sit down. The dog slipped inside and slinked over to lean against him. There was much talk, while Collins sat quietly. Afraid of Beavers returned and squatted down beside him, reaching to pat the dog fondly. In a short while, Wakalyapi came through the entrance in the company of a stocky Indian man with a pronounced limp.

"This is *Phá Thánka,*" she told him. "He is known as Big Head by the whites. He can speak Sioux and Cheyenne languages. This way we will be able to talk with everyone."

C.W. nodded to the man and smiled. Big Head nodded back in a friendly manner. Wakalyapi spoke to him and he translated to Feathered Dress Woman.

"Please find out where the boy took our horses," Collins said.

"They are picketed outside. He has unsaddled them and watered them. All your possibles are there."

Somehow, he felt he had been uncouth. "I am sorry. I should have known."

She gave him a quick smile then spoke again to Big Head. He passed her message on to the Cheyenne woman who spoke in turn.

When Big Head had translated her words, Wakalyapi said, "Morning Star is here. They have seen him. He is very weary and ill. I will ask Afraid of Beavers to see if he is willing to meet with you."

She passed the message on and the boy got to his feet and ducked out of the lodge.

"We have been asked to stay here for the night."

"What do you think we should do?" he asked.

"I think it would be impolite to refuse."

"Then we must share the elk meat and other food, for I do not believe these people have much."

"This is the lodge of the woman's uncle. Many of the *Šahíyela* are related to these people here. Everyone is poor now and supplies do not come when promised."

Collins became acutely aware that all the other people in the tipi were watching them closely. "Should I hand out some food now?"

"That would be courteous."

She spoke to *Phá Thánka,* who then spoke to the others. Collins stepped outside and found where the boy had placed their belongings. He uncovered the food pannier and took out a tin of hard biscuits, a large portion of dried meat and a tin of raisins. He also brought out the cups, grinder, some coffee beans and his coffeepot and filled the pot from his canteen. There was a hearth ring in front of the lodge, but the fire was almost out. He built it up using wood and dried cow manure from a small pile at hand, ground the coffee and placed the coffeepot on to boil. When he rejoined the small group inside the lodge, he gave the food to Wakalyapi to distribute. All was shared with much comment and palpable delight.

In a while, he checked on the coffee and brought in the pot to fill his two solitary cups. They were passed around along with a sack of sugar he had purchased at Camp Sheridan. He kept filling the cups until all was finished. Wakalyapi spent much of the time speaking to Big Head. Afraid of Beavers finally came back after a protracted absence. He reclaimed his place near Collins and spoke animatedly. After much discussion, Wakalyapi told C.W. what had been decided.

"Morning Star will see you. Afraid of Beavers has convinced him. It is fortunate you had met this boy and his mother before. The chief would not have been willing without their good opinion."

"I am glad to have met them," he said. "Shall we go now?"

"Tomorrow. The sun is almost down and his lodge is a good distance away."

"Should we set up camp?"

"We are expected to be guests in this lodge."

Big Head, along with the other man and his women companions, took his leave and Wakalyapi told Collins he had promised to return in the morning to guide them to Morning Star's camp and interpret for them. She was able to communicate in signs with the Cheyenne woman and her son and they spent the early evening eating roasted elk meat, drinking more coffee and listening to drumming and singing coming from a distant tipi.

Some of the women who had survived the escape from Camp Robinson heard of a sympathetic white man in camp. After the sun had set, they came with their children to see Collins and to show their wounds and attempt to explain their terrible experiences. It was all done with expressive acting and signs, but, with Wakalyapi's assistance, Collins comprehended and did his best to convey genuine compassion and sorrow.

Many of them wept and spoke imploringly, but he was unsure of what they were seeking from him. The description of their numerous wounds was distressing, especially when referring to the children. Many of them must have died excruciating deaths. He was profoundly appalled that soldiers would once more brutally attack vulnerable Indian people in this way, leaving them dead or permanently maimed and enduringly distraught. It was intelligence he would definitely provide to Schurz.

The next morning, Big Head arrived early and assisted in communicating a request that Afraid of Beavers take charge of the mules. When Collins and Wakalyapi rode out, the boy attempted to get Gal to stay with him, but she broke away. They followed Big Head, who rode a shaggy black pony. He led them along the creek.

"It is said that *Tašúnke Witkó* was brought by his parents to this place," Wakalyapi told Collins.

"Where?"

"*Čhankpé ópi Wakpála.* He rests near here."

Collins raised an eyebrow. "Do you mean his remains, then?"

"Yes. They removed him from the burial near Camp Sheridan on Beaver Creek and brought him here."

"It is quite sad that he was murdered. I found him to be a formidable leader and honorable man."

"This is true," she said. "Lakota people all mourn him, except for those who were jealous of his influence."

"Really?"

"Perhaps. Perhaps I am talking about *Mahpíya Lúta.* There is talk he caused *Tašúnke Witkó* to be killed."

"To whom are you referring?"

"Someone who makes himself important with Washington. The one who has had many agencies named after him."

After a couple of hours of following the creek, they

came to a sandstone bluff and in a shallow defile at its base was a lone buffalo hide lodge, darkened with smoke. A brown mongrel dog barked, then ran over to sniff at Gal. They walked stiff-legged around each other, but did not fight. The trio reined in their horses and sat waiting, as was polite when visiting a remote camp, until some-one acknowledged their presence. The flap on the lodge was thrown back and an older woman emerged. She was very thin and bore the appearance of having recent-ly endured great physical trials. She wore a threadbare army blanket around her shoulders and over her head.

Big Head dismounted and walked to her. They spoke and C.W. could see her nodding her head. Coming back to where they sat on their horses, Big Head spoke to Wakalyapi.

"*Phá Thánka* tells me Pawnee Woman is the wife of Morning Star," she told Collins. "She says she will let her man know we are here now. We must wait."

They swung down from their horses and Collins of-fered his canteen to Wakalyapi and Big Head. The dog withdrew from social interaction with the other canine and trotted over to sit near Ulysses. The few clouds that had filled the morning sky burned away and the sun shone warmly. After a prolonged delay, a blan-ket wrapped figure came out of the lodge, leaning on a middle-aged Indian man and followed by Pawnee Wom-an. The individual was lowered onto a pile of blankets in front of the tipi and the blanket fell away from his face to reveal strong, chiseled features; careworn and stalwart. The younger man, also exhibiting signs of re-cent and arduous privations, summoned them to come nearer with a wave of his hand, then sat down. Pawnee Woman tucked blankets around the older person on the ground and retreated back into the lodge. The blanket had slipped from her head and Collins noticed her hair was cut short and ragged.

"Dull Knife?" Collins asked his companion.

"Yes."

They ground-tied their horses and C.W. followed Wakalyapi and Big Head closer to the two men sitting in front of the lodge. Big Head made an extended speech, gesturing with his hands toward Wakalyapi and Collins. The younger man then spoke. Big Head translated for Wakalyapi. She in turn passed the information on to Collins.

"This is Dull Knife and his son, Buffalo Hump. His mother was killed on the journey from the south. There are others of the family who have also walked on. Buffalo Hump's wife and boy are here but do not desire to see you."

Collins wondered briefly whether the woman that Woodchuck had spoken of, trampled and buried near Ladder Creek, could have been Buffalo Hump's mother. "Please thank them for speaking to me," he said.

The message was passed on. Dull Knife finally spoke at length. His words made their way back to C.W. through the two interpreters.

"He says that if you are seeking knowledge about the deaths of Cheyenne people or soldiers at the fort, they are too afraid of saying. The soldiers are still looking for him and he hopes you will not bring them here."

"Tell him that I do not want to bring him any trouble, but I only want to know if he can give me directions to where Little Wolf may be hiding. Tell him I want to help Little Wolf to not be killed by the soldiers, as many of the other people have been."

Wakalyapi gave the words to Big Head in her own dialect and he passed them on in the Cheyenne language. The chief sat and considered for an extended period, then spoke.

"Morning Star says he is reluctant to tell you where Little Wolf may be hiding. He has lost faith in white men words." Wakalyapi told Collins. "Perhaps I may talk?"

"Yes please."

Walking slightly closer to Dull Knife and his son, Wakalyapi engaged in a lengthy monologue, which Big Head then passed on. Buffalo Hump spoke, then he and his father seemed to have a discussion. After this dialog, Dull Knife sent a protracted message back to Collins.

"I have given my word that you can be trusted," Wakalyapi said. "I told him of our time together before and your loyalty to *Tatánka Íyotaka*. He is now willing to say that Little Wolf might be found around the stream the whites call the Snake Creek. There are some lakes and much wildlife. The white people get lost in there, he says, and they do not like to go in there." She paused. "I do not believe they will say more. These people are in mourning and in a bad way."

"I brought some food as gifts. Shall I get it?"

"Yes."

Walking back to his gelding, Collins untied two grain bags hanging from his saddle and carried them back to where Wakalyapi stood. He placed the bags on the ground and pulled out sacks of sugar, rice and flour, tins of hard biscuits, tea and molasses, a slab of pork side meat, some of the dried venison and a small sack of beans, placing the items on the ground near the fire ring in front of the lodge.

"I feel this is quite inadequate," he said. "The post trader had very little in the way of portable foodstuffs."

Dull Knife and his son took turns speaking. Big Head translated.

"They say they are very grateful for your generosity," Wakalyapi told him.

Dull Knife called to someone and Pawnee Woman came out with a blanket to gather up the provisions. She smiled timorously at Collins and Wakalyapi and toted the blanket back into the tipi.

"A finger on her left hand has been cut off and appears to be rather painful," C.W. said.

"Yes. It is the custom when mourning. You do not recall this?"

He thought back to his time with her people; when death and starvation had been relentless. "Yes. I had forgotten."

"They have lost important family members. They have lost too much." She spoke to Big Head. "We must go." She signed to Dull Knife and Buffalo Hump and they made signs in response.

"Make your hands do this," she told Collins and showed him a gesture that resembled an abridged breaststroke.

He attempted to emulate her movement and smiled at the chief and his son. They squinted their eyes in amusement, nodding.

Riding away from the camp, Collins asked, "What did I say, exactly?"

"You thanked them."

"Did I do this correctly?"

"It is of no consequence," she said inscrutably.

38

When they had parted ways with *Phá Thánka*, after having given him a gift of tobacco, Collins and Wakalyapi went hunting. They traveled farther down Wounded Knee Creek, away from the small camps situated here and there, and almost into the northwestern periphery of the sand hills region. In the brakes along the creek, they came upon a herd of deer and each of them brought down a doe. When the carcasses were eviscerated, loaded and secured on their saddles, they headed north, back toward the encampment where Feathered Dress Woman had her lodge. Ulysses crow-hopped desultorily in protest at the scent of blood and unaccustomed weight, but Collins lined him out and the gelding acquiesced.

The sun had almost set by the time they returned to the lodge. Afraid of Beavers helped them unload and unsaddle their horses in the remaining daylight, visibly excited about the fresh meat. Collins suspended both the deer from the drying rack beside the lodge to protect the meat from roving packs of dogs. Gal sat beneath, lapping up the blood that dripped down and fiercely guarding her prerogative. Wakalyapi cut choice slices from a carcass and brought them to Feathered Dress Woman. C.W. fried potatoes and made coffee while their hostess roasted the meat. Wakalyapi left the camp, returning a short while later with a bundle of firewood from the creek bottom.

Early the next day, Collins and Wakalyapi saddled the horses and mules and packed up their belongings, dwindling dry goods and two hindquarters of venison. They gave the remaining meat to Feathered Dress Woman and her son, who expressed heartfelt gratitude through signs and overall demeanor. As they rode away, it saddened Collins that he would not know the ultimate fate of the Cheyenne family and sincerely hoped they would eventually be allowed a modicum of security and contentment. Given the caprices of the U.S. government and its representatives, it did not seem likely to be so.

The weather had turned cold and unsettled. A bitter wind blew from the west and heavy clouds obscured the sun as the day advanced. They followed Wounded Knee Creek until it forked and then traveled along the waterway that angled in a southeasterly direction. Wakalyapi had expressed a general knowledge of the region mentioned by Dull Knife, but was not in certainty they would be able to find Little Wolf nor whether they would survive the encounter. With confidence born of experience, C.W. was willing to gamble his time and welfare on his valued friend.

Around midday, the creek they were following diminished and they rode into the threshold of the sand hills country. The landscape quickly became an undulation of grassy and monotonous knolls, interrupted here and there by shallow bodies of water. Collins could easily comprehend the ease with which someone could become lost upon such repetitive terrain. He was compelled, however, to acknowledge the beauty of the locality. Buttery grasses adorned the hills in flaxen tresses, which the escalating breeze rippled in waves. Abundant grouse, pheasants and meadowlarks populated the landscape and he frequently sighted antelope and mule deer when they had climbed yet another elevated vista before descending once more into an ensuing hollow. On his voyage from Ireland to America many years before, the vessel had encountered violent weather. The topography they now traversed reminded him of the peaks and valleys of water over which the ship had been tossed, while he and his mother clung to each other in certain knowledge they would not survive.

On the brink of a larger sized lake, they stopped to permit the horses and mules to drink. Wakalyapi knelt to taste the water before allowing the animals near.

"It is salt. We must find another."

After a short distance, they came to another smaller lake and she found it was fresh. They dismounted and let the animals drink, while they shared a canteen containing water from the Wounded Knee Creek. C.W. never cared to drink from standing water unless obligated by circumstances.

"We should come to the *L'Eau Qui Court* by end of day," Wakalyapi told him.

"The water that runs?"

It is the river which travels east and west. The river called Running Water or Niobrara by the *wašíču*."

"Oh of course. I crossed it when I rode up from the Platte to the White River."

"Yes."

As the afternoon wore on, Collins grew jaded with the reiterative scenery and sought to inspire a discussion with his companion.

"Do you plan to remain in Canada?" he asked.

She thought about his question for a moment. "It is not my home country. It is acceptable for now."

"Do you plan to remain with Sitting Bull?"

"It is what Kinealy wants and I am with him now. It is where he has safety from the soldiers."

A few light flakes of snow began to fall. "And afterward? Where will you go?"

"The Hunkpapa agency is at Standing Rock. These are my *thiyóšpaye*. My band."

"You will not go back to hunting for the soldiers?"

"No. I am through with that."

"Lieutenant Bradley was killed two years ago."

"Yes. I heard this," she said flatly.

The dog began to bark agitatedly, dodging back and forth in front of a cluster of dried bunchgrass. A bobcat issued forth, snarling and hissing, with its ears pinned back on its head. Gal withdrew with a yelp and Collins dropped the lead rope in order to prod his gelding at the animal to drive it off. The cat stood its ground an instant, then evaded the horse and disappeared into the tall grasses. He rode back and Wakalyapi handed him Molly's rope. When he smacked his thigh, Gal jumped into the saddle.

"You trained that dog?"

"No."

"Damn clever."

Snow was falling harder. Collins was grateful they were riding with their backs mostly to the wind.

"Are you very angry?" he asked after a while.

"Angry?"

"At the whites. At the loss of so much."

She hesitated. "I am angry that white people believe they can tell us where to live…how to live. I do not see that the white way is superior to the Indian way. I have seen how the *wašíču* are greedy and do not like to share. They starve us and kill us and then beat their chests and brag of their worth."

This was an exceptionally long oration for his friend and C.W. waited to discover if she had more to say. After a period of silence, she continued.

"The *Šahíyela* wanted to go home. They were hungry and sick. If the whites want us to live in a different way, can we also tell them they must live in a different way? No. There is no balance. Always there should be balance."

The simplicity of her words struck his heart. The British behaved similarly in his native Ireland and in all parts of their empire. Colonizers always espoused their own superiority and always as harbingers of benevolent civilization among savage peoples. The hypocrisy was colossal.

" 'Bearing their own misfortunes on the back, of such as have before endured the like.' "

Wakalyapi thought about this. "It has happened before."

"Yes."

"I once met a Shawnee person. He was always angry. He told me something of his people and other tribes farther east. Then I understood why he was always angry. But we should be known by our courage ... not our suffering."

"Injustice is a beast that rends the spirit."

"Shakespeare?"

"No," he said simply.

They camped that evening on the banks of the Running Water. Snow covered the ground and was still coming down, whipped about by a stout wind. Collins feared they might be facing a bout of hostile weather along with their other challenges. He insisted that Wakalyapi share the tent and in the morning, they had to dig their way out of drifts that had banked against the canvas shelter. Snow continued to fall and he had to use some of the remaining paraffin to start a fire.

"We are in for it, I think," he told his friend.

"Perhaps," she said, cradling a steaming cup of coffee in her hands.

"I wish I had more grain for the animals."

"We must be cautious now. That is my worry."

"Little Wolf?" he asked, finishing his breakfast of venison and dried apples.

"He and his people have been hunted and wounded. They will not be easy to approach. They will be on the fight."

"Have I been lunatic to make this attempt?" He packed and lit his pipe.

"Why do you risk yourself?"

"Why?" He smoked and considered his answer. "I will tell you. I am working for Secretary Schurz. He is the overall head of the Indian Bureau and wants to remain so. General Sherman, the main general of the army, wants to take over the Indian Bureau. This would be very unfortunate for the Indians. I am attempting to give ammunition to Schurz so he can remain in charge."

"What of Little Wolf?"

"I am not certain, but I believe that by reaching out to Little Wolf, he hopes I can convince him to surrender and end the violence. The army has already made a meal of the Cheyenne and the soldiers are not popular among the whites in the east. If Schurz can bring a peaceful resolution, he will be a hero."

"And if you are killed?"

He grinned and shrugged. "Then you may have my horse and mules."

Nodding as if seriously regarding this as a possibility, she said, "I would take very good care of them."

The snowfall dwindled and quickly ceased. Collins watched an owl preening high up in the grey branches of a leafless cottonwood tree. "How will we communicate with Little Wolf if he does not kill me first?"

"There may be a person who speaks my language. Or that of the Crow. Or else, I may be able to sign sufficiently to make myself known. I have not learned that skill well."

"If only we had more food to offer."

"You are offering your honor. This may be enough."

39

Kneeling in the snow and breaking ice on the edge of a narrow stream with a rock, Collins made a hole from which they could fill their canteens and the animals could drink.

"This is *Phežúta Wakpála*," Wakalyapi said. "Medicine Creek. I believe this is Medicine Creek."

"Does that mean we are lost?" he asked, getting to his feet and brushing snow from his clothing.

She gave him an impenetrable glance. "It means that just beyond here are some lakes and two lonely valleys. I remember them. We should look there."

Riding southeast of the stream, they shortly came upon horse tracks. Near a small lake, they found a herd of several unshod ponies foraging among the dried grasses along the perimeter. Ulysses began to nicker softly and C.W. tugged on the reins to quiet him.

"We have been seen," the woman said.

They climbed an elongated hill and dropped down into an open flat with two more small lakes. Cautiously following a narrow coulee leading south from the lower lake, they rode into an attenuated valley that extended east to west. Directly in front of them lay several lodges. Almost immediately upon their approach, they were confronted by a number of well-armed warriors, running toward them, shouting and making threatening gestures.

Dismounting swiftly, Wakalyapi began to speak with her hands, executing a sweeping movement with closed fists, then placing an open right hand in front of her mouth followed by an outward motion. The men pulled up short and stood, watching her. She pointed at Collins and signed again, drawing a line across her forehead and then delivering a soundless monologue with supplemental gestures. The aggressive anger of the warriors appeared to subside. One of them spoke and simultaneously made a sign.

"You may dismount now," Wakalyapi told Collins.

He slowly swung down from his horse, keeping his hands in plain sight. The dog, as if sensing the tension, took refuge under the mules. "Shall I come forward?"

"Yes."

Guardedly, Collins walked to stand beside his friend. Another warrior arrived and spoke.

"This is good," Wakalyapi said. "This man speaks my language."

The two of them conversed at length and then the man spoke in the Cheyenne tongue to his comrades. At last, he beckoned them to follow, as he made his way toward a lodge on the edge of the small camp. A slim, imposing warrior stood in front of the tipi, watching them.

"This man is *É'oestóonáhe*," Wakalyapi explained. "Broken Jaw or *Ičhéte Kawéǧa* in the Lakota language. The other one is Little Wolf. I do not know how to call him in the Cheyenne way. I have known *Ičhéte Kawéǧa* before, many years ago. He stayed with my people while he was interested in a woman."

"Pass on whatever you think my words should be," C.W. told her.

She spoke to Broken Jaw and he, in turn, addressed Little Wolf. The chief listened blankly, then went into the lodge with only a brief word or two. Collins thought it was an indication that they should depart, but Broken Jaw said something to Wakalyapi.

"We are to enter," she said.

Broken Jaw went into the tipi first, followed by C.W. and the woman. Many of the people in the camp had come to gather around the lodge. Little Wolf was already seated by a small fire of weed stalks and dried buffalo chips. Two women sat behind him, shyly looking at the ground. Collins knew enough to walk behind everyone to a place indicated by Broken Jaw. He had learned it was impolite to pass between a person and the fire ring at any time. Wakalyapi remained on her feet, standing behind Collins.

"The Cheyenne do not hold their women in esteem as the Lakota do," she explained quietly. "It is best I am like a shadow."

"Explain through Broken Jaw that I am here to bring a message from Washington. It is a request to surrender before the soldiers kill them. Also, say that if he surrenders, the army will not be allowed to take charge of all Indians and always treat them as criminals. Tell him I know the situation is bad, but it could be worse if the army is in charge of everything."

The statement was passed along to Little Wolf. The chief sat silently for a long while. C.W. studied his face, impressed by the strength and resolve he found there. He appeared to be around sixty years old, but youthful in vigor. Not surprisingly, the people in the camp seemed to be in better health and spirits than the survivors of the Fort Robinson breakout. Finally Little Wolf spoke at length.

"He says there are soldiers hunting for him in this rough country," Wakalyapi told Collins when the chief's words were translated. "He plans to take the people to the *Nóávóse*. This is *Mató Pahá* in my language and Bear Butte for the whites. It is a holy place for both Cheyenne and Lakota people. From there, they will try to reach their home on the north rivers, in the country of Bear Coat Miles. Little Wolf once served as a scout for the army. Perhaps Miles will let them stay if they scout. In this way, he will try to surrender."

"So he wants to make it to the Powder River country?"

"Yes."

"Tell him he must be careful not to be caught before he reaches his destination. Tell him to hold his warriors back from raiding whites and I will tell Washington he must not be attacked."

"I will tell him."

When his advice had been passed to the chief, Little Wolf studied Collins closely, almost as if measuring his integrity and veracity. After several minutes, he responded, still looking directly at Collins.

"Little Wolf says he will hold back the young men. It is difficult now that they are so angry. They have heard what has happened to Dull Knife and his people."

"How did he hear?" Collins asked incredulously.

"Broken Jaw told me that one of the men who escaped from the soldier prison found his way back here. Little Wolf also says he will avoid mining settlements in the *Paha Sapa* and trusts that you will not betray him to the soldiers. He is grateful for your words and whatever help you can give in allowing them to go home."

"Tell him I will do what I can and that I know what happened to Dull Knife was unjust and shameful."

She rephrased his words in the Lakota language to Broken Jaw. Little Wolf listened attentively to the translation and nodded solemnly. He rose to his feet.

"It is time for us to leave," Wakalyapi said.

Collins got to his feet and followed her out, exiting the lodge in the proper manner. Almost instantly, the group of people that had gathered outside were clutching at him and jostling him, speaking in loud and angry voices. Wakalyapi and Broken Jaw shoved into the crowd in an effort to extricate him. When Little Wolf emerged from the lodge, he spoke sharp and forceful words. Reluctantly, the men and women backed away, sullenly watching as Collins walked back to where they had left the horses and mules. The packs were intact and unmolested, but his Winchester was missing from the scabbard and he pointed this out to Wakalyapi. She passed this information on to Broken Jaw, who went to speak to Little Wolf. After much wrangling, a young man grudgingly brought the rifle and handed it to C.W.

"We should leave. We should leave now," Wakalyapi said.

Mounting up, Collins said, "I do not see the dog."

"We must leave," she said again.

Without a display of unseemly or fainthearted haste, Wakalyapi led the way out of the encampment. Collins fought down an urge to look back. In spite of the implied danger, more than anything he was concerned for his dog and her whereabouts. They departed along the same route by which they had arrived. When they were out of sight of the camp, Wakalyapi kicked up her dun mare and guided Collins swiftly beyond the immediate range of the embittered Cheyenne warriors. Heading due west, they finally slowed their animals to a walk. Collins was sick at heart, searching the surrounding landscape for his lost dog.

"That dog is clever," Wakalyapi said. "She will find us."

"Unless someone hurt her. Perhaps she tried to protect the horses when the boy stole my rifle."

"I am sorry," she said solemnly.

Angling slightly to the north, they broke out of the sand hills and came upon the Niobrara River by late afternoon. They found a clearing along a wide pool with good cover and plenty of forage for the livestock. Snow was drifting down and the wind had ceased.

As they unloaded the mules, Collins said, "I had tobacco and some other goods. I wished to give them to Little Wolf."

"It is of no consequence. He saw the threat."

After caring for the horses and mules and giving them each a small portion of oats, Wakalyapi built a fire while Collins put up the tent and arranged a comfortable camp. When they had finished a simple meal, they drank coffee and smoked their pipes. Collins was distracted and did not foster conversation. His spirits were utterly cast down, pondering the tragedies suffered by the Cheyenne people in their bid for freedom. His personal loss weighed heavily but paled in comparison. He was gravely concerned that Little Wolf and his people would not make it safely through the Black Hills. As the fire died down, he walked off into the brush to relieve himself. Standing among the tall cottonwoods, he tipped his head back and savored the cool light flakes of snow that caressed his cheeks.

"Charles?" Wakalyapi called from the camp.

"I am here."

"You must come."

Fearing intruders, he hastened back. In the dim light he saw that a small, furry bundle was enfolded in the woman's arms as she knelt upon the snowy ground. Moved beyond speech, Collins fell to his knees and embraced the shivering animal when she bellied over to him. In a moment, she was wriggling in delight.

Wakalyapi placed a hand on his shoulder. "Your friend has found you. I am glad."

He built up the fire and examined the dog. She was wet to the skin and had a bloody graze on her shoulder. He dried her with a saddle blanket while Wakalyapi cut a hunk of venison for the animal, which she ate hungrily. Plainly, Gal would surely recover from whatever tribulations she had endured. Where Collins had so recently been bereft of felicity, he was now overwhelmed with it. Sleep would not be elusive, after all.

40

"I wish to find the location of the final conflict between Dull Knife's people and the soldiers," C.W. told Wakalyapi the next morning.

The temperatures had dropped sharply and clouds of steam rose from their exhaled breath and cups of coffee. Gal lay at his feet, curled on the saddle blanket he had placed on the ground for her.

"Why would you wish this?"

"To be able to report as a witness to the totality of aggression."

"And this will be good for the Cheyenne people?"

"I truly believe that if the Indian Bureau is transferred to the War Department, the plight of all Indians will be made unbearable."

Wakalyapi gave him a disparaging look. "It is not bearable now."

"However bad a situation may be, it can be made worse," he said, shrugging his shoulders. "*Bíonn an chomhchosúlacht ann.* Coming events cast their shadow before. Have not the soldiers revealed their purposes when dealing with Indians? I hope to provide additional evidence to Secretary Schurz that the army acted in a dishonorable and criminal manner. He is sincere in his desire to prevent General Sherman from taking over." Collins reached down to pet the dog.

"Is this for the Indians or for him? White men place much importance on being the head man."

"That might be part of it," he said, smiling. He sensed he was happily exempted from her censure. "But I do believe the Indian is generally safer under the protection of anyone other than the soldiers."

It was still early when they rode out of camp, the dog cradled in front of Collins on his horse. They headed due west along the river, planning to arrive at the Sidney and Black Hills Trail and follow it back north to the fort. They traveled with determination, making rudimentary camps, and by the morning of the third day, they came to the Running Water stage station. Wakalyapi remained behind in a grove of trees, keeping the dog with her, while Collins went to resupply.

The burly station tender was undoubtedly suffering from a recent debauchery and was none too friendly as Collins gathered necessary goods from the inventory of supplies. The place was remarkably well stocked and he was able to replenish many necessities and procure some indulgences that would make the remainder of his journey quite comfortable. He meticulously loaded the goods on the mules, balancing the weight and securing everything compactly. He was nearly out of funds, having spent the banknotes sewn into his coat. It would be necessary to seek out a financial institution before he could rejoin civilization.

He found Wakalyapi napping in the noonday sun, leaning against a wide cottonwood for a back rest with Gal snuggled in beneath one arm. He tethered the animals to a tree and eased the cinches. Reaching into a pannier, he took out a large tin of pipe tobacco and walked over to the woman. The dog ran to him, wagging her stumpy tail in enthusiasm.

"I thought perhaps you had given me your dog," Wakalyapi said, getting to her feet and stretching.

He handed her the tobacco. "I bring gifts, but you may not have my dog."

Chapter 40

"I already have your other dog," she said. "Thank you for the *čhanlí*."

Collins watered his horse and mules, adjusted the packs, tightened cinches and prepared to depart. They made it to the White River before dark had settled, making camp, west of Fort Robinson and the old Red Cloud Agency, on an isolated stretch of the stream.

"I think it best for you to avoid any unintended meeting with soldiers," Collins told his companion.

"Yes."

They built a comfortable camp, proposing to rest the animals for part of the next day, prior to setting out for the site on Indian Creek. That evening, Collins produced bread and jam, canned peaches, smoked ham and an entire apple pie. When they had concluded their feast, they smoked and drank coffee. The horses and mules were grained and provided with ample fodder along the river bottom. Collins took time to pull matted hair from Ulysses' mane and tail and rub down Joey and Molly. Gal received her own portion of meat and bread, then fell asleep beside the fire, her belly round and serried.

With a renewed supply of paraffin, Collins lit the lantern and read the beginning of Act 3 of *Richard II* to Wakalyapi.

Needs must I like it well. I weep for joy
To stand upon my kingdom once again.
Dear earth, I do salute thee with my hand,
Though rebels wound thee with their horses' hoofs.
As a long-parted mother with her child
Plays fondly with her tears and smiles in meeting,
So, weeping, smiling, greet I thee, my earth,
And do thee favors with my royal hands.
Feed not thy sovereign's foe, my gentle earth,
Nor with thy sweets comfort his ravenous sense,
But let thy spiders, that suck up thy venom,

And heavy-gaited toads lie in their way,
Doing annoyance to the treacherous feet
Which with usurping steps do trample thee.
Yield stinging nettles to mine enemies,
And when they from thy bosom pluck a flower,
Guard it, I pray thee, with a lurking adder,
Whose double tongue may with a mortal touch
Throw death upon thy sovereign's enemies.
Mock not my senseless conjuration, lords.
This earth shall have a feeling, and these stones
Prove armèd soldiers, ere her native king
Shall falter under foul rebellion's arms.

"It is a king saying this?" she asked when he had finished reading.

"Yes."

"He wishes that the earth help him fight his enemies?"

"That is it, exactly."

Wakalyapi became thoughtful. "The *makhá* cannot be made to fight as a slave. It is what feeds and cares for us."

"Such is the arrogance of the white men."

"I admire the words. I enjoy hearing them."

"I am glad."

They sat quietly for a while. Collins wanted to query his friend about a delicate subject, but was unsure how to broach the topic.

"I must ask you a question," he finally said.

"Yes?"

"Do you believe it is possible that in the midst of a desperate escape from the pursuit of soldiers, Cheyenne warriors would pause to rape white women and girl children?"

Wakalyapi gazed long into the flames as if seeking her answer there. "Did this occur?" she asked.

"Such assertions have been made by the victims of

raiding in Kansas."

She paused, then said, "I would not believe it was possible. But anger and hatred may cause a person to behave very badly."

"Enough to outrage children?"

She shook her head. "This cannot be so. I cannot think it would be so."

After a leisurely morning, they broke camp and followed a trail through a gap in northern ramparts of sandstone that gained elevation and brought them to open country of yellow grasslands broken by narrow valleys and punctuated with banks of snow and dark green pine trees. Higher ridges lay to the east, the rugged foreground of the distinctive buttes that overshadowed the White River and through which the Cheyenne had made their desperate escape. Collins' old map provided immaterial assistance, as they strove to find a route through the fragmented terrain that lay north of them. Finally, they came to a narrow pass through which a tentative path made its way toward their general destination.

They followed the circuitous route down through a tapering ravine and eventually emerged again into open vistas of prairieland. Collins attempted to lower the dog to the ground so she could run, but she struggled to remain in the saddle. He noticed Wakalyapi watching him.

"Yes, we are ... what was that word?"

"*Wóiha.*"

"That was it. Humorous."

"Yes. But I would let that dog ride with me."

When they came to a substantial stream, Collins suggested they make camp. The day was already waning and dark blankets of clouds lay upon ridges to the west. They took refuge in one of the tight bends of the creek, choosing a site in thick brush. A driving wind brought icy sleet as they were gathering wood and arranging the camp. Collins tethered the horses and mules so they would not drift with the storm and together they pitched the tent within a thicket of boxelder trees. The squall expended itself quickly and a watery sun set undramatically as a persistent breeze turned the evening frigid.

"How will we know this place?" Wakalyapi asked, as they rode north from the camp the next morning. A punishing wind battered them and she was forced to speak loudly to be heard.

He shrugged expressively.

After a while, they came to another negligible stream lined with spindly cottonwoods. They seemed to be drawing closer to the imposing timbered ridge in the west as it angled toward their course. Ahead, arose a crest of low and barren hills, after which they rode onto a broad expanse reaching far to the north. In the distance, they could see an intermittent line of trees that foretold another creek bisecting their path.

Collins reined in Ulysses. "I am unsure as to how to proceed," he said. "I was certain there would be a few ranches out this way and there would be someone who could direct us."

"I saw smoke to the southwest."

"Do you believe it was from a house?" he asked hopefully.

"Perhaps."

Taking the lead, Wakalyapi turned into the wind and they backtracked, bearing toward the pine covered ridge. Ahead, Collins could just make out puffs of smoke emanating sideways from a cluster of trees nestled at the base of the sandstone rim. As they drew closer, he could see buildings, one a sod house and the other a log structure. Smoke was coming from a tilted tin pipe poking out of the roof of the soddy. A few cattle were scattered among the trees along a creek that wound desultorily nearby. The wind was greatly mitigated in the location, making it a desirable setting.

"You go. I will stay here," Wakalyapi said.

"May I leave the dog with you?"

"It is best."

Having secured the mules and handed Gal over to Wakalyapi, C.W. rode toward the ranch buildings. He could easily observe that the operation was fairly embryonic, but generally in order. A tidy stack of firewood covered one entire wall of the sod house and whatever tools in evidence were free of rust and misuse. A couple of robust draft horses stood within a buck and rail corral by the barn. He dismounted near the house and called out a greeting. Abruptly, the door swung open to reveal a sizable man holding a double barrel shotgun. An unruly ring of red hair crowned his uncovered head and his eyes were buried in creases that bespoke humor. His upper lip was adorned with an abundant russet moustache.

"Who the hell might you be?" he asked with the accent of a Highland Scot.

"My name is Charles Collins. I am seeking directions and hoped you may be able to assist."

The man lowered the shotgun. "I am Angus Brewster. My partner, Nathan Emmons and I run this place. You are in an out of the way province to be asking directions."

"I am searching for the locus of the final conflict between the Indians and the soldiers last January."

The big man snorted derisively. "Och aye, what a damned cock up that turned out to be. We had troopers and Indians scrambling all over us. Lost a few beeves. Those blue bellies finally ran their prey to ground a few miles from here. I and Nate went to look, after all was done, and 'twere a sorry sight and no mistake." He crossed his arms and gazed at the barn.

"So you are able to direct me?" Collins chose to ignore the man's use of distinctively rebel terminology for the soldiers. He knew that quite a few Scottish immigrants had joined the Confederacy.

Brewster squinted at him. "What in hell do you want

to go there for?”

“I am on an assignment from Washington to investigate.”

“Not much left to see,” the Scotsman said.

“Perhaps, but I must complete my commission.”

“You might as well come in, then. Have a wee nibble of something.”

Collins shook his head. “I really must keep on. I am required to be in communication and therefore must make haste to Deadwood and the telegraph. But thank you for the invitation.”

Looking slightly crestfallen, Brewster said, “It is rare that a body passes by here. I would have liked the company. Emmons has left to Cheyenne a fortnight ago.”

“Very sorry, Mr. Brewster,” Collins told the man. He swung into the saddle. “Will you direct me to the site?”

“Follow yon beck to the northeast about seven or eight miles. You will find it along the same waterway and know it by the freshly dug soil. There is a feeling about the place and not a happy one, I can tell you. A goodly quantity of shell casings are scattered about and a few scraps of this and that.” Brewster paused a moment. “Takes a hell of a man to pour lead down on helpless women and bairns.”

Collins thought he detected a tightening in the man’s speech. “It is disgraceful, no doubt.” He paused. “This creek hard by ... is it Indian Creek?”

“Some call it that. Others call it Antelope Creek. There is some confusion. And Hat Creek stage station is nowhere near Hat Creek, you ken?”

Smiling, he turned Ulysses to go and said, “I am grateful, Mr. Brewster. Good luck to you.”

“Wait a moment. You should know there is a telegraph at Hat Creek station, if you are of a mind to save a few miles.”

Collins reined in his horse. “What route would I take?”

“Ride due west to join up with the Cheyenne Deadwood Trail. You should come upon the place easily enough. Unless you have business that takes you to Deadwood, of course."

Pulling down his hat against the wind, he thanked the man once more and went to rejoin Wakalyapi. C.W. braced himself for the next leg of his disheartening expedition. He sincerely hoped his efforts would somehow improve the destiny of the Northern Cheyenne or, he mused sadly, produce at least one small effect that would help prevent further abject butchery of Indian people. His experience with the vagaries of bureaucracy told him this was a derisible ambition.

PREY

41

Standing beside the mound of earth, sunken in places from the settling of topsoil, Collins could not help but mourn. The wind howled and shook skeletons of gangly trees that grew irregularly along the stream banks. They were stunted and twisted and seemed appropriate as markers for the tragedy that had so recently taken place at this terminus of a desperate and calamitous odyssey. Shell casings and other battlefield detritus lay about; silent testament to the determination of the 3rd Cavalry to exterminate these last defectors from the tender mercies of the U.S. Army.

Wakalyapi had refused to come closer than a few hundred yards away, unwilling to make herself vulnerable to the dread and desolation that shrouded the environs like a palpable vapor. He fell victim to it, immobilized by the ghostly cries of children, the rage of men who have been thwarted in their duty to protect, and the despair of women who have had all they hold dear torn from them by brutal hatred and sanctimonious politics. The bleakness of the scene, heightened by grey skies and grey muddy clay, nearly choked him with grief and he fell to his knees, unused to the loss of control over his emotions and somehow abandoning any attempt at repossession of it.

When he had, at last, ascended from the quagmire of intolerable anguish, he regained his feet. A whitish sun had emerged to replicate the distorted trees in shadows upon feeble yellow grasses that blanketed the rounded banks of the waterless creek. Here and there, he noticed excavations authored by coyotes or other scavengers and he chose to avoid investigation, lest he make an unwanted discovery. It did not seem as if the burial had been either painstaking or thorough. The dog had joined him and sought to offer solace by the pressure of her small body against his leg. He reached down to pat her head and rub an ear, grateful for her invitation to extract himself from the echoes of heartrending slaughter and rejoin his companions in the here and now.

Swinging onto Ulysses, who seemed restless and keen to depart, he rode to where Wakalyapi awaited him. She studied his face and did not speak, but handed him Molly's lead rope and turned her dun mare to ride away. Collins followed her docilely, unwilling to assert any plan or destination. He felt hollow and brittle, as if the substance of his corporeal flesh had relinquished quiddity and likened to a husk. The sun retreated again behind thin and hesitant clouds, mottled and misshapen as they scurried across the sky, driven by a resolute breeze. He paused a moment to let the dog mount up and she tentatively licked his chin.

After they had travelled a short distance, Wakalyapi reined in her horse and turned to look at him. "You are done here?" she asked.

"I am done."

"How is it, Charles?"

He gazed off at the exposed stretches of country to the north. "I cannot say. I am simply beaten down by it."

"And now you will go on the Thieves' Road to the *Paha Sapa?*"

"There is a telegraph line to the west of us. I will go there."

"We will have to part soon."

Already downcast, Collins was not ardent to quit his dear friend. "Let us find a genial location for a camp and discuss our leave-taking tomorrow. I cannot consider it at the moment.”

They rode west until, by late afternoon, they came upon another stream. It was swift enough to provide open water and offered abundant shelter amid trees and undergrowth. They built camp, cared for the livestock and settled themselves by a roaring fire with a generous meal and strong coffee.

“I must return,” the woman said, stirring the fire with a stick. Night had fallen and they sat quietly within the halo of golden light, casting incandescence upon the spectral trees surrounding them.

“I know.” Collins sat on the ground with the dog, smoking his pipe.

She rested her hand on his shoulder. “It has been good, Charles. And we will see one another again.”

“Yes.” He touched her hand, pressing it a moment. “I have no words.”

In the morning, he gave her the gifts he had purchased in Chicago, always intending to give them to her when next they met. There was a walnut pipe with silver inlay, a Webley “Bulldog” revolver with a box of cartridges and a leather-bound copy of *The Lady of the Lake* by Sir Walter Scott. He also gave her the flint spearhead he had found in Kansas and two gold double eagle coins.

“This is very generous,” she said quietly.

“Your assistance and friendship is priceless,” he told her. “This is not enough by far.”

Their eyes met a moment. She smiled her crooked smile. “And the dog?”

“I will keep the dog.”

After furnishing her with ample provisions for the journey north, they saddled the animals and packed and secured the loads. When the time arrived, they clasped each other’s shoulders briefly, then separated diffidently.

“Soon,” Collins said, firmly. “I promise.”

"I know this to be true," she told him.

They rode west together for a couple of miles, then Wakalyapi abruptly began to angle her horse away to the north. "*Tókša akhé*," she said and rode once more out of his fellowship.

Confident that thrashing wind gusts produced the tears in his eyes, he travelled until he came upon the perceptible track of the road to the Black Hills. Not far to the south, he espied a rambling log building among a few trees. There were corrals with horses, men employed by various activities and two or more wagons harbored nearby. Telegraph wires and poles ran to and from the edifice, demonstrating the veracity of Mr. Angus Brewster.

Riding into the trampled yard of the stage station, Collins dismounted and tethered his horse to a rail. He looped Molly's lead around the horn and directed the dog to remain safely in the saddle. One of the hands approached him.

"Want me to put up your animals?"

"No, thank you. I will not be staying."

"Good 'nuf," the scraggly man said and returned to his chore of mucking out a manure-filled pen.

Looking around, C.W. noted what appeared to be a blacksmith's yard, a butcher shop, stables and a half-buried stone structure with port holes; apparently a fortification against attack. Incongruously, an impressive rack of elk antlers adorned the center of its conical roof.

Collins opened the door and entered the confines of the low L-shaped log building. It was tremendously warm inside and surprisingly well lit. A tall man emerged from a side room, carrying a ledger book in his hand.

"Well hello," he said to Collins. "What might I do for you?"

"I wish to send a telegram," he said.

"Of course. Right over here."

The man led him toward the back of one leg of the

building. They stepped into a small room wherein the telegraph apparatus was visible on a table in the rear.

"My name is John Bowman," the man said, turning to shake hands. "My wife, Sally, and I run the place."

"Charles Collins. And you know telegraphy as well?"

"I do. Jack of all trades, as they say," he said, grinning and grasping the lapels of his waistcoat comically.

C.W. smiled. "Very well ... I assume I will be capably served."

"You will, sir, you will," he said, jovially, sitting down at the table and providing Collins with a blank form and pencil. "The Cheyenne and Black Hills Stage Company guarantees it."

Stepping over to a narrow counter below a window, he composed his telegram.

> Hat Creek Station Feb 27 1879
> To Herr Burschenschaft
> Willard Hotel Washington DC
> Have completed commission
> Imperative that Little Wolf be allowed to surrender
> at Fort Keogh
> Avoid military interference at all costs
> En route to Ft. Laramie and thence to Wash DC
> Full report on arrival
> CWCollins

Handing the form to Bowman, he awaited the tally of his fee. He paid the amount from his depleted funds and thanked the man.

"Will you not stay for a meal or night's respite?"

"I fear I must make for Fort Laramie."

Bowman scratched his head. "No way you will get there today. It is around sixty miles."

"Then it is imperative I travel as far as possible with the remaining daylight. I thank you."

When Collins walked back out of the building, he saw that a small group had gathered around his animals. A woman and a handful of men were admiring Joey, his mule, and appeared to be fascinated by Gal, still crouched upon his saddle and visibly fearful of the proximity of strangers.

"Pardon me," Collins said, pushing through.

"Is this your dog?" asked one young man, not more than thirteen or fourteen years of age.

"It is," he said, moving toward his horse and reassuring both animals. Molly and Joey stood stoically, enduring the intrusion of curious bystanders with aplomb.

"That is the biggest damn mule I have ever seen," one of the men opined.

"Yes," Collins said politely, while checking his cinches and preparing to depart.

"Is the dog some sort of circus animal?" the woman asked.

"No, just a dog," he answered, swinging into the saddle and settling Gal upon his lap. "Please make way. I am in haste."

The covey of onlookers parted to allow him to pass. He tipped his hat and headed south along the stage road, pleased to be shed of the company of people. At the moment, he cared only for the amity of his beloved animal companions and his melancholy reflections.

42

The train rolled through open country along the South Platte River, past the vicinity of Annie Guthrie's homestead and through Ogallala and various rudimentary towns, as it sped toward Omaha and the great cities of the east. His cherished horse and mules were safely boarded at Fort Laramie with Major Evans and Gal was in the admirable care of a young woman, the daughter of a Captain William Collier, an acquaintance from the war. As much as it aggrieved him to separate from his dog, he knew she would be in excellent fettle when he returned to claim her.

Looking out the window, Collins barely registered the scenery, absorbed as he was with the events of the past several weeks. The tragic consequences of the Northern Cheyenne people's flight from internment in the south were almost beyond belief. Beyond belief, that is, if one was not conversant with the lamentable parade of events that constituted the colonization of North America. And, he thought, given the innumerable Indian casualties throughout the past two centuries, the ruthless depredations committed in Kansas hardly outweighed the brutality inflicted upon generations of indigenous Americans.

Knowing his opinions were not in accordance with the majority of white citizens or even his employer, C.W. would not be sharing them with anyone except Wakalyapi when next they met. The thought of his friend made him smile. He glanced up to see a fellow passenger, a disagreeable looking man in a blue tricot suit, observing him closely. Not in the least bit inclined toward cordiality, he stared the man down, deriving guilty satisfaction from this puerile victory. He was not eagerly anticipating a descent into oceans of humanity in overcrowded cities after so many days of solitude and isolated hinterlands. His burgeoning intolerance of the general populace made him uncivil in the extreme.

His days of railroad travel were consumed with reading newspapers and composing a detailed report of his activities for Secretary Schurz. Replenished funds, acquired at the Bank of Rogers and Company in Cheyenne, meant he could afford himself every desired comfort and the journey from Omaha to Washington D.C. was not unpleasant. On arrival in the capital city, Collins obtained accommodations at the Arlington Hotel and sent a telegram to Secretary Schurz' office to alert him of his arrival.

He greatly enjoyed the luxurious furnishings of his rooms and by the time he was notified of a proposed appointment with Schurz, he had shaved, bathed and was outfitted in a new wool Harris Cassimere suit. His Stetson hat had been thoroughly brushed and C.W. felt he was more than respectable enough for the overweening gentry of downtown Washington. He walked to the building that housed Schurz' office, since the weather was unusually mild and it was early afternoon, all the while admiring beautifully attired women doubtlessly en route to social calls or visits to museums.

He was kept waiting in an anteroom for only a matter of minutes before he was escorted into the office of the Secretary of the Interior. Schurz met him just inside the room to shake his hand.

"Mr. Collins, so good to meet with you again. Come, sit." He gestured toward a chair positioned beside the colossal desk.

Noting that he was not to be seated across from Schurz like a naughty schoolboy, he sat down and waited for the man to begin the conversation.

"I have appreciated your telegrams and the information they proffered, but I fear they were rather too succinct and arrived too belatedly to provide me with prior knowledge as the situation advanced."

"I was in territory that offered few opportunities for communication," Collins said mildly.

"Of course, of course. I quite understand." Schurz removed his pince-nez. "And do you now have further intelligence for me?"

"I believe so."

"Pray, begin. I am desirous to hear it," Schurz said and took a seat in the leather upholstered chair behind the desk.

"Firstly," C.W. said, crossing his legs and placing his hat on a nearby side table, "I am of the confirmed opinion that the military mismanaged the entire affair from start to finish. I am especially convinced that, despite protestations to the contrary, no attempts were ever made to mitigate violence toward women and children, notwithstanding individual beneficent acts by specific personnel."

Schurz stroked his beard meditatively. "What makes you say this?"

Smiling sardonically, Collins said, "I do not believe it is possible to fire forty rounds of shell and solid shot into a ditch full of women and children and call it humane and tender dealing."

"*Nein.* I quite agree."

"Secondly, it is beyond comprehension that approximately three hundred Indians could evade several companies of cavalry and infantry across three states, despite their intimacy with the landscape. Albeit heroic on the part of the Indians, this does not speak well for the

Division of the Missouri under the auspices of General Sheridan."

"Again, I agree," Schurz said, nodding.

"Furthermore, withholding food and water from the Indians as a means of persuasion, the indiscriminate slaughter and subsequent unrelenting pursuit of the fugitives, not to mention the mutilations and looting of bodies by civilians, all speak to a distinct lack of adequate leadership by officers of the 3rd Cavalry."

"I certainly do not espouse the notion that freezing and starving the Indians was the way to reconcile them to their fate. Nor am I comfortable with the resolute destruction to which they were subjected."

"I should think this would all present compelling evidence that the War Department is ill-equipped to take over the administration of the Indian Bureau."

Schurz appeared a trifle disconcerted. "As it happens, Mr. Collins, there was a recent vote in the House that put an end to the debate and Phil Sheridan's interference."

Collins was quite taken aback. "Does this mean my commission was inconsequential?"

"On the contrary. I believe you have more information to report, do you not? What of the depredations?"

"There was irrefutable destruction…not to mention loss of life and property. I remain unconvinced about the rest."

"To what are you referring?"

"The claims of outrages to women and children. I believe some men are requesting monetary recompense for such deeds? It is difficult to countenance that Indians in full retreat from combined military forces would take the time to violently assault women. There were no reported mutilations or scalps taken."

Schurz thought a moment. "I take your meaning." He leaned back in the chair. "And the events that took place in Nebraska? What did you learn?"

"Are you not in possession of the testimony from the inquiry held at Fort Robinson?"

"I am, but please indulge me. I crave your perceptions into the totality, especially from the perspective of the Indian. It has been my understanding that you are uniquely advantaged in that area."

" ' That I may pour my spirits in thy ear, and chastise with the valour of my tongue,' " he quoted, smoothing the knee of his trousers pensively.

"I do wish to be privy to your insights, Mr. Collins."

Looking up, he said, "Dull Knife is alive. He and his people suffered gravely and they remain in desperate straits." Collins struggled to keep his anger in check. "Some of the Cheyenne women at the Red Cloud Agency imparted to me the full extent of their injuries and those of their children. It was simply beyond comprehension." He sighed loudly and shook his head. "When they were finally driven to ground, it was in the most desolate and unremarkable of fields. That they should have found their end in this dreadfully ignominious setting ... Mr. Secretary, there is absolutely no justification on earth to authorize the pitiless subjugation of one group of people by another in such a manner. I simply do not accept that God's mandate can be the excuse."

Schurz rose to his feet and paced about. "We are a civilized nation, Mr. Collins. This was an unfortunate anomaly."

Knowing he was bested by unwavering and facile conviction, Collins retreated into silence. He reached in a vest pocket for the round stone given to him by Woodchuck and held it in his hand.

Schurz walked over to lean on the desk near Collins' chair. "We are creatures of the times," he said gently. "I am sympathetic to your animus, but we must needs maneuver as best we can."

Regretting his temporary lapse in composure, C.W.

looked up at the man. "Has Little Wolf been intercepted? I have not heard."

The Secretary of the Interior walked back to his chair behind the desk. The leather creaked as he sat. "I heeded your advice and have expressed my desire to see that he is allowed to surrender on his own. Unfortunately there have been incidents of raiding attributed to him."

"Recent?"

"Quite recent, but, in truth, Sheridan has expressed disgust with the manner in which the whole Cheyenne business was conducted at Fort Robinson. I have reason to believe that he will not dismiss my recommendations out of hand."

Collins weighed his words carefully. "Mr. Secretary, there must be an end to the policies of extermination and confinement. Do not Indian peoples deserve our aid and compassion?"

Schurz regarded him earnestly. "I do appreciate your candor, Mr. Collins. I am surfeited by lackeys and charlatans." He toyed with a glass paperweight that appeared to house a gold nugget. "General Sherman has voiced the opinion that the Indian can never be civilized and should be confined to reservations under strict military supervision. He expects that over time, they will become extinct by virtue of their own incurable barbarism."

Collins did not respond, but sat quietly, examining the floor in consternation. He placed the stone back in a pocket.

"Now that the Indian Bureau will remain safely within the administration of the Department of the Interior," Schurz continued, "I propose to begin policies of education, self-support through agriculture and animal husbandry and to promote exposure to uplifting contact with benevolent white society." The man adopted a grandiloquent air. "In point of fact, I am sponsoring the creation of a specialized government-run school for Indian children in Carlisle, Pennsylvania. Lieutenant Richard Henry Pratt has formulated a laudable campaign with which to bring the Indian fully into the 19th century."

The proposal was shaded with portents of the English statutes that forbade the use of the Irish language and were intended to anglicize the Irish people. Collins was distinctly uneasy, not the least because he had acquaintance of Pratt and found him to be a bombastic fool. His participation in the battle of Washita did not further recommend the man in C.W.'s esteem.

Schurz again fidgeted with the paperweight. "Do I take your silence for repudiation?"

"It is not my place to repudiate the plans of great men, Mr. Secretary. I only know from cruel experience that forcing a people to renounce their chosen way of life is unconditionally devastating."

Appearing categorically rankled, Schurz said, "It is that or annihilation. We must be practical."

"Yes, of course." Collins perceived no advantage in continuing to articulate his misgivings. He came to his feet. "I have taken enough of your time. Was there any further intelligence you require?" He placed a notebook upon the desk. "I have written a full report of my activities and all aspects of my investigation."

Clearly prepared for the interview to be at an end, Schurz stood and walked around the desk. "I believe this will be sufficient. Full remuneration for your services awaits you at the National Savings Bank. If I require additional elucidation of the facts, I will be in communication through the Pinkerton Agency. I thank you, Mr. Collins, for your diligence and conscientious veracity."

They shook hands and Collins left the office. He slowly descended a wide staircase to the ground floor, thinking that the ranch near Deer Lodge would be a distinct possibility if the amount of compensation for his employment was as substantial as expected. The sale of his farm on the coast would not be an impediment, since its location was desirable and the buildings were in excellent condition. He smiled in anticipation.

As he emerged onto a bustling walkway, brimming with the fashionably attired elite of the nation's government, Collins was suddenly overcome by contrition that he should profit while so many were destined for ruination. He was at liberty to make plans and choose his own destiny, possessing the autonomy to be his own master, when all was said and done. Indian peoples would only be allowed to subsist at the behest of the U.S. government and public policy; forced to dwell in questionable conditions...expected to become counterfeit beings and adopt an existence diametrically opposed to their natural and authentic way of life.

Collins experienced tangible remorse, while navigating the crowded sidewalks and traversing streets congested with horse-drawn conveyances of every type and style. Nevertheless, he supposed Schurz had been correct. He was, after all, a creature of his times. *Is fear filleadh as lár an áthe ná bá sa tuile,* he thought, making his way toward the imposing edifice of the National Savings Bank. It is better to turn back from the middle of the ford than to be drowned in the flood.

The End

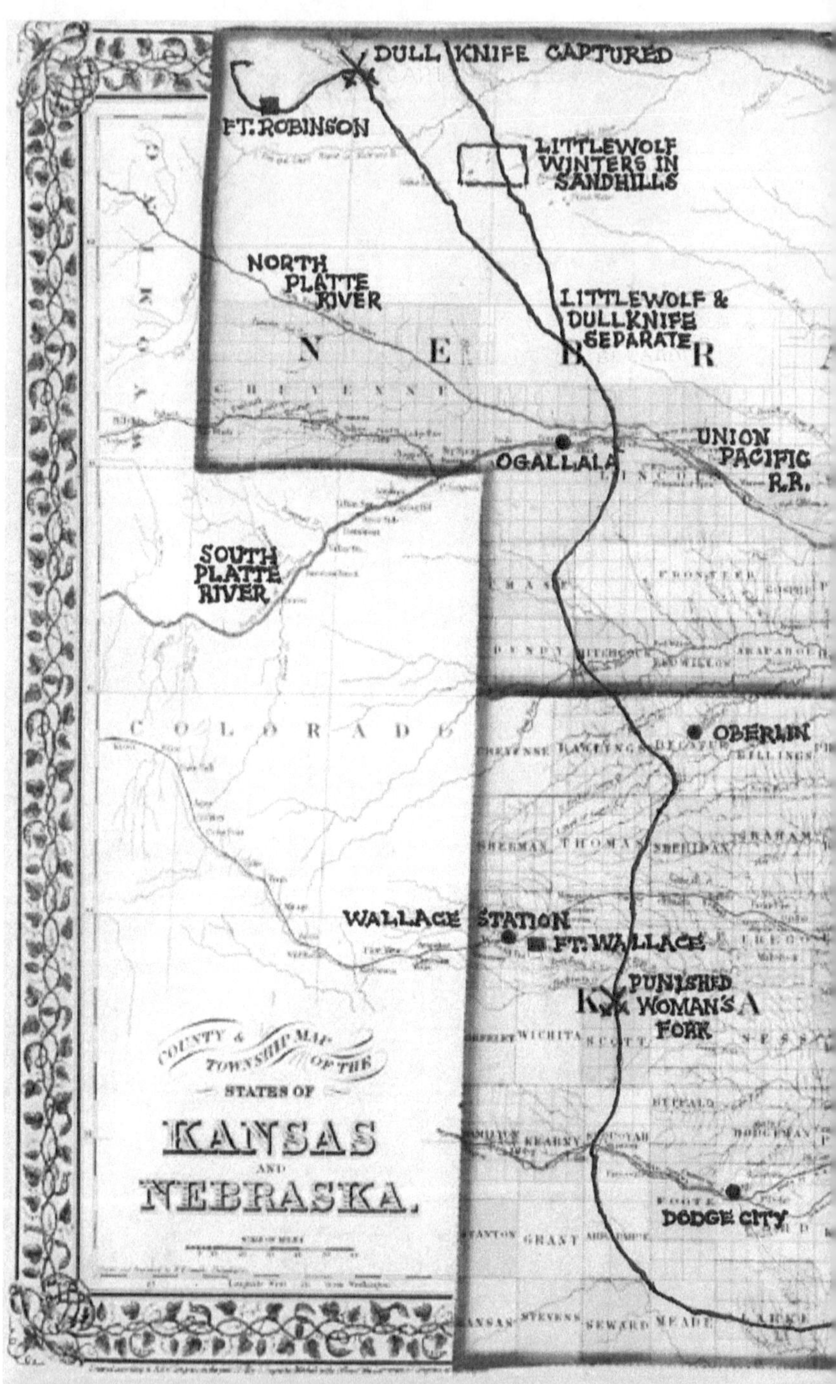

APPROXIMATE ROUTE OF NORTHERN CHEYENNE.

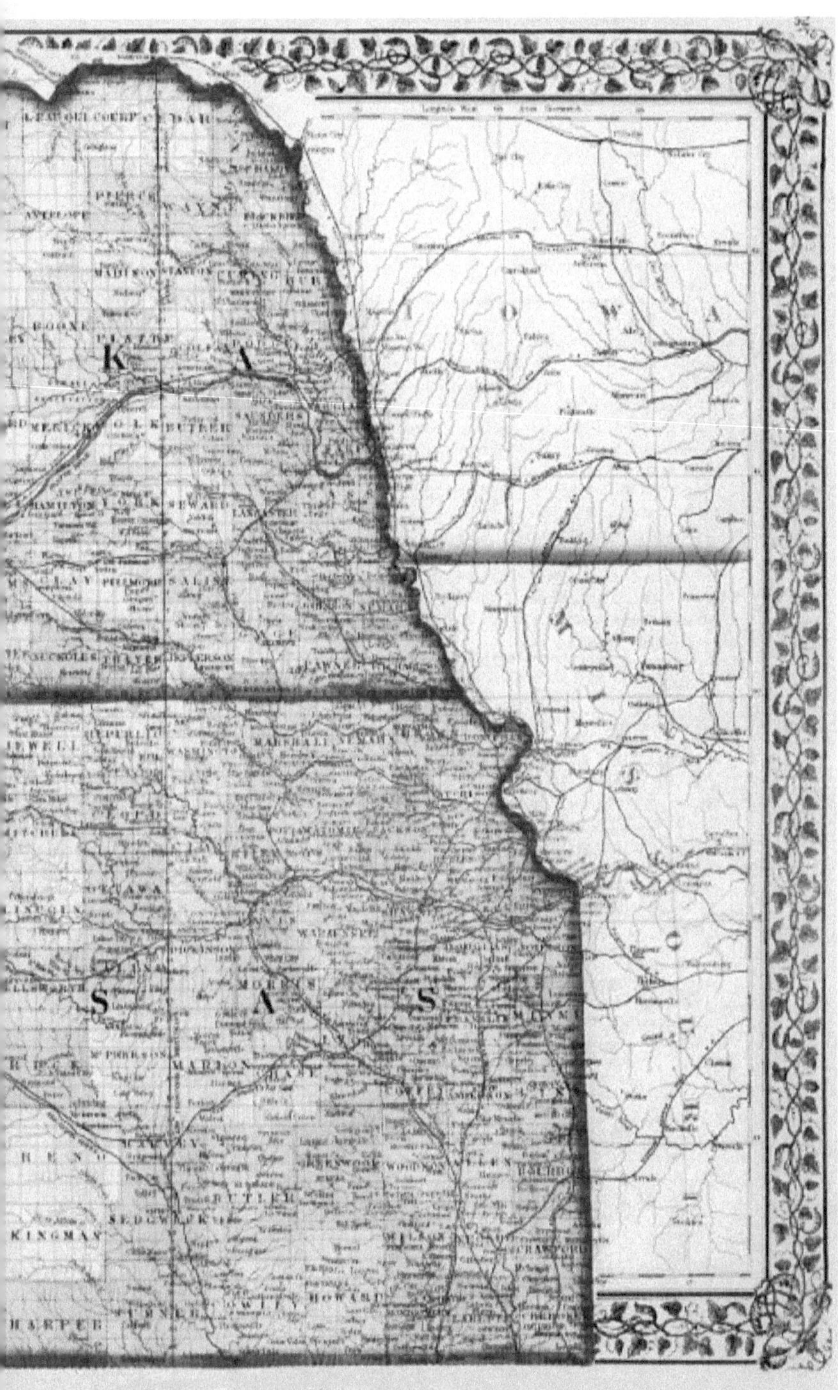

MAP ANNOTATIONS: ROBERT SZUCS

er.
ler
of
fe-
the

ice
ark
of
aid
de-
ad
ily
ing
ur-
his
per
for
ver
or
ce-
ler
ds-
nd
ap-
ces

gs
en.

of
y:
of
fc-
us-
pi-
99
le-
B.

baronet and major of artillery. He has been arrested.

SENATOR SAUNDERS voted in committee against the transfer of the Indian bureau from the Interior to the War Department. It is understood that Senator Saunders favors authorizing the president at his discretion to turn over to the war department the control of any tribe that might be in rebellion, or giving trouble, or such tribes as the president may think best at this time, and that he was in favor of the Sioux being transferred at once with the reservation that such transfer shall not affect the schools or farming interests, &c.

THE news from Ft. Robison, under date of the 23d, brings word that the escaping Cheyennes were pursued by Capt. Wessell's command, and overtaken about forty-six miles from Ft. Robison, where a severe battle was fought, strewing the ground and killing twenty-three Indians in their rifle pits. Three of our troops only were killed, Sergeant Taggart, privates Brown and Nelson. Capt. Wessells was wounded in the scalp, but not dangerously. Ambulances will bring in the dead and wounded and the captives.

THE numerous western murderers, horse thieves, "road-agents" and desperadoes are just now having a lively time to escape the vigilance

DEAR
Legislat
and nu
through,
ator Cla
the con
senator
(that w
juryman
the cou
be disqu
years, th
professic

Senato
mined to
J. C. M
managei
keeps n
what Mc
save exp
the peop
fault wit

At th
Wednese
ment, th
Finch, g
crowded
ing on W
House T
ler of t
good ad
prohibiti
islature.

Next v
from Bol
ton *Hai*
all Linco

NEBRASKA NEWSPAPER

Epilogue

The balance of people included in this work of fiction were historical figures and much of the dialogue assigned to the most prominent individuals was taken from actual historical records; military and otherwise.

"Little Wolf and his people surrendered to First Lieutenant W.P. Clark of the 2nd Cavalry on March 25, 1879, near the Yellowstone River. With him were thirty- three men, forty-three women, thirty-eight children and approximately three hundred ponies. Lieutenant Clark reported to his superiors that, "No fears need be entertained of treachery or an attempt escape. They are weary with constant fighting and watching. They want peace, rest and a home somewhere in this country where they were born and reared."

(Taken from "Official Copy Respectfully Forwarded to Headquarters Military Division of the Missouri" by Lieutenant Colonel Whistler, Headquarters Department of Dakota, April 3rd, 1879.)

As reported by Lieutenant Clark on April 2nd, 1879, Little Wolf made a statement that included the following:

> "… our hearts looked and longed for this country, where we were born. There are only a few of us left and we only wanted a little ground where we could live … My Brother Dull Knife took one half of the band and surrendered near Camp Robinson … They gave up their guns and then the whites killed them all."

Little Wolf's people were taken to Fort Keogh and held as prisoners of war. On April 28, 1879, Secretary of the Interior Carl Schurz recommended they be sent to the Shoshone Agency in Wyoming Territory. In response to the proposed plan of providing all confiscated Cheyenne horses to the 5th Infantry, Schurz recommended that the ponies be sold and the proceeds applied to the purchase of cattle for use by the Northern Cheyenne.

On May 5th, 1879, Lieutenant Clark reported the following statement made by Little Wolf:

> "Ask the Great Father to give us all a home here in the north. Perhaps if we could see him and plead with him for a little ground and for life he would heed our prayers. We are poor but we are brave and we can die. We ask for pity-hope-and life."

Lieutenant Clark reported that the Northern Cheyenne remained afraid of being sent back south and expressed his belief that should this be the case, many would make their escape by seeking death.

The Office of Indian Affairs (variously known in the 19th century as the Indian service, the U. S. Indian department or the Indian bureau) gave permission for Dull

Knife and his people to move from Pine Ridge to Fort Keogh in November of 1879.

The Northern Cheyenne Indian Reservation was created near the Tongue River by Executive Orders on November 26, 1884, and March 19, 1900, [1 C. Kappler, Indian Affairs 860-861 (1904)], and it was confirmed as property of the Tribe held in trust by the United States by the Act of June 3, 1926, [c. 459, 44 Stat. pt. 2, 690].

On January 21, 1879, the day before the final massacre east of the Hat Creek Breaks, a Board of Officers was charged with examining and reporting "the facts attending the arrest, confinement, disarmament, escape and recapture, of a number of Cheyenne Indians, recently at and in the vicinity of Fort Robinson, Neb." The proceedings convened on January 25th, 1879 and adjourned on February 7th, 1879 *sine die*. It is not clear how many of the fourteen days were employed in recording testimony, although over two hundred pages of testimony were documented.

The Board of Officers was assembled at the behest of General Crook and consisted of Major Andrew Evans, 3rd Cavalry, Captain John Hamilton, 5th Cavalry, and First Lieutenant Walter Schuyler, Crook's aide-de-camp. These officers were required to investigate, record and, finally, "express an opinion as to who, if any person in the military service, is to blame in the matter" and recommend what further action, if any, would be deemed necessary.

(Taken from Special Order No. 8. Headquarters Department of the Platte. Fort Omaha, Nebraska, January 21, 1879. By Command of Brigadier General Crook.)

Several pages of the Board's findings are concerned with the capture of the 149 Northern Cheyenne men, women and children near Chadron Creek and their possession or acquisition of weapons before and after their imprisonment. They seemed more interested in how the Northern Cheyenne had retained or acquired the weapons used in the breakout than in assigning guilt to military personnel for perpetrating a massacre and a grave miscarriage of justice.

That they were convinced the Cheyenne people were determined to die, rather than return to Darlington Agency in the south, was made clear. In reference to the breakout of January 9th, 1879, the Board found that "the statements of the Indians were not brag...they literally went out to die."

Interestingly, the officers of the board reported over a dozen mutilations to the Cheyenne dead and that many women had been "indecently exposed." Blame for the barbarities was attributed to a group of civilians that had been observed robbing the dead, going so far as to remove the blankets covering the bodies, placed there by military personnel. First Lieutenant Edward Mosely, Assistant Surgeon, reported several bodies shot in the head, hours after death.

Regarding the Northern Cheyenne's fear of being returned to Indian Territory, the Board concluded that "the return of these Indians to the south could only have been accomplished by bloodshed" and the "recourse to measures of starvation bears too strong an analogy to the ancient ... practice of torture."

While the Board felt duty bound to "call attention to what it deems errors of judgment by Captain Wessells," they also placed responsibility at the feet of Major Carlton, his predecessor as post commander. Beyond that, the Board attached no blame to anyone in the military due to "the manifest fact that collision with these Indians and consequent loss of life was unavoidable." The Board recommended that no further action was to be taken.

According to the Board's findings, the casualties were as follows:

SOLDIERS KILLED: 11

OFFICERS WOUNDED: 1 (Captain Wessells)

ENLISTED MEN WOUNDED: 9

INDIANS KILLED: 64 *(Many of these were women and children, especially considering that of the 149 Northern Cheyenne people captured and taken to Fort Robinson, only 49 were men.)*

CAPTURED AND IN CONFINEMENT: 78 *(There is no mention in the Board's records of the great number of the recaptured Northern Cheyenne people's injuries, some of which were truly appalling. According to medical records, many children suffered from serious gunshot wounds, some as young as six years old.)*

STILL UNACCOUNTED FOR: 7 *(This number would have included Morning Star, his wife, his son Buffalo Hump and family.)*

Regarding the Northern Cheyenne people killed in the massacre northwest of Fort Robinson, the Board finds,

"Of the 32 Indians in the pit 17 men 4 women and 2 children were killed 1 man, 1 woman and 1 child mortally wounded, died next day. That women and children should be killed, however much to be regretted, was simply unavoidable in the assault of this small hole."

(All the above information was taken from the "Proceedings of a Board of Officers to Investigate Cheyenne Outbreak 1878, 905 Mil. Division of MO 1879" NARA)

Major Andrew Evans ordered the burial of the Cheyenne fatalities of the final conflict, after the removal of a handful of dead and wounded military personnel. The bodies were buried *in situ,* but were not to remain inviolate.

A medical officer from Fort Laramie was directed to the site almost two years later.

The following is from the Post Medical History of Fort Laramie for September of 1880:

> "Detached service. Asst. Surgeon Carlos Carvallo, U.S. Army, pursuant to S.O. No. 169 C.S. Post Headqrs. went Sept. 23d to…80 miles north of Fort Laramie, to seek the Indian Skulls of the Cheyenne which escaped from Fort Robinson, January 1879, and returned Sept. 27th with 4 complete skulls and fragments of ten more, also long bones representing 19 Indians - obtained for Army Medical Museum at the instigation of Col. Geo. A. Otis, Surgeon, U.S. Army."

As a result of the deadly reprisals for the breakout from Fort Robinson, fewer than 20 Northern Cheyenne men had survived. Of these, Tangle Hair, Strong Left Hand, Old Crow, Porcupine, Wild Hog, Noisy Walker and Blacksmith were transported in iron manacles to Fort Leavenworth to await trial for the depredations that allegedly took place in Kansas. These men and their families left Fort Robinson on February 4, 1879 and arrived at Fort

Leavenworth, Kansas on February 11, 1879. Plans for their arrest had begun in the previous November.

To George McCrary, Secretary of War, the governor of the state of Kansas, wrote the following:

"November 11, 1878. Sir: On September 9, past, a band of Northern Cheyenne Indians escaped from their reservation at Fort Reno, Ind. Ter., and took up their march northward. In their passage across this State, which covered a period of nearly thirty days, they not only evaded capture by the United States military forces, but they committed crimes against life and property savage and revolting in their character, and disastrous in pecuniary loss. More than forty men were murdered, and many women ravished and worse than murdered. An Indian invasion, so unexpected and so revolting in its fiendish details, has awakened a feeling of profound anxiety and a rightful demand for the adoption of extreme measures to prevent a recurrence. If this band can be permitted to flee its reservation and traverse two States, plundering and murdering at will before even a portion of their number is captured, and not meet with exemplary punishment, then the reservation system should be abandoned as a failure and the frontier citizen surrendered to a condition of perpetual peril. To end such undertakings on the part of the Indians, and protect the future from their consequences, an example of adequate punishment should be made in this case. To return this band to their reservation, with its chiefs and leaders, would be a wrong to this State against which I protest in the name and on behalf of its entire population. I cannot believe such a thing will be seriously contemplated. On mature reflection, and with thoughtful reference to the demands of law and justice, as well as the end of public safety, I feel it an imperative duty to call upon you for a surrender to the proper officers of the civil courts of the State of Kansas, for trial and punishment under its laws, the principal chiefs, Dull Knife, Old Crow, Hog, Little Wolf, and others whose identity can be established as participants in the crime of murder and woman-ravishing: I believe there is a precedent for this demand in the surrender to the civil courts of Texas of Satana and one other chief in the year 1872. But if there were no precedent, public necessity and simple justice would, I believe, be ample justification for this demand. The laws of Kansas work a practical abolition of capital punishment; but the fact of surrender to the civil authorities for trial, with a conviction, followed by a sentence of death or imprisonment for life, would have a salutary effect, and, as I believe, work protection and comparative security.

Very respectfully, GEO. T. ANTHONY,
Governor of Kansas."

Also to McCrary, Secretary of War, the Secretary of the Interior, Carl Schurz wrote:

"November 22, 1875. Sir: I have the honor to acknowledge the receipt of your letter of the 11th instant, transmitting a copy of telegram dated Chicago, November 8, 1878, from General Sheridan, urging that some disposition be made of the Cheyenne prisoners at Camp Robinson; and in reply would respectfully state that the matter was duly referred to the Commissioner of Indian Affairs for an expression of his opinion, and that officer, in reply thereto, under date of 16th instant, recommends that all of the Cheyennes in the custody of the military, who were engaged in the recent hostilities, be taken to Fort Wallace or some other military post in Kansas, with a view to the identification of such as committed outrages in said State, and their delivery to the proper civil authorities for trial; and that the remainder of said Indians be returned to their agency in the Indian Territory. The recommendation of the Commissioner has the approval of this department.

Very respectfully, C. SCHURZ, Secretary."

(Taken from: THE MISCELLANEOUS DOCUMENTS OF THE SENATE OF THE UNITED STATES FOR THE THIRD SESSION OF THE FORTY- FIFTH CONGRESS, 1878 - '79)

The prisoners were subsequently transferred to Dodge City on February 17, 1879, where they languished in jail, shackled and suffering from wounds and desolation. After they were charged with first-degree murder, J.G. Mohler volunteered to defend the Cheyenne men and in June of 1879, he had the trial relocated to Lawrence, Kansas in the name of impartiality. The court case was delayed throughout the summer for various reasons and, finally, the defendants were freed due to the failure of the prosecuting attorney and any witnesses for the prosecution to appear in court on October 13, 1879, the first day of the proceedings. They were returned to Indian Territory, but later were allowed to return home with their families after the establishment of the Northern Cheyenne reservation.

General Phil Sheridan articulated the potent reasoning behind the government's resistance to allowing the

Northern Cheyenne to succeed in their escape and return north. In a communication to the Adjutant General of the Army, he wrote the following:

> "November 5, 1878. It looks to me as if there was an unnecessary amount of sympathy in the Department of the Platte for these Cheyenne prisoners, and I wish to state also that I have had my suspicions that these Indians had some encouragement to come up before they even started. I sympathize with the Indians as much as anyone, but I think that to encourage Indians in opposition to the policy of the government is a matter of doubtful propriety. The condition of these Indians is pitiable, but it is my opinion that unless they are sent back to where they came from the whole reservation system will receive a shock which will endanger its stability. Most of the reservation Indians are dissatisfied, and if they can leave without punishment or fear of being sent back, they will not stay long. These Indians certainly should be sent back to their reservation, or those at the reservation should be permitted to come north.
>
> P. H. SHERIDAN, Lieutenant-General"

(Taken from: THE MISCELLANEOUS DOCUMENTS OF THE SENATE OF THE UNITED STATES FOR THE THIRD SESSION OF THE FORTY- FIFTH CONGRESS, 1878 - '79)

On April 6, 1879, First Lieutenant W.P. Clark wrote a letter to the Adjutant General of the Department of Dakota containing the ensuing passage, referring to the mutilations of the Northern Cheyenne dead, strewn upon the field following the breakout from Fort Robinson:

"On the morning of the 10th when the bodies of the dead Indians were collected for burial, it was found ...civilians had committed these barbarities upon the dead and the evidence shows that one at least had boasted of having arrived in time to 'kill a squaw.' Civilized warfare is supposed to be many removes from the savage but in all the accounts of atrocities committed by these Cheyennes en route, is there a picture with darker or more wretched coloring than this?"

MANIFEST DESTINY

Author's Note

Native American readers will hopefully understand that any denigrating or otherwise objectionable terminology in this text is used to illustrate prejudices and attitudes of the historical period within which this story occurs.

It is disrespectful to refer to the escape from the barracks prison at Fort Robinson as an "outbreak" due to the relationship the word has to disease and pandemics. The proper term is "breakout," although the prior designation was used in all military documentation of the time and in contemporary newspaper references.

It is the author's considered opinion that the gross mismanagement of military response to the Northern Cheyenne's resolute journey back to their home in Powder River country, as well as the army's violent and pitiless reply to the Cheyenne people's unyielding defiance of orders to return south to Indian Territory, led to the decision that the War Department would not be given authority over the Office of Indian Affairs. If this is correct, then the courage and determination of the *Tsétsêhéstâhese/ So'taahe'* are pivotal in improving whatever chances *all* Native peoples of the United States had for surviving the antagonism of military administration.

General William Tecumseh Sherman did, in fact, voice the opinion that "the Indian" could never be civilized and should be confined to reservations under strict military supervision and that over time, they would become extinct by virtue of their own incurable barbarism. Adolf Hitler professed an admiration for the manner with which the U.S. had dealt with Native Americans, using the policies as inspiration for the "Final Solution."

Readers may notice the use of both "Camp Robinson" and "Fort Robinson" throughout the book. This is because there was a transition in designation of the military post from Camp to Fort during this time period and the term was used in documentation interchangeably.

Women homesteaders were common in response to the Homestead Act of 1862. They were eligible to file claims if single, divorced or widowed. Many of these women were successful in pursuing economic security, adventure and independence. The suffrage movement gained traction in the West due to intrepid and sturdy women homesteaders. The name Annie Guthrie was taken from a contemporary Nebraska newspaper with notice of her filing on land.

All Cheyenne words were respectfully sourced from the online Cheyenne Dictionary copyright (c) 2003-2021 by Chief Dull Knife College

Special thanks to professors emeriti Jeff Sanders and Bruce Johansen for their support, interest and keen insights, Holly Federle, who was invaluable as my research pal, Hymn Alexander for the stimulating discussions, Judge Peggy Nelson for her advice and friendship, and

to my husband for his unerring reinforcement and in-
credible artistic talent.

And, of course...the dogs.

Much appreciation to the staff of the El Rito Public Library
for their vital assistance in accessing interlibrary loans.

LIBERTY

Additional Reading

Wooden Leg: A Warrior Who Fought Custer, Interpreted by Thomas B. Marquis, 2016, University of Nebraska Press

The Fighting Cheyennes, by George Bird Grinnell, 2018, C. Scribner's sons

Cheyenne Memories, by John Stands in Timber and Margot Liberty, 1998, University of Nebraska Press

A Century of Dishonor, by Helen Hunt Jackson, 2016, University of Oklahoma Press

Voices of the American West, Volume 2, The Settler and Soldier Interviews of Eli Ricker, 1903-1919, Edited by Richard E. Jensen, 2012, University of Nebraska Press

The Dull Knifes of Pine Ridge: A Lakota Odyssey, by Joe Starita, 2002, Berkley Books

Sweet Medicine: The Continuing Role of the Sacred Arrows, by Peter J. Powell, 1969, University of Oklahoma Press

People of the Sacred Mountain: A History of the Northern Cheyenne Chiefs and Warrior Societies, 1830-1879, by Peter J. Powell, 1981, HarperCollins College Div

The Reminiscences of Carl Schurz: Illustrated with Portraits and Original Drawings, Volume 3, also by William Archibald Dunning and Frederic Bancroft, 2015, Doubleday, Page & Co.

Cheyenne and Sioux: The Reminiscences of Four Indians and a White Soldier, by Thomas B. Marquis, 1973, University of the Pacific

Various resources: https://history.nebraska.gov

Juliana "Hoolihan" Clayton

About the Author

Juliana "Hoolihan" Clayton is an indigenous woman of Turtle Island (First Nations Plains Cree/Nehiyawak) who was adopted by a white family and raised on a cattle ranch in Wyoming. She has lived and worked with Native Americans and cowboys throughout the West during her years as a ranch hand and wildland firefighter. With a degree in history and education from the University of Montana, it has long been her goal to create a series of entertaining novels that are rife with impeccable research, unflinching veracity and forthright cultural perspectives on American history.

A member of Western Writers of America, J. Hoolihan has been published in western historical magazines, such as "True West" and "Wild West." During her extensive research, she continues to accumulate an abundance of topics for a succession of factual stories pertaining to the 19th century American West. Her first novel, *Commendable Discretion* was published in January 2021. *With Great Discretion* is the second book of this series.

"Throwing the hoolihan" is a technique that old time cowboys used for roping horses. It has been Juliana's nickname for many years.

CARLISLE SCHOOL

List of Illustrations

Illustrations from *Harpers Weekly* are used with explicit permission, and are available through the Library of Congress (LOC) Prints & Photographs Reading Room, Prints and Photographs Division, Prints & Photographs Online Catalogue.